Flames of Rebellion

Book 2 of the Shadows of Rebellion series.

by David Lingard

<u>A note from the author</u>

I just wanted to say here, thank you, whoever you are for however you have arrived at this book and my story. It makes a big difference to authors like me, who like to feel as though their hard work and dedication is appreciated when our work is read.

Your investment of your own time and money is as always, well appreciated. It takes a long time and a lot of effort to write, edit and release a book, so please, I ask that you **rate** and **review** everything that you read – and not just this book, so that lesser-known authors can grow their audience and gain the credibility that they deserve.

Also, I have a website that is usually kept up to date with current works, reviews and a few extra little bits. You'll find it at: www.davidlingard.com

Prologue

The Pit was a place where young fire mages came to hone their skills, push their limits, and compete against each other. It was a place where a Journeyman, master, Archmage or Grandmaster with the affinity for fire mana could rise to greatness, but it was also a place where dreams could be crushed, bones broken, and flesh burnt.

With each new week, new competition was brought to the Brotherhood of the Flame, and with it, new opportunities to prove how strong a fire mage had become.

Kai had always wanted to become a great fire mage. Since the Great Rebellion, as it had become to be known had failed three years ago, the central city of the Kingdom of Avondale had become entirely off-limits for any mage or anyone with the light of mana shining in their eyes. That was of course except for any who practised the Cyclonic Essence, or air mana who had chosen to ally with the tyrant King Roderick.

Kai had arrived at the Brotherhood of the Flame soon after the failed rebellion in the city. It hadn't been his intention to join with the other fire mages to fight for a higher cause, but after searching for safety within the Forbidden Forest with a small group of others, it soon became clear that they would either have to join a faction that already had a home base, or go back to the city. It was an easy choice really. Nobody was going to go back to the city.

They'd had no idea where to go once they realised the Forbidden Forest was not the place for a young fire mage and his Apprentice-ranked parents. His parents had mana within them of course, though without ever having any guidance, all that they had ever had within them was a definite spark, and a deep red hue to their eyes.

Kai's parents could control no mana and cast no spells, but within a few weeks of his own mana awakening, Kai had been able to summon a single bright flame in the palm of his hand. He had been briefly told about how mages were ranked by his parents, and although he had no official title, he had chosen to call himself a Journeyman, because in his eyes, that's what he was, as he could cast a spell.

Out of the Forbidden Forest and to the arid desert sands to the north, the Brotherhood of the Flame had built their home. An old, abandoned fort that had stood in ruin for hundreds of years sat within a vast stone wall that had half-fallen down and half-filled with sand. With no trade routes or water sources for miles around, it was clear why the place had been abandoned.

But the Brotherhood of the Flame saw potential where others saw only desolation. They had cleared out the sand, reinforced the walls, and made the fort into a home. It was a harsh and unforgiving place, but it was theirs, and they were determined to make the best of it.

Kai had been training at the Pit for two years now, and he had worked hard to control his mana as best he could. But it was difficult. Where others had described the feeling of their mana within, he found no comparison. It was as though the flames within him were unruly, petulant and no matter what he did to try to coax them into obeying him, into casting a spell, any spell except the small flame he could conjure, they simply wouldn't comply.

But in the end, Kai knew that whatever he was doing to try to better himself, he and the other fire mages were not content with just training in the desert. They wanted to take back what had been taken from them. They wanted to show the world that fire mages were not to be trifled with, and that they could be powerful and respected.

The kingdom of Avondale was once a prosperous and peaceful land, ruled by a benevolent King, with his Queen by his side and who had the support of all the mages in his kingdom. However, things had changed when the Queen had passed through sickness and the King had been killed in a failed attempt to communicate with his deceased wife.

Prince Roderick, the only son of the King, quickly took hold of the kingdom with an iron fist; he hated mages in every form and had outlawed them from the kingdom. Ransoms were placed on the mages of note and each had been executed as soon as they had been caught. If anyone within the kingdom had been found to have mana within them – denoted by a colourful glow in their eyes – then they too were sentenced to death.

This is where the city guards' favourite phrase came from: 'Open your eyes'.

The phrase 'Open your eyes' became a reminder to all the citizens of the kingdom to keep their magical abilities hidden, and for others to be on the lookout for anyone who might have mana within them. This led to a culture of fear and mistrust within the city, with many people turning in their friends and neighbours to save themselves from the harsh punishment that came with being caught with magic within, or even befriending those who did. Coupled with the increasing rewards for any who turned in a mage, and the ever-increasing taxes tightening the king's grip on the citizens, it was the perfect storm.

Of course, many mages had fled the city and sought refuge in different kingdoms, but the journeys were long and difficult as foreign lands were distant, so frequently it was better for families to simply do their best to conceal the mana that some of them had within. After all, anyone could have their mana awoken at any point, it was what came next that would be the real choice to make, and could bring about the dangers they would have to face.

Kai and his family were among the many non-cyclonic mages who were forced to flee the kingdom and seek refuge in the Forbidden Forest . It was a difficult time for them, as they struggled to survive in the harsh wilderness without any guidance or support for a long time. They had been a part of a large group who all left the city together, though it quickly became apparent that the two leaders of the group were anything but exceptional. If anything, they were simply concerned parents who were looking for their child within the forest, and anything else that wasn't related to that task was irrelevant.

Within the group had been a mix of mages, of earth and fire affinities, and it quickly became apparent that groups of each formed and clung together. It did make sense though, because in their own groups, they could teach and learn from each other.

But Kai and his family did not care about the internal politics of mages and their systems. They needed a safe place to live, away from the city and the oppressive regime of King Robert. This was why they eventually left the group and settled with the rest of the fire affinity mages to the north in their stone fort.

When his group eventually stumbled upon the Brotherhood of the Flame, Kai knew immediately that he'd found a place where he could hone his skills and learn from other like-minded mages. The Brotherhood of the Flame quickly became his new home, his new family and he spent every waking moment training and practicing how he was supposed to, hoping to one day become a great fire mage and to show the world that non-cyclonic mages were not to be underestimated. The problem was though, that no matter how hard he trained, no matter how many questions he asked, his mana within would still do nothing but light a tiny flame in the palm of his hand.

It was a frustrating and disheartening experience for Kai, who had always dreamed of becoming a great fire mage. He began to doubt himself and his abilities, wondering if he was simply not cut out for magic, or mana.

Yet despite his doubts, Kai refused to give up. He continued to train and practice, seeking guidance and advice from the other fire mages in the Brotherhood. He knew that becoming a great fire mage would not be easy, but he was determined to see it through to the end, for better or worse; after all, he had nothing to lose.

His end could have come sooner than expected though, for the Brotherhood of the Flame had some peculiar ways of pushing the limits of their members. First of all was this place, what they called 'The Pit'.

The Pit was the backbone of the Brotherhood of the Flame, a society of fire mages who competed against each other week on week to learn, grow, and get stronger. Each week, a new competition was brought to the Brotherhood, and with it, new opportunities to prove how strong a fire mage had become. In The Pit, you fought as though your very life depended on it, and in most cases the competition would result it bloodshed, and in a fleeting few occasions, even death.

It was a competitive society, but also one that was based on camaraderie and support. The mages of the Brotherhood were all united in their passion for magic, and they worked together to help each other improve and reach their full potential.

The main problem with all of this, was that Kai was not just someone who had no spells to wield as of yet, but also he wasn't a great fighter, and if anything, he was kind of weak. This problem was exacerbated by the fact that in the Brotherhood of the Flame, everybody had to fight, with no exceptions.

Despite the fact that Kai was unable to control his magic, he still threw himself into the competitive society of the Brotherhood of the Flame. He watched as the other mages battled it out in The Pit, their flames hot and their spells powerful. He fought and lost battle upon battle, week upon week and never seemed to show even the slightest signs of improvement.

As much as he tried, Kai found himself lacking in the fighting department. He was small and thin, with no real experience in combat. He wanted to compensate with his magic, but even that seemed to be failing him. He knew that one day if he could just get his mana to obey him, then at least he'd stand a fighting chance against the others.

It was a frustrating and disheartening experience for Kai, he felt like he was constantly falling behind the other fire mages in the Brotherhood and as time passed he continued to doubt whether he belonged there, whether he was cut out for magic at all.

And then of course there was the torture. It wasn't just torture for the sake of torture, or so that the residents of the Brotherhood of the Flame would remember who their betters were or anything like that. No, if that was the case then people would leave as they were free to do so. This kind of torture had a purpose: to increase the pain threshold and elemental resistances of the members of the Brotherhood.

The Brotherhood called them 'tolerance training sessions', and essentially it involved a group of mages being bombarded by painful fire spells, or even simply just regular fire until they could bare it no more. It sounded barbaric and by all accounts it was, but Kai couldn't help but feel that sometimes, the end goal could be worth it.

It had been waning in popularity over the last year or so though and had all but disappeared, but every now and then, it would rear its ugly head again and some member of the Brotherhood would become bed-ridden for some period of time. Above most else, this method of training was shunned because it meant that the mage in question needed to take some time off training, and that was something they simply couldn't abide.

Chapter 1 – A Beating

Kai was fourteen when he had joined the Brotherhood, and now at sixteen he still had no real clue what he was supposed to do in life. He was determined to be the best that he could be, though in his teenage years and surrounded by a world of pain and heartache, he wasn't quite sure what that was supposed to look like.

Standing in the middle of the arena, watching as the other mages went through their training routines, Kai saw that as usual there were mages of all ages and levels from Apprentice to Master, but Kai knew that he couldn't even begin to compare to them; they all just seemed to know what they were doing, where they fit in and if anything, it made him feel like even more of an outsider.

The Archmages would train only with each other, and their battles each week would leave the spectators wide-eyed and open-mouthed.

As Kai looked around, he could see the determination in the eyes of the other Journeyman mages, like him. They all wanted to be the best, to prove themselves worthy of becoming a Master mage. Deep down inside, as he did frequently, he knew that he was no real Journeyman. He had no real spells and couldn't control his mana properly; he could just summon and nurture this little flame in the centre of his palm. In some ways it made him a Journeyman, but in reality, he was a poor facsimile of the other mages of his rank.

Kai took a deep breath and stepped forward, his hands raised before him. His desire was for flames to erupt from his fingertips, and for them to dance and flicker in the air like he'd seen a couple of the other mages do. He closed his eyes and focused, imagining the heat of the flames against his skin, and the feeling of letting the power flow through him. He felt the fire weave itself through his body, twisting and turning through his veins, leaving a trail of smoke in their wake. He felt the fire burst forth from his physical presence and erupt into a show that would make even the Masters step back away from him.

As he opened his eyes again, he saw that in reality, the other mages had stopped their training and were watching him, some with hope and some with devious grins on their faces.

With a practised flick of his wrist, Kai tried to cast his spell, and where a wave of flames should have surged towards the target on the far side of the arena, engulfing it in devastating heat, nothing happened, and Kai could once again hear the laughter cascade around the training arena from the other mages. It didn't matter. He was used to it by now.

Kai felt his face flush with embarrassment, and he lowered his hands. He knew he wasn't the strongest mage here, but he had hoped to at least show some progress one day, to show everyone he wasn't entirely useless. Obviously today was not to be that day and he turned to leave the arena with his shoulders dropped and his eyes fixed on the ground, but a voice stopped him in his tracks.

"Not bad for a beginner," the voice said, and Kai turned to see a tall, muscular man with fiery red hair and a thick beard approaching him.

Kai recognised him immediately as one of the Archmages, and he felt a surge of nervousness course through him. He knew how tough the Archmages could be and he didn't know why the man would even bother talking to someone like him, he hadn't before.

The Archmage just smiled and clapped Kai on the back. "You've got potential, kid," he said, before his face twisted into a look of exaggerated pain. "But you need to work on your spell face. You know, when you scrunch your face up like this, you kinda look like you're in pain!"

The other mages around them chuckled at the Archmage's joke, and Kai felt a flush of embarrassment rise to his cheeks. He knew he was way behind the curve, and he couldn't afford to let his guard down in front of the other mages, especially not the Archmages.

"Sorry, sir," Kai said, trying to keep his voice steady and his gaze up. "I'll work on it."

The Archmage simply shook his head and walked away. He was shortly followed by a group of three young mages with looks of absolute glee on their faces.

"Hey, I may have a candle back in my room if you need something to practise on," the boy in the centre said. Marcus was his name, and his two companions were Nathan and Owen. Marcus was a strong looking boy of about sixteen with sharp features and short dark hair. Owen and Nathan were both average-looking, and always seemed to follow Marcus around anywhere he went. And as a Master-ranked mage, whilst Nathan and Owen were still Journeymen, Kai could see why they idolised Marcus. If the boy wasn't so pompous then Kai could've seen himself idolising the Master too.

Kai pushed his hands into the pockets of his jet-black robes, which were trimmed with a vibrant red to denote his membership with the Brotherhood.

"Thanks, I appreciate it," Kai said with a small smile. "Maybe I'll take you up on that offer."

Marcus' face twisted into an angry smile and any sense of a jovial back and forth instantly disappeared.

"Watch your tongue, boy," he snarled and took a single menacing step towards Kai. He was quickly joined by his two minions and Kai felt his entire body tense.

The thing was, as weak and powerless as he was, Kai could never seem to back down from a fight. It was a sad fact that had earned him a beating fairly regularly.

Kai took a step back, his eyes narrowing as he prepared for whatever was about to come. He could feel his heart racing in his chest, and he knew that he was in for another tough fight. Marcus was a Master-ranked mage, and he knew the other two could be particularly vindictive if they so chose to be. He wouldn't stand a chance one on one with any of them though and three together? He only hopes that they wouldn't hurt him too bad.

But Kai refused to let them intimidate him. He refused to let anyone intimidate him and he raised his hands before himself, ready to try to cast a spell, but before he could do anything, Marcus began to laugh.

"Oh look everyone," Marcus chuckled. "Kai's going to try to cast a spell! Maybe we should ask him to open his eyes while he does it so we can see if he really does have any magic in there!"

There were a few chuckles from the other mages in the arena, but then Marcus knocked on Kai's forehead with a balled fist and peered into his eyes theatrically.

Kai gritted his teeth and tried to push Marcus away, but the older mage was too strong. The other two mages laughed along with Marcus, and Kai felt his face flush with anger and humiliation.

As Marcus continued to taunt him, Kai's anger boiled over. He knew he was weaker than the other mages, but he refused to let them belittle him. In that moment, he decided that he simply wasn't going to take it anymore.

This was his time to show everyone what he was truly capable of.

With a surge of anger and a cry of defiance, Kai lunged forward, throwing a punch at Marcus. It wasn't a particularly well-aimed punch, and Marcus easily dodged it, but the action caught the other mages off guard.

Suddenly, fists were flying, and the other mages rushed to join in the brawl. Kai fought with everything he had, his body moving on instinct as he tried to hold his own against his more powerful and numerous enemy. He didn't care that he was outnumbered or outmatched, he was going to fight until he couldn't fight anymore. That was the way of the Brotherhood.

The fight went on for all of thirty seconds and where Kai had hoped that he would have the upper hand, all that eventually had happened was that Marcus had easily tackled him to the ground, and he and his two friends then proceeded to punch and kick him over and over. Past the first few hits though, Kai could no longer feel anything; he simply slipped away into unconsciousness and his vision faded to black.

Within the darkness though, Kai could hear a voice. It wasn't the taunting tone of Marcus, nor anyone else that he recognised, but he was sure that he heard the incorporeal words reach him.

"Weak… disappointment."

And whatever or whoever this was, the voice told the truth. He was an embarrassment to the Brotherhood and all of the fire mages he lived with in The Pit.

When Kai eventually woke up, he was lying on his small cot in the corner of the dormitory. His body ached all over, and his head throbbed with pain. He sat up slowly, wincing at the soreness in his muscles and as he looked around the room, he saw the other fire mages going about their daily routines, ignoring him completely.

Kai felt a sense of shame wash over him. He had let himself down *again*, but more importantly, he had let down the other mages in the Brotherhood. He knew that he needed to do something to redeem himself, to prove that he was worthy of being among them, otherwise he may as well have packed up his things and turned himself into the city guard to be dealt with as the other mages were.

He had tried so hard to become a great fire mage, to control his mana and cast spells like the others in the Brotherhood. But no matter how much he practiced or how hard he begged his mana to obey him, it simply wouldn't listen. Some days he could barely even feel it within him.

He had always thought that being a fire mage was his destiny, that he was meant to wield the power of the flames and become one of the greatest mages in the kingdom. But as he lay there, his body aching and his spirit broken, he began to wonder if he had been wrong all along.

He closed his eyes and focused on his mana, trying once again to coax it into obeying him. There was nothing else that he could do. But just like before, there was no response. Today it was as if his mana had a will of its own, and it was *choosing* not to listen to him.

Tears began to stream down Kai's face as he lay there in silence, feeling more alone and powerless than ever before. He couldn't help but wonder if he would ever be able to control his magic, or if he was destined to be a failure as a fire mage.

"Why do you do it to yourself?" a voice came from behind Kai's tightly closed eyes.

"Hey, you're awake," the voice said again, interrupting Kai's thoughts. "Are you feeling any better?"

Kai opened his eyes and saw his only friend in the Brotherhood of the Flame, a fellow Journeyman fire mage named Elijah, sitting beside him. He tried to sit up, but winced in pain and settled back down.

"I'll take that as a no," Elijah said with a small smile. "What happened out there, Kai? I heard that you got into a fight with Marcus and his friends."

Kai gritted his teeth, feeling a mix of shame and anger. "I was stupid," he admitted. "I teased Marcus into a fight, thinking I could hold my own. But I couldn't. I got beaten pretty badly."

Elijah shook his head. "You know you can't win against them, Kai. They're too powerful and too experienced. Why do you keep trying to fight them?"

Kai shrugged, feeling helpless. "I don't know, Elijah. I guess I just wanted to prove to myself that I'm not weak, that I can fight back. But every time I try, I just end up getting hurt."

Elijah sighed and placed a hand on Kai's shoulder. "You're not weak, Kai. You have a strength that they don't have. You just keep trying to fight everyone and everything all at once!"

Kai looked up at his friend, surprised. "What strength? I can't even control my magic."

Elijah smiled. "You have a kind heart, Kai. You care about others, and you stand up for what you believe in, even if it means putting yourself in harm's way. That's a rare quality in this world, and it's something that they don't have. Don't let them make you think that you're weak just because you can't fight like they can."

Kai nodded slowly, feeling a flicker of hope in his heart.

Elijah stood up and stretched. "Anytime, Kai. Just remember, you don't have to prove anything to anyone. Just be yourself, and the rest will fall into place."

Kai watched as Elijah walked away and eventually sat down on his own small cot in the dorm. The room housed eight members of the Brotherhood, all Journeyman ranked – or under as Kai's case may have been – and not many of them interacted with each other much. It was no surprise though; being a part of the Brotherhood of the Flame was neither pleasant nor easy, and if a mage could make it through an entire week without being badly burnt, then they had managed a lucky week.

Kai lay back down on his own cot, contemplating Elijah's words. Maybe he didn't have to be like the other fire mages, maybe he didn't have to be a great fighter or a powerful spell caster to belong in the Brotherhood of the Flame. Maybe there was something else that he could offer, something that was just as important as physical strength or magical ability. After all, his parents still hadn't learnt a single spell and they had become useful in travelling the roads to and from The Pit to gather food and water. Perhaps he could do that, and then maybe people would take him a little more seriously. And if they didn't, then maybe he just wouldn't give Marcus and his friends any food or water. That would show them who held the power.

Whatever he decided though, it wouldn't change what he had to do tomorrow. It was the end of the week, and that meant that he would be facing off in a tournament against the other mages of his rank.

There had always been around thirty Journeyman mages within the academy and not all of them around Kai's age; some were even in their forties and had their mana awoken in later life. None were younger than Kai though, and he was pretty thankful that he didn't have to lose in the first round of the tournament week on week to mages who were years his junior.

Chapter 2 – Round 1

When Kai awoke the next morning, the pain he felt had dulled somewhat, but it was still there and as he attempted to move, his body resisted with aches and pains all over. He was just about to roll out of his bed so that he didn't have to bend, when Elijah ran over to him and dropped himself heavily onto the bed. In his hand was a single piece of white paper, and Kai knew exactly what it was; he'd seen this every single week since he'd arrived at The Pit.

"The pairings are in!" Elijah announced with glee.

Kai didn't know why Elijah was always so excited about the tournaments though, his friend never having been past the third round.

"Paired me with one of the good ones then have they?" Kai grumbled, not even looking at the paper. "Dex maybe? Aiden? No wait, don't tell me, it's Nathan or Owen again, isn't it. I bet they'd love that."

"Nope," Elijah said. "I've got Owen in the first, and if I win that I'll have Nathan in the second… kinda sucks actually," he trailed off and looked thoughtful for a moment.

"Well?" Kai asked. "Who have I got?"

"It's Lyra," Elijah said with a smile.

"Lyra?" Kai repeated. "But she's an Apprentice, isn't she? Or has she now surpassed me too?"

Elijah shook his head with a smile. "They've demoted you to Apprentice!" he announced happily.

Kai rolled his eyes but couldn't help but feel a wave of disappointment within himself. Being demoted to an Apprentice meant that he was now ranked below all the other Journeyman mages in the Brotherhood, including his current tormentor Marcus' crew: Owen and Nathan. It was a blow to his ego, but at the same time, he couldn't deny that it was probably where he belonged. He hadn't made any progress in his magic, and he couldn't even win a fight.

But Lyra... that was a surprise. The small, brown-haired girl was his own age, she was kind and gentle, with a smile that could light up a room. She was also one of the few mages who had never made fun of him or treated him like he was weak. Kai felt a glimmer of hope, maybe he could win this fight, and maybe he could prove to himself that he was still a fire mage, even if he wasn't the strongest or the most powerful.

"Thanks, Elijah," Kai said, managing a small smile. "Do you think they'll make me change dorms though?"

Elijah shook his head. "Nah, don't think so. I mean I've never heard of a mage being demoted before so you know, don't quote me on it. But I reckon it'd be too much hassle." Then he looked thoughtful again. "Anyway, what do you think? You can beat Lyra, right? She's been here what, a month?"

"Two," Kai said as he looked back at Elijah. The boy was a couple of years his senior but always had the time to talk to him or help him out. He wasn't popular, but had the ability to drift between cliques, making friends and acquaintances along the way. He had dark brown hair like Kai, and his eyes shone with a deep red that betrayed his mana within.

Kai shrugged. "I don't know, Elijah. I mean, I've never seen her fight before, but I don't think she's the type to go all out. She's not like the others."

Elijah nodded. "Yeah, I get what you mean. But don't underestimate her, Kai. She might surprise you."

Kai nodded, feeling a sense of determination wash over him. "I'll do my best," he said. "Besides, it's not like I've ever won a single fight anyway, why should this be any different?"

Elijah grinned. "That's the spirit, Kai. Just remember, you don't have to be the strongest or the most powerful to win. Sometimes, all it takes is a bit of strategy and a lot of heart."

Kai smiled back, feeling grateful for Elijah's support. "Thanks, Elijah. You always know how to make me feel better."

Elijah patted Kai on the back and the gesture hurt Kai more than he wanted to admit. "Anytime, man. Just don't forget to eat something before the tournament. You need all the energy you can get."

Kai nodded, though his thoughts had already turned to the tournament.

After eating a small breakfast of eggs and bacon – the Brotherhood of the Flame always seemed to have a way of getting hold of the best food - Kai found himself standing in front of the large iron gates that led into the arena, where the tournaments were held each week. He took a deep breath and entered the arena, where he was greeted by the sight of dozens of other mages, all gathered in the stands to watch the fights.

Kai made his way to the seating area, where he immediately ran into Lyra, who must have been waiting for him. She smiled at him, and Kai felt a strange mix of nerves and excitement.

"Hey, Kai," she said, her voice soft and kind. "I heard we're fighting each other in the first round."

Kai nodded, feeling his throat go dry. "Yeah… I guess we are. Sorry about that."

Lyra tilted her head, studying him for a moment. "Are you okay? You look a little nervous. And why are you sorry?"

Kai shrugged, trying his best to play it cool. "I'm fine. Just ready to get this over with. And I mean I'm sorry because you have the pleasure of fighting the very first mage to have ever been demoted."

Lyra smiled again. "Don't worry, none of that ranking stuff really makes a difference anyway, does it? Anyway, good luck, Kai."

Kai watched as she walked away, feeling a strange sense of admiration for her. She was everything he wasn't – confident, friendly, and no doubt skilled with magic even for an Apprentice. He couldn't help but wonder what it would be like to be like her. But then again, after a few years in The Pit, she probably wasn't going to be that cheery either anyway.

Kai took his seat in the stands, watching as the other mages made their way into the arena, ready for their fights. The air was filled with the crackle of magic and the smell of burnt wood, and Kai couldn't help but feel a little overwhelmed. He had never been good at controlling his magic, and he knew that in a fight, that could be a major disadvantage. But he was determined to try his best, to show everyone – including himself – that he was still a fire mage, no matter what his rank said.

The Grandmaster of the Brotherhood was an imposing figure, standing tall and broad-shouldered with a regal bearing that commanded respect. His dark hair was streaked with silver, and his eyes shone with a sharp intelligence and a bright red glow that seemed to pierce through anyone he looked at. He wore long, flowing robes of deep red, embroidered with gold thread that glinted in the light of the arena.

As he stepped forward to address the assembled mages, the Grandmaster as usual took the time to introduce himself as Master Orthos, though he needed no introduction as the most powerful mage in the Brotherhood by far. His reputation preceded him, and many of the mages in the audience looked up at him in awe and reverence.

Grandmaster Orthos' voice was deep and commanding, and he spoke with a confident and measured tone that only years as a skilled and powerful mage could generate. He laid out the usual rules of the tournament, reminding the mages that the use of deadly force was strictly prohibited, and that any who broke the rules would face severe consequences. Torture and excessive force, though, was not strictly against the rules and by most accounts, it was widely encouraged.

"My brothers and sisters. Today, we begin the weekly tournament, where we will test our skills and prove ourselves worthy of the Brotherhood of the Flame. As usual, we will begin with the Apprentices, followed by the Journeymen, Masters, and finally the Archmages." He looked to the stands where the mages sat and smiled. "This week, we have six brave Apprentices who will fight for their place in the Brotherhood. Next, we have thirty-four Journeymen who will battle it out to prove themselves worthy of advancing to the next rank. We have twenty-two Masters who will face each other in a true test of skill and power. And lastly, we have four Archmages who will compete for the title of the strongest mage in the Brotherhood, beneath myself of course. But remember, my fellow mages, this is not just about winning, but about showing our strength, skill, and honour. May the flames guide you all in your battles and may the best mage win. So let the tournament begin!"

With those words, the Grandmaster stepped back, and the arena erupted with cheers and applause from the gathered mages, all eager to prove themselves in the coming battles.

As he finished speaking, Archmage Orthos surveyed the audience with a piercing gaze, and Kai felt a shiver run down his spine. He knew that he was in the presence of a true Master of the flame, and he couldn't help but feel a sense of awe and fear.

The arena was essentially a large sand pit with sheer stone walls on three sides and stone stands on the fourth. Overhead hung a long tapestry on hoists that held the names of the mages currently competing and although each of the mages knew who they'd be competing against, they didn't know in what order the matches would come. They would have to await their name on the tapestry.

Kai watched as the first names were revealed, and breathed a sigh of relief when his name wasn't shown. He didn't mind the tournament, but he certainly didn't want to go first.

As the tournament began, Kai watched as the first two Apprentices stepped into the arena, both looking nervous and unsure. They were both young, probably only a year or two older than Kai himself, and they looked like they had never fought before.

The audience watched and cheered politely as the two Apprentices awkwardly circled each other, neither one sure what to do. Kai couldn't help but feel a little sorry for them, knowing exactly how it felt to be so inexperienced.

After a few tense moments, one of the Apprentices made a move, throwing a clumsy punch that missed its mark. The other Apprentice retaliated with an elbow and the first Apprentice stumbled back but managed to keep his balance.

The fight continued in a similar manner for a few more minutes, with both Apprentices trading clumsy blows and looking more and more worried as time passed. Eventually, the second Apprentice managed to land a solid punch, knocking his opponent to the ground. The audience cheered as he was then declared the winner.

Kai watched as the defeated Apprentice was helped up by the Brotherhood's doctors, feeling a pang of sympathy for the young mage. He knew that feeling all too well – the feeling of defeat and humiliation. But he also knew that it was all part of the process of becoming a better mage.

As the next pair of Apprentices stepped into the arena, Kai couldn't help but feel a little more confident. If they all fought like that, surely, he had a chance. He just needed to focus, and remember what Elijah had said – sometimes, all it took was a bit of strategy and a lot of heart, not how well you could cast a spell. Apprentices couldn't do any spells anyway, so the playing field had been well and truly levelled for him.

Then the next fight came and went, and that just left Kai to descend the stone steps and take to the arena for his bout. As he walked, he couldn't help but overhear Marcus say quietly as he passed: "Try not to die out there, Apprentice."

Kai tried to ignore Marcus' taunting, knowing that he had bigger things to worry about. He took a deep breath as he stepped into the arena, feeling the sand crunch beneath his boots. The audience was a blur of faces and voices, and Kai tried to focus on the task at hand.

Kai's heart was racing as he stood on one side of the arena, facing Lyra on the other. He could feel the eyes of all the other mages upon them, watching intently as they waited for the fight to begin.

Lyra looked calm and collected, with a small smile on her face as she stared back at Kai. He couldn't help but feel a little worried that he would once again make a fool of himself, but he tried his best to keep his nerves under control.

Then the match began, and Kai and Lyra both took a step forward, their eyes locked on each other. They circled each other for a few moments, sizing each other up, and then Kai made the first move.

He closed his eyes and held his hands out before him as he had tried so many times before. He imagined his mana deep inside swirling, growing like a tornado made of fire and willed it to reach out, cast a spell, make a huge flame – anything - and then all he heard was laughter.

Kai opened his eyes and he saw what was happening. Once again, the only thing that his mana allowed him to do, was conjure a small orange flame in the centre of his hand.

Lyra raised an eyebrow, amused, but not surprised. "Is that all you've got, Kai?" she asked, her tone friendly but with a hint of challenge in her eyes.

And there it was, another mage who had teased him, and no doubt another that he was going to lose to in the tournament.

Or was he?

Kai was bigger than Lyra and probably stronger. She was an Apprentice rank which means she knew no spells, so he could just beat her the non-magical way, couldn't he?

Kai rushed forward, trying to grab Lyra, but she was too quick for him. She easily sidestepped him, and then grabbed his arm and twisted it behind his back, causing Kai to wince in pain. He tried to break free, but Lyra had him in a tight hold.

Kai stumbled as Lyra swept his legs out from under him, and he fell to the ground with a thud. He tried to get up, but Lyra was already on him, pinning him down by mounting him where he had fallen. The crowd cheered loudly at the smaller girl holding Kai down.

Lyra then took a hold of Kai's arm and he struggled to break free, but he simply couldn't and as he tried to fight back, Lyra twisted his arm slowly away from her and he began to feel the pain radiating from his shoulder. He tried with all his might to fight back, but the more he tried to move, the more the hold hurt.

"Tap out, Kai," Lyra practically whispered. "I really don't want to hurt you."

Kai gritted his teeth, feeling frustrated and embarrassed. He didn't want to tap out, but he knew he had no other choice. He tried to hold on for a moment longer, but eventually he had no choice but to tap the ground with his hand, and Lyra released him from the hold. Kai could hear laughter coming from Marcus above everything else.

Sitting up, Kai looked at Lyra with a questioning expression on his face and saw that she was now standing over him with a smile.

"Nice try," Lyra said, extending her hand to help him up. "But you need to work on your technique a bit more. You're stronger than me, but strength alone isn't enough to win a fight."

Kai took her hand, feeling a mix of relief and embarrassment. He had underestimated Lyra's skills and had paid the price for it. He had always thought that brute strength was all that was needed to win a fight, but Lyra had shown him that there was much more to it than that.

"Thanks," he said, standing up and dusting himself off. "I'll keep that in mind."

Lyra nodded, and then turned to leave the arena. As she walked away, Kai heard Marcus call out: "You got your ass kicked by a girl, Kai! How pathetic!" And the rest of the crowds laughed again. Kai clenched his fists, feeling anger rising up in him, but managed to push it away as he walked away from the sands and back to his seat. He knew that starting a fight with Marcus again would do him no good. Especially not here, and right now.

Chapter 3 – How It Should Be Done

With the Apprentices done with their own bouts, next up came the Journeyman-ranked competitors, and first up was Elijah. This was a fight that Kai was especially interested in, because his friend was about to face off against Marcus' friend Owen.

Kai watched eagerly as Elijah stepped onto the sands, a serious look on his face. He knew that his friend was a decent mage, and had been looking forward to seeing him in action again, especially if he planned on casting more of those spells that still seemed so out of reach for Kai.

As Journeyman ranked mages, they could usually cast a moderate spell or two, so the bouts weren't going to be ground-breaking, but watching them still filled Kai with jealousy.

Owen, Elijah's opponent, was average sized Journeyman with dark hair and piercing red eyes. He had a reputation for being one of the more skilled fighters in his rank, and Kai knew that Elijah had a tough fight ahead of him.

The two mages faced off, and the arena fell silent as they prepared to begin. Elijah held his hands out in front of him, his eyes focused and intense, while Owen stood relaxed, a small smile playing on his lips.

Then, without warning, Owen made his move. He lunged forward, his hand outstretched and sent a burst of bright orange flame towards Elijah. Elijah was quick to react and deflected the spell with a wave of his hand, sending the flames harmlessly off to the side.

After the opening salvo, the two mages circled each other, their eyes locked in concentration. Owen made the next move, sending a barrage of tiny, pea-sized fireballs towards Elijah. But Elijah was ready for this, and he responded with a powerful wave of heat, which snuffed out the flames and sent Owen stumbling backwards.

The fight continued like this for several more minutes, with both mages trading spells and trying to outmanoeuvre each other. It was clear that they were quite evenly matched, and the audience was on the edge of their seats, waiting to see who would come out on top. The problem was though, that the spells they could each cast were limited.

Finally, after what felt like an eternity, Elijah managed to land a decisive blow. He conjured a ball of fire the size of his fist, which he hurled towards Owen with all his might. Owen tried to dodge, but it was too late. The fireball struck him in the chest, and he was thrown backwards with a loud cry of pain.

The audience erupted into cheers and applause as Elijah was declared the winner and Kai could see the relief and joy in his friend's eyes as he stepped off the sands, victorious.

As the fights continued, Kai watched in awe as now everyone was able to cast spells with their fire mana: the Eternal Flame within, and he felt the familiar jealousy wash over him again.

But as impressive as their spells were, Kai couldn't help but think back to Lyra and Elijah's words. Strength alone wasn't enough to win a fight. It was all about strategy, technique, and heart. He knew that Elijah had a lot of heart, so with a little strategy and a lot of luck, he would have a good chance of winning his next round.

Elijah had to wait a short while until he would fight in the next round, so he retook to the stands to sit next to Elijah, and the pair spoke about Elijah's fight.

Kai turned to Elijah with a grin. "Nice job out there, man," he said, clapping his friend on the back. "You had him on the ropes."

Elijah chuckled. "Thanks, Kai. It was a tough fight, but I managed to pull it off. I think I got lucky with that fireball, though."

Kai nodded. "Yeah, it was pretty impressive. But I think Lyra was right - strategy and technique are just as important as power."

Elijah looked at Kai, his eyes sparkling with interest. "What do you mean? Do you have any strategies in mind? And Lyra?"

Kai shrugged. "Not really, but I'm thinking that if we can't beat them with our magic, we'll have to outsmart them some other way. She did beat me and with some moves I haven't seen before... it was hard!"

Elijah grinned. "I like the way you think, Kai. Maybe we could try some non-magical moves or even create distractions. No-one above Apprentice really fights with their hands so it could be a surprise kind of thing."

Kai nodded. "Yeah, and if all else fails, we can always just run away," he joked.

Elijah laughed. "Hey, it's not cowardice if it works."

Kai chuckled. "True, true. But I'm not giving up on using magic just yet. I just need to figure out how to use it better."

Elijah nodded. "Of course, and I have faith in you, Kai. You've got a lot of potential, you just need to find the right way to channel it."

Kai smiled, feeling encouraged by his friend's words. "Thanks, Elijah. I'll keep trying."

The two friends sat in comfortable silence for a few minutes, watching the other fights unfold in the arena. Kai found himself studying the other mages, trying to figure out their strengths and weaknesses. Even though he hadn't ever been able to cast any spells of note, if there was one thing he was good at, it was studying.

He had read every book that the small library had to offer on mana, magic, spells and the Eternal Flame – even if the works were limited due to the persecution of mages by King Robert and the city.

He had studied the battles in the arena to see what the other mages did, how they moved and what spells they relied on. He had always just figured that one day he'd get it, and when that day came, he'd have a wealth of knowledge to fall back on.

As the next fight ended, the announcer's voice boomed through the arena, calling out the next pair of competitors and Elijah stood up, ready to make his way back down to the arena.

"Good luck, man," Kai said, clapping Elijah on the shoulder.

Elijah grinned. "Thanks, I'll do my best."

Kai watched as Elijah made his way down to the sands, his heart racing with excitement and nerves. He knew that his friend was a skilled mage, but he also knew that anything could happen in the arena.

The crowd hushed as the announcer called out the names of the two competitors, and then the fight began. Kai watched with bated breath as Elijah and his opponent circled each other, both waiting for the other to make the first move.

His opponent as Elijah had said was Marcus' other crony, Nathan.

Kai's eyes narrowed as he watched Nathan, remembering how he had taunted him before and had even thrown a few punches and kicks at him as he had laid on the ground. He could see the smug grin on Nathan's face as he sized up his opponent, and it made Kai's blood boil. He wanted nothing more than to see Elijah take down Nathan and wipe that grin off his face.

The two mages circled each other warily, their eyes locked in a silent battle of wills. Nathan was slightly taller than Elijah, with broad shoulders and what would clearly grow into a muscular build given a little ,more time. He had a cocky smirk on his face, as if he already knew that he was going to win.

Elijah kept his expression neutral, his eyes focused on Nathan's every move. He knew that Nathan was skilled, but he wasn't going to let that intimidate him.

The first few moments of the fight were tense, with neither mage making a move. Finally, Elijah decided to take the initiative. He raised his hand and conjured a small flame, which he balled and hurled towards Nathan. Nathan easily dodged the spell, and then countered with one of his own. He conjured a blast of heat, which he directed towards Elijah, trying to knock him off balance.

Elijah managed to stay on his feet and then launched another spell. This time, he conjured a slightly larger ball of fire, though it looked as though it took some effort to do so, which he then threw towards Nathan. Nathan managed to deflect the spell with another blast of heat, but then Elijah launched another spell, this time a column of fire from his hand.

Nathan was caught off guard, and the fireball struck him in the shoulder with a crack and a sizzle. The robes of the Brotherhood that they all wore went some way to absorb the flames and heat, but they weren't entirely impenetrable and it caused the Journeyman to stumble backwards with a cry of pain. Elijah saw his opening and rushed forward, trying to follow up with another ball of fire. But Nathan was quick to recover, and he countered with a blast of heat again, which knocked Elijah off his feet. Kai could see just how limited Nathan's attacks were, and although he had a very powerful heat blast spell, it was beginning to get old and surely Elijah would soon find a way to bypass it.

Kai watched as the two mages continued to trade blows, each trying to gain the upper hand as heat and flames lit up the arena as the spells flew, the smell of burning robes and singed flesh too began to fill the arena.

It was clear that the pair were evenly matched, with neither able to gain a clear advantage. But then, as the fight wore on, Elijah seemed to be getting tired. His spells were becoming weaker and less precise, and Nathan was starting to take advantage of this. Physicality, it seemed was playing a part in the battle.

Finally, after what felt like an eternity to Kai, Nathan managed to land a decisive blow. He conjured a huge blast of heat with renewed vigour, which he directed towards Elijah, knocking him off his feet and leaving him gasping for air.

The audience erupted into cheers as Nathan was declared the winner. Kai could see the disappointment in Elijah's eyes as he stepped off the sands, defeated. But despite the loss, Kai knew that his friend had fought with everything he had, and that was something to be proud of. Besides, it wasn't like Kai could do any better.

"He was so strong," Elijah said as he slumped down next to Kai. His robes were still smoking and if Kai was in his place, he was sure he would've gone to see the doctors.

You did great, Elijah," he said, trying to offer some comfort. "You'll get him next time."

Elijah managed a small smile, still clearly disappointed. "Thanks, Kai. I really thought I had him for a moment there, but I just couldn't keep it up."

Kai nodded, understanding the feeling of disappointment all too well. "Don't worry about it. He had one good spell and that's never a good thing. He relies on that blast of heat way too much, you'll see."

The rest of the fights passed in a blur, with Kai studying each mage carefully, trying to learn from their strengths and weaknesses. By the end of the next round, he once again felt as though he had a much better understanding of the Journeyman-ranked mages, and what they had been concentrating their training on in the last week.

As the next round began, Kai and Elijah took to the edge of their seats in the stands once again, eager to see who would come out on top. They watched as the next pair of competitors stepped onto the sands, including Nathan, the mage who had defeated Elijah in the previous round.

Nathan was up against a skilled Journeyman mage named Alina, who seemed to be well-rounded in her abilities. Again, they circled each other, both wary of making the first move. Nathan raised his hand, conjuring his trusty blast of heat, but Alina was ready for it, having seen what he had done in the last fight. She sidestepped the spell with ease and then launched one of her own, a tennis-ball sized ball of fire that struck Nathan on his cheek. The spectators let out a sympathetic groan as Nathen shrieked in pain.

Nathan stumbled, clearly caught off guard by Alina's quick reflexes. He tried to recover and launch another blast of heat, but Alina was too fast. She dodged the spell again and then conjured another ball of flame, which she hurled towards Nathan.

Nathan tried to dodge, but he was too slow. The fireball struck him in the chest this time, and he was thrown backwards with a cry of pain. The audience gasped as Alina then began to raise a small carpet of flame from the ground beneath where Nathan lay. But then it quickly disappeared.

"Alina is the winner!" The Grandmaster's voice came above the sounds of the confused crowds, and it quickly became clear that the battle had been forcibly ended so that Nathan wouldn't be cooked alive right in front of everyone.

Alina was rightly declared the winner, and Nathan stumbled off the sands, defeated, with a very angry look on his face.

Kai turned to Elijah with a grin. "See? I told you he relied on that blast of heat too much."

Elijah laughed. "Yeah, you were right. It's always good to have a backup plan."

Kai smiled. "Exactly. It's all about being well-rounded and prepared for anything."

As the fights continued, Kai and Elijah watched with renewed interest, both studying each mage carefully and trying to learn from what they could see in the fights.

They could see that the successful mages were the ones who were able to adapt to their opponents and use a variety of spells, rather than relying on just one. Kai took mental notes on the different spells he saw, trying to commit them to memory so he could practice them later on. He knew that it was no use to him right now, but he couldn't help but hope that one day he would be at their level. Deep down he knew that he had never really been a Journeyman.

As the final round of the Journeyman-ranked fights passed, Alina proved to everyone that she was not to be messed with, as she used the same spells and quick reflexes to best her opponent once again, but also by using two more spells she hadn't showcased before.

The first spell that Alina hadn't used before was a spell that conjured a wall of fire. As her opponent launched a spell towards her, she quickly raised her hand and conjured a wall of flames that blocked the spell and sent it harmlessly into the air. The crowd gasped in awe at the impressive display of magic.

The second spell that Alina used was a spell that created a dome of fire around herself. As her opponent launched a barrage of spells towards her, she raised her hands and created a shimmering dome of flames that surrounded her, protecting her from the attacks. The dome then dissipated, leaving Alina unscathed and ready to launch her own counterattack.

Kai and Elijah both cheered as Alina was declared the winner of the Journeyman-ranked fights. They were both impressed by her skill and adaptability in battle, and Kai couldn't help but feel a sense of awe and admiration for her.

As the Journeyman fights ended, the next group of fighters would be the

Master-ranked mages, and that was always an impressive showing of might and magical ability.

Chapter 4 – Hostile Tactics

The first two Masters to step onto the sands were Masters Isaac and Helena. Both were known for their mastery of the flame and their devastating offensive spells.

Isaac was a tall, imposing figure with a stern expression on his face. He was dressed in the normal dark robes of the Brotherhood and held his hands in front of him as though he was holding a ball that only he could see. Helena, on the other hand, was a petite woman with long, flowing hair and a serene expression. She wore a simple black gown and let her hands hang down beside her waist.

The crowd fell silent as the two Masters took their positions on opposite sides of the arena. There was an air of tension and excitement, as everyone knew that this would be an exciting bout. They always were though, because once a mage became Master-ranked and beyond, it was because they really knew what they were doing.

Isaac and Helena began to circle each other, their eyes locked in concentration. Suddenly, Isaac launched a massive fireball towards Helena, who deftly dodged it with a quick sidestep. She responded with a spell of her own, creating a swirling vortex of flames that headed straight towards Isaac.

Isaac countered with a another spell, creating a wall of fire that absorbed Helena's attack. The two Masters continued to trade spells, each one more impressive and deadly than the last. The crowd watched in amazement as they unleashed the full extent of their mastery over the element of fire.

It was a battle of power and skill, with neither mage giving an inch. The air around them crackled with energy as they exchanged spells at lightning-fast speed. Finally, after a fair amount of back and forth, Helena landed the final blow. With a powerful incantation, she conjured a massive column of flame that engulfed Isaac and sent him flying backwards.

The audience erupted into cheers and applause as Helena was immediately declared the winner of the match. She took a deep breath and bowed to Isaac, who returned the gesture with a respectful nod.

Kai and Elijah looked at each other in awe, amazed at the sheer power and skill displayed by the two Masters.

Up next though, was Marcus. And if there was anyone that Kai would have liked to have seen beaten to a bloody pulp, it was him.

Marcus stepped onto the sands with an air of confidence, his eyes fixed on his opponent, Master Ariana. She was a stern-looking woman with short, silver hair and a determined expression on her face. Kai knew that she had some powerful magic, though she was not his first choice for someone to bring the pain to Marcus.

The audience fell silent as the two mages took their positions. Kai could feel his heart racing as he watched, still hoping that Marcus would finally get what was coming to him.

The match began, and Marcus wasted no time in launching a barrage of fire spells at Ariana, over and over his hands moved swiftly and released fireball after fireball at his opponent, and Kai couldn't help but think that if these spells were coming towards him, he would've been killed in an instant. But Ariana was quick and nimble, dodging each spell with ease and when she saw a tiny opening, she then retaliated with a spell of her own, conjuring a burst of flames that engulfed Marcus and sent him tumbling to the ground.

Marcus quickly righted himself and although he still had a smile upon his face, it seemed a little more forced than it had been previously.

Kai couldn't help but feel a sense of satisfaction as he watched Marcus struggle. For once, he was the one on the receiving end of a powerful spell, and it was clear that he wasn't enjoying it.

Ariana continued to launch spells at Marcus, and he struggled to keep up, constantly dodging and weaving to avoid being hit.

Then Marcus cast a wall of fire that started to move and slowly worked its way across the arena, and Kai couldn't see how Ariana was going to avoid it. The flames were intense, their heat causing beads of sweat to form on Marcus' forehead. Then Kai watched, mesmerized, as Ariana calmly walked towards the wall of fire, her eyes fixed on Marcus. Just as the flames were about to engulf her, Ariana raised her hands and closed her eyes. Kai could practically feel the energy building around her, and then suddenly, she opened her eyes and walked straight *through* the spell that threatened to engulf her.

Marcus looked surprised for a moment, but then he quickly regained his composure and launched another barrage of fireballs at Ariana, but they seemed rushed, like he was worried that after everything he had tried so far, he had been unable to harm her. Ariana dodged and weaved, her movements graceful and fluid. Kai could see that she was just waiting for the right moment to strike.

Suddenly, Ariana raised her hands and conjured a massive ball of fire between them. Her spell was so quick and so perfectly executed that Marcus had no chance to stop her. The ball grew larger and larger, until it was the size of a boulder, and then she hurled it towards Marcus. The ball struck him squarely in the chest, knocking him off his feet and sending him flying backwards with a surprised look upon his face.

The audience gasped as Marcus crashed to the ground, and for a moment, there was silence.

Then, as if on cue, the crowd erupted into cheers and applause. Kai felt a sense of satisfaction wash over him as he watched Marcus struggle to get back to his feet and the crowd turned silent.

Marcus was not defeated yet. He stood back up and for some reason that Kai couldn't fathom, Ariana waited for his to do so.

With a now very angry expression, Marcus launched another barrage of fire spells at Ariana and as he did so he let out a fierce cry of determination.

Ariana ducked and dodged as best she could, her movements becoming more erratic as the wave of flames and heat continued. But it was clear that she could not stand against this for much longer.

Kai could see now that Ariana was tiring, and he knew that she couldn't keep this up forever. He watched, helpless as Ariana retreated further and further, until Marcus simply let his spells dissipate and he ran at her at full speed. Marcus launched himself at Ariana and clasped her around the waist, the pair tumbling to the ground and as soon as Ariana's back had hit the sand, he had straddled her with a bright orange flame held to the ready in his hand, aimed menacingly in her face.

In that moment, Kai, Elijah, and the entire crowd saw the look of absolute hatred in Marcus' eyes. Not hatred for Ariana, who looked scared beyond all belief, but hatred for the audacity that someone had thought they could best him in a fight.

Marcus let the spell disappear and stumbled to his feet, looking confused and disoriented, and perhaps a little sheepish. Kai watched as he made his way off the sands and although he was the victor, the crowd remained silent after the anger they'd all just witnessed.

"A great show of force!" the Grandmaster announced to bring the spectators back to a state of enjoyment. "Let's just hope nobody wakes Marcus up too early, hmm?" there were a few nervous laughs returned, but at least the silence had been broken.

As the Grandmaster tried to bring the crowd back around to the fun side of the tournament, Kai couldn't help but feel disgusted by what he had just witnessed. He had wanted Marcus to lose, but he had never expected him to turn into whatever that was.

Then he felt something deep down inside of him stir. Like it had just felt something that it recognised, and Kai didn't know what it was. A moment passed and the feeling disappeared and Kai turned his attention to the next fight about to begin on the arena sands.

During the next fights, Kai couldn't stop thinking about what he'd seen in Marcus' eyes. The anger and hatred, it almost made him shiver.

Of course, Kai knew that there was more to being a mage than just raw power and strength. It was about control and discipline, and Marcus had shown none of those traits in his fight with Ariana.

As the Masters' fights continued, Kai watched in newfound amazement as they conjured up spells that were beyond his wildest imagination. They were able to create massive pillars of flame that reached towards the sky above, as the arena had an open ceiling. They could summon infernos that could engulf entire companies of soldiers, and would manipulate flames into intricate patterns and shapes.

But even as he watched in amazement, Kai couldn't help but feel a sense of envy. He had taken a step backwards, and it made him feel sick.

The fights eventually came to an end, and the Grandmaster declared the winners of each category. All but the Archmages who would fight in a four-way battle royal for the ultimate title of arena champion. Of course, the title was usually short-lived as each week a new Archmage would take the title, having developed a tactic to beat the previous winner, but it was a solid title nonetheless.

Kai felt a mixture of excitement and nervousness as he watched the Archmages step onto the sands. These were the most powerful mages in the arena, and they were all vying for the same title. That was of course except for the Grandmaster, who seldom actually fought in front of the others.

The four Archmages were: Master Lucas, a tall, muscular man with a fierce reputation for his powerful spells; Master Sofia, a serene-looking woman with long, curly hair and a reputation for her precise and calculated attacks; Master Alexei, a young and brash mage who had recently made a name for himself with his unorthodox tactics; and finally, Master Malik, a wise-looking elder who had been a staple in the arena for years and was known for his knowledge and experience.

The crowd was buzzing with anticipation as the four Archmages took their positions, each one eyeing their opponents warily. Then, with a sudden burst of energy and a fanfare of flame, the fight began.

Kai watched in amazement as the incredibly skilled fighters launched spells at each other with incredible speed and precision. The spells themselves were much larger and faster than any that ever Marcus had cast, and as they flowed freely from the Archmages, the arena filled with heat and smoke because of the sheer volume of fire mana that was on display.

Master Lucas conjured up massive walls of fire that towered over the other mages and high into the air, while Master Sofia created intricate webs of flames that ensnared her opponents and burnt their flesh without prejudice. Master Alexei was constantly on the move, his spells smaller but quicker than the blink of an eye – which was unpredictable and hard to counter, while Master Malik seemed to be everywhere at once, his spells striking with deadly accuracy before he launched himself away again to find his next vantage point.

The tension in the arena was palpable, and Kai felt his heart racing as he watched the mages weave their spells with incredible skill and finesse.

It was difficult for Kai to keep track of the action as the four Archmages darted around the arena, launching spell after spell at each other. He could see that the other spectators were also struggling to follow the action, with gasps and cheers erupting from different sections of the crowd as various spells connected or missed their mark.

Master Lucas' wall of fire was an impressive sight, towering high above the other mages and sending waves of heat throughout the arena. But even as the other mages struggled to find a way around it or in some cases *through* it, Master Sofia's intricate webs of flames proved to be just as deadly, ensnaring any of her opponents unlucky enough to get in its way.

The Archmages were clearly evenly matched, each one displaying an impressive amount of control and power as they fought. It dawned on Kai though, that these Archmages weren't actually trying to kill each other – if one were to be in an actual fight, he didn't know how anyone at all would stand against them.

Suddenly, a massive explosion rocked the arena, sending flames and debris flying in every direction. For a moment, the arena fell silent as everyone looked around in shock and disbelief, trying to figure out what had happened. Then, as the smoke cleared, Kai could see that it was Master Alexei who had caused the explosion. He had conjured up a massive ball of fire and launched it at the ground beneath himself, causing a chain reaction of spells that had resulted in the explosion.

The audience erupted into cheers and applause as Master Alexei smiled as he watched the other three Archmages fall to the ground, but his expression quickly changed when all three of them returned to their feet. The battle hadn't been won yet.

The three Archmages then launched their own barrage of spells at Master Alexei all at once, who deftly dodged and weaved his way through them. It was like watching a dance as the four mages moved around each other, spells flying in every direction.

It was then that Kai noticed something strange. It wasn't a three-on-one between the Archmages, as Master Malik had been slowly moving around the arena. Master Malik had been biding his time, waiting for the perfect opportunity to strike. And when that moment finally came and he was out of sight of Master Alexei, he launched a powerful spell that impacted and sent Master Alexei tumbling to the ground.

Master Malik then turned his attention to the other two archmages, but they were ready for him. Master Sofia launched a barrage of fireballs at him, while Master Lucas conjured up a massive wall of flames to trap him. But Master Malik was too quick for them still, dodging and weaving his way through their spells with incredible agility.

Master Sofia though took a newly found advantage and turned to weave a spell around her momentary comrade, Master Lucas. She was simply too close and Lucas was too preoccupied with Alexei to have done anything about it. Master Sofia's web had quickly entangled Master Lucas and removed him from the battle.

And then there were two. Masters Sofia and Alexei took a moment to peer across the arena sands at each other for a long moment, each of the mages' shoulders rising and falling as they breathed heavily after the toll of the battle so far had been paid.

Then with a powerful incantation and an ear-piercing scream, Master Sofia conjured up a massive ball of fire that she hurled towards Alexei with all her might. He managed to mostly dodge the great fireball, but it glanced his chest, sending him spinning backwards and crashing to the ground before he righted himself again, still panting.

Master Alexei, still reeling from the impact, struggled to regain his footing as Master Sofia closed in on him. He raised his hands in front of him, ready to defend himself as she launched another spell in his direction.

But just as the spell was about to strike him, Master Alexei conjured up a powerful wall of flames that shielded him from the attack. Master Sofia's spell dissipated harmlessly against the wall, and she looked surprised for a moment before launching another attack.

The two mages continued to exchange spells, each one trying to gain the upper hand. But as the battle continued, it became clear that Master Alexei was slowly losing ground. His spells were becoming weaker and slower, and he was beginning to tire.

Then, with a final burst of energy, Master Sofia launched a powerful fireball at Master Alexei's head.

But Kai noticed something about this spell and it took him a moment to realise what it was. The spell had been aimed slightly higher than he would've expected, the ball of fire not sent hurtling towards Master Alexei's face, rather at the very top of his head. He couldn't figure out what had caused the misaim, but he didn't have to wait very long to find out. Master Alexei ducked the spell easily as though on instinct, and as he did so, Master Sofia called forth a tendril of red flame to erupt from the ground and wrap itself around Alexei's neck.

Master Alexei brought both his hands up to his neck to tug on the flames, and he screamed with effort as he tried to pry the spell free. But it was no use and after a few tense moments, he dropped to his knees and ceded the fight.

The crowd erupted into cheers and applause as Master Sofia was declared the winner of the battle. She took a deep breath and bowed to her opponents who had awaited the end of the battle, acknowledging their skill and strength. Kai watched in awe as the Archmages stepped off the sands, their heads held high and their spirits unbroken.

As the audience began to disperse, Kai and Elijah made their way towards the exit from the arena, their minds still reeling from everything they had witnessed.

"That was insane!" Elijah said, breaking the silence between them.

Kai nodded enthusiastically. "Yeah, it was. So amazing! I still can't believe how powerful the Archmages are. Every week they just get better and better, don't they?"

Elijah grinned. "Just wait until you become a Master yourself. You'll be even more powerful." Then he winced, remembering that Kai's next steppingstone on his path was not Master rank, rather Journeyman.

Kai ignored the slip of the tongue and chuckled. "I've still got a long way to go."

Chapter 5 – Friends

Kai and Elijah stood at the edge of the arena, watching as mages began to take to the sands to begin their training for the day. As usual, the ranks seemed to remain segregated, with Apprentices staying with Apprentices, Journeymen with Journeymen and Masters with Masters.

As Kai watched, he noticed Lyra standing on the sand facing off against another Apprentice, a large boy who looked fairly confident that he would be able to best the smaller girl.

"I can't believe she beat me," Kai said somewhat distantly as he took in her stature once again. A Apprentice, and small, he should've been able to hold his own with her at least.

But before Elijah could reply, the pair watched as Lyra's opponent flung himself at her, and she simply stepped out of the way. It was actually quite amusing to watch Apprentices train as without any spells to call upon, they usually just fought with their fists and hoped for the best. Sometimes it would end up in one of those awkward headlocks where nobody knows quite what to do.

Elijah chuckled. "Well, maybe she just caught you off guard. And Alina beating Nathan? That's impressive too."

Kai shook his head. "I still can't believe it. Nathan is one of the strongest Journeymen I've seen. And Alina, I didn't even know she was that good. Has she always been able to do those things?"

Elijah shook his head. "Just one of those things I guess. People can change so fast and learn new spells and techniques, it's what this place is all about, right? Plus, it just goes to show that you can never underestimate your opponents. Everyone has their own strengths and weaknesses, and you never know what they might be hiding."

Kai sighed. "I guess you're right. I just need to focus on my own training and get better. I can't let myself fall behind like that again.'

Elijah gave him a reassuring smile. "You'll get there, Kai. Just keep pushing yourself and you'll be right back with us in no time. But… if you fall back again… I don't think there's a rank for that!" Elijah smiled and Kai threw him a very small smile. It was a funny statement, but what Elijah had said was the truth.

Then the pair watched as the fight between Lyra and the larger boy continued, though like a raging bull and with each of his unsuccessful charges, the boy seemed to get more and more annoyed.

Lyra remained calm and collected, dodging his attacks with ease and striking back with precise hits that sent him stumbling backwards. It was clear that she was well-trained and had honed her skills to a fine point and it filled Kai with awe and wonder.

Kai couldn't help but also feel a twinge of envy as he watched her move with such grace and confidence. At least the longer he watched her fight, the better he felt about losing to her.

The larger boy charged again, throwing a wild punch that Lyra easily dodged. She ducked under his arm and wrapped her arms around his waist, then lifted him off his feet and slammed him to the ground. The boy grunted in pain, but before he could react, Lyra had taken his back and applied a rear-naked choke.

The boy struggled to free himself, but Lyra held on tight, her arms squeezing his neck with incredible force. After a few moments of struggling, the boy went limp, and Lyra released her hold, standing up and brushing off her clothes as if nothing had happened.

Kai and Elijah watched, mouths open as Lyra walked away from the boy, who was now being attended to by a medic. "Wow," Kai said, "I had no idea she had those kinds of skills."

Still watching Lyra as she walked, Kai then realised that she was walking towards *them*.

Lyra approached them, a small smile on her face. "Hey, guys," she said. "How's training?"

"Just watching some of the fights," Elijah replied. "And we just saw you take down that big guy. That was pretty impressive."

Lyra chuckled. "Thanks. I guess I just got lucky."

Kai shook his head. "It wasn't luck. You clearly know what you're doing."

Lyra shrugged. "I've been training for a while now. And besides, size isn't everything in a fight. I just hope that when I learn some spells soon, it's all still useful stuff to know."

Kai nodded, still impressed. "Yeah, I can see that. I guess I still have a lot to learn."

Lyra grinned. "We all do. That's the beauty of being a mage. There's always something new to discover."

Kai looked at Lyra for the first time. Really looked. She had long brown hair tied into a tight pony-tail and bright red eyes that seemed to sparkle with energy and excitement. There was just something friendly about her that made Kai feel totally at ease in her presence.

Then another female voice reached the three as they stood to the side of the training arena.

"Everything OK, Lyra?" Alina asked as she walked over to the group.

Lyra nodded. "Yeah, just talking to Kai and Elijah. How about you?"

Alina smiled. "I'm still going strong. I've got a couple more fights to get through before I can call it a day."

Kai looked at Alina with newfound respect and just couldn't help himself: "I heard you beat Nathan. That's pretty impressive."

Alina blushed. "Thanks. Nathan is a tough opponent, but I managed to catch him off guard."

Elijah spoke up. "It seems like the two of you are really making a name for yourselves in the ranks."

Lyra and Alina exchanged a look before Lyra spoke up. "We're just trying our best. It's not about making a name for ourselves, it's about improving and becoming the best mages we can be."

Kai couldn't help but smile at her words. "You know, you're both pretty inspiring. Maybe I'll start training a little harder."

Alina and Lyra both laughed. "That's the spirit, Kai," Alina said. "We're all in this together, trying to improve and become the best mages we can be."

Kai took a moment to appraise Alina as she spoke. She had long, flowing black hair and bright red eyes that betrayed inner fire. Her skin was smooth and unblemished, and she had a lithe, athletic build that suggested she was in excellent shape.

"Hey," Lyra said suddenly. "Why don't we all train together? I mean, Kai and I are Apprentice ranked and you two are Journeymen, so we might all have something to learn, right?"

Kai and Alina both looked at Lyra, considering her suggestion. It seemed like a good idea, and they were all here to improve their skills.

"I'm up for it," Kai said, glancing at Alina to see if she was interested.

Alina nodded. "Sure, let's give it a try."

Lyra grinned. "Great! Let's go!"

Kai, Lyra, Alina, and Elijah quickly made their way to the centre of the arena, where they began to set up a makeshift training area in a wide circle. Lyra explained that they would be doing a type of training called "Shark Tank," where two fighters would be in the centre, and the others would take turns fighting them one at a time until they were beaten. It sounded exhausting to Kai, but he was prepared to do whatever he could to get some progress.

Lyra stepped forward and offered to be the first fighter, while Alina and Elijah began to warm up and practice their fireballs, juggling small balls of fire as though it was the easiest thing to do in the world. Kai tried his best not to look too envious.

Then Kai turned his attention back to Lyra, as she began to demonstrate some hand-to-hand, grappling style moves. The first was something she called a double-leg takedown, that made dropping a larger opponent to the ground so much easier.

It sounded simple, but as Kai watched and tried the move for himself on Lyra, he realised that he had a lot to learn. Where she had moved with fluidity and grace, her movements calculated and efficient where his were clunky and unrehearsed. She effortlessly took down Kai in a matter of seconds, but he was unable to return the favour.

With Kai soundly defeated, it was now Elijah's turn to face Lyra. Elijah, aware of Lyra's limitations, focused on his basic fire spells, launching small fireballs at Kai to keep her at bay.

Lyra skilfully dodged the fireballs, closing the distance between herself and Elijah and as she moved in for a strike, Elijah used his magic to enhance the force of a punch of his own, forcing Lyra to block the punch by crossing her forearms.

Then Lyra moved to the offensive and began to strike out at Elijah with her hands and feet, forcing him to constantly adapt his defences. Lyra feinted a punch and then quickly switched to a leg sweep, causing Elijah to stumble.

Seizing the opportunity, Lyra then executed the double-leg takedown on Elijah, bringing him to the ground.

Panting from the exertion, Lyra released Elijah and stood over her fallen opponent, who grinned and gave him a thumbs up.

"Nice work, Lyra! You're a stone-cold killer!," Elijah said, clearly impressed. "Where did you learn all that?"

Lyra smiled, her eyes gleaming with pride. "Thanks, Elijah! I learned these moves from my older brother. He's a skilled martial artist, and he used to train me when we were younger. I figured it would come in handy someday, even though I can't cast magic like you guys yet."

Kai, who had been watching the bout, couldn't help but feel inspired by Lyra's performance. It was clear that even without magical abilities, Lyra was a formidable fighter.

Alina stepped forward to challenge Lyra next and it was clear that Lyra was tiring. Instead of relying solely on her fire spells this time, Alina decided to incorporate some hand-to-hand combat techniques as well. She launched a few small fireballs at Lyra, who deftly dodged them, before moving in close to engage her physically.

The two exchanged a flurry of blows, their movements fast and fluid. Lyra managed to block most of Alina's strikes, but Alina's magical enhancements gave her a definite edge. With a well-timed punch, Alina knocked Lyra off balance and followed up with a swift kick, sending her tumbling to the ground.

"Great fight, Lyra!" Alina said, offering her hand to help Lyra up. "You're really tough, even without magic. I had to give it my all to keep up with you."

Lyra accepted Alina's hand, grinning despite her defeat. "Thanks, Alina. You're an amazing fighter too. I'm glad we're all on the same team!"

The friends continued to take turns in the Shark Tank, each round pushing them closer and closer to fatigue, but with each new battle, they all learned something new.

The only problem was that Kai didn't win a single round. In fact, he didn't even come close. He did his best not to let it get to him, but deep down, once again he felt ashamed.

After a few more rounds of fighting, it was Kai's turn to step into the ring again. He was still nervous, but he would press on nevertheless.

Lyra was the previous victor and already proved herself a formidable opponent, so he knew that he would have to do something special to stand a chance.

Kai squared off against Lyra, taking a few steps back before launching himself at her in an attempt to catch her off guard. She had been on for a few rounds in a row now so at least she would be tired, and hopefully a little slower than before.

Lyra quickly dodged Kai's attack, grabbing him by the arm and flipping him onto his back. Kai scrambled to his feet, but before he could react, Lyra had taken him down again, this time applying a choke hold that left him gasping for breath.

In the entirety of the training session, Kai lost every single fight he was a part of. But in truth, against Alina and Elijah, he would have no chance as their magic would be able to best him every single time. He had hoped to at least pose Lyra a threat, but the smaller girl was just so technical that he had no idea where he would even begin with her.

Eventually, the group finished up their training and made to leave the sand in search of dinner.

Lyra turned to Kai as they walked. "So, what did you think of the Shark Tank training?"

Kai grinned. "It was intense, but I loved it. I feel like I learned a lot from you and everyone else, but I feel like I'm always going to be behind."

Lyra smiled reassuringly and patted Kai on the back. "Don't worry, Kai. We'll always all be better at different things. It's true that you don't have the magic abilities that Alina and Elijah have, but that doesn't mean you can't become an excellent fighter. You just need to focus on honing your own skills and developing your own unique fighting style. Trust me, you'll catch up. I mean when I first started, I'd have no chance against anyone out there. But it's about practise, not about natural ability."

Kai nodded, appreciating Lyra's encouragement. "You're right, Lyra. I can't compare myself to you guys all the time. I need to focus on improving myself. I think I can do that."

As they walked together towards the large dining hall, the group continued to chat and share their experiences from the Shark Tank training. They discussed new strategies and techniques they could incorporate into their training sessions, as well as ways to support each other in their growth as fighters and mages.

Chapter 6 – Revenge

The dining hall was a large room with stone walls, floors and even tables. On the walls, someone had managed to hang deep red tapestries which did go some way to at least cheer the place up a bit, otherwise it would simply be a sea of grey. Three stone tables had been filled with a veritable banquet by the workers in The Pit as they usually were around meal times, and the group took their seats at the end of one, as far away as they could be from everyone else in the hall.

As they settled into their seats, the aroma of the delicious food filled the air, causing their stomachs to grumble in anticipation. Roast meats, fresh vegetables, and warm bread filled the tables, as well as an assortment of fruits and desserts. It was clear that the workers at The Pit took great care to provide hearty meals for everyone, despite the rough environment.

The friends filled their plates and began to eat, enjoying the food and each other's company. Laughter and conversation filled the space around them, creating a sense of camaraderie that extended even beyond their small group.

Then somehow the air around them all turned stale, and their conversation was interrupted by the arrival of a group that Kai had rather not have seen. Marcus, the Master-ranked mage, led the group, followed by Nathan, the Journeyman-ranked mage who had been beaten by Alina in the tournament, and Owen, also a Journeyman-ranked mage who had lost to Elijah in the previous tournament.

The trio approached Kai, Lyra, Alina, and Elijah with smug expressions, clearly intending to intimidate them. Marcus folded his arms across his chest and looked down at the group disdainfully.

"Well, well, if it isn't the Apprentices and their little Journeyman friends," Marcus sneered. "I heard you were all training together today. How cute."

Nathan chimed in, his eyes narrowing at Alina. "It's nice to see you're taking pity on the weaker ones, Alina. But don't forget, there's a reason they're still Apprentices."

Owen glared at Elijah, the memory of his defeat still fresh in his mind. "You just got lucky last time, Elijah. Don't think it means you're better than us."

The atmosphere at the table had turned tense, as Kai and his friends exchanged glances, trying to gauge each other's reactions. Instead of rising to the bait, Alina spoke up calmly.

"We're all here to learn and grow as mages," she said, her voice steady. "There's no need for hostility. We're all on the same side, after all. We are all here to eventually lead the fight against King Roderick and his stupid laws against mages, right?"

Marcus scoffed, shaking his head. "You're all so naïve. In the end, only the strong survive. Remember that. It doesn't matter how noble your cause is. If you're weak, you die, it's as simple as that."

With that, Marcus turned as if to leave, but then seemed to change his mind half way through the motion. Instead, he leaned in closer, his eyes fixed on Kai. "You know, it's a shame you couldn't win a single fight in your little training session. What a disappointment you must be."

Kai clenched his fists under the table, trying to control his anger. Lyra placed a reassuring hand on his arm, but her eyes were also filled with rage. Alina and Elijah exchanged worried glances.

Nathan, eager to join in the mockery, smirked at Alina. "I guess you really do have a soft spot for the weak, don't you? Must be hard to be stuck with a bunch of losers."

Owen's gaze settled on Elijah, his voice dripping with contempt. "Yeah, it's not like you're anything special either, Elijah. You'll never be as strong as us. It's a shame really…"

Marcus, Nathan, and Owen laughed cruelly, their laughter echoing through the dining hall. The other occupants of the room had become silent, watching the confrontation with a mixture of curiosity and concern.

Elijah's eyes narrowed, but he kept his voice calm and measured. "Look, we're not interested in fighting with you guys. We're here to eat and have a good time with our friends. Can't we just let it go and move on?"

But Marcus wasn't ready to let it go. He slammed his hand down on the table, making plates and cups rattle. "Oh, we'll let it go, all right. But only after we teach you all a lesson you won't forget."

Nathan and Owen nodded agreeably, cracking their knuckles menacingly. They seemed eager to escalate the situation further, and it was clear that they wanted a physical confrontation.

Alina sighed and stood up, her eyes filled with determination. "Fine. If you want a fight so badly, then let's do this. But not here. We'll meet you out in the training grounds. We don't want to involve innocent people in your petty squabbles."

The bullies grinned maliciously, accepting the challenge. "You're on. Meet us in fifteen minutes. We'll be waiting," Marcus said, his voice dripping with anticipation.

Kai, Lyra, Alina, and Elijah exchanged a glance, knowing that they couldn't back down now and each of them couldn't help but feel like they'd made a terrible mistake. They quickly finished their meals, their appetites diminished by the prospect of the upcoming fight. As they left the dining hall, they could feel the eyes of the other mages on them, whispering about the impending confrontation.

Once outside, the four friends huddled together to discuss their strategy. "We need to be smart about this," Alina said, her voice serious. "They're strong, but they're also arrogant. We can use that to our advantage."

Lyra smiled. "Yeah, we need to work together and use our strengths. We may not have the same magical abilities as them, but we're resourceful and determined. We can do this."

Elijah clenched his fists, his eyes filled with resolve. "Let's show them that we won't be intimidated or bullied. We're stronger than they think."

Kai took a deep breath, trying to calm his nerves. He knew that this fight would be tough, but he also knew that he couldn't let his friends down. "Together, we can do this," he said, looking at each of them in turn.

With their resolve steeled, the four friends headed towards the training grounds, ready to face the bullies and prove their worth.

As Kai, Lyra, Alina, and Elijah reached the training sands, they slowly walked out into the centre of the arena but their three opponents were nowhere to be seen.

Suddenly, Marcus, Nathan, and Owen appeared from the far side of the sands, Marcus, with a definite cruel grin on his face. Before anyone could do or say anything, the Master-ranked mage quickly conjured a wall of flames around Alina, separating her from the rest of the group.

"You'll have to deal with Nathan alone, Alina," Marcus taunted, his voice echoing through the wall of fire. "We'll see how strong you really are when the stakes are a little more realistic, right?"

Alina's eyes narrowed, and she steeled herself for the fight, peering through the flames. Kai, Elijah and Lyra called out to her, but they all knew that there would be no passing through this spell for them.

Nathan didn't have the same issue though, and he approached her, walking straight through the flames with a smug expression on his face.

Kai, Lyra, and Elijah could think of only one thing to do: they had to face Marcus and Owen as Alina and Nathan replayed their duel, but as they moved to approach the Master-ranked mage, he summoned another flame wall that kept everyone separated. Owen watched the wall of flames with a shocked expression, clearly not expecting Marcus to take things this far. Marcus, however, seemed to revel in the chaos he had caused. It seemed like Marcus didn't care if he had help in this fight or not; he was content to deal with everyone in whichever way he saw fit.

Back within the ring of fire, Alina and Nathan exchanged a flurry of blows, their magical abilities clashing fiercely. Nathan was powerful, but Alina's skill and determination gave her the upper hand once again. She dodged and countered his attacks, gradually wearing him down. She also had some newfound experience with hand-to-hand combat to draw upon, which would no doubt be a game-changer for her. She'd beaten this fool once already anyway, so she knew she could do it again.

Nathan started by launching a series of fireballs towards Alina, trying to keep her at a distance. However, Alina was quick on her feet, dodging the projectiles with ease and moving closer to the Journeyman. Instead of relying on magic, she decided to close the gap between them and engage in hand-to-hand combat.

Nathan, caught off guard by her sudden approach and wild change of tactics, tried to create a barrier of fire to keep her at bay. But Alina anticipated his move and swiftly slid under the flames, emerging unscathed on the other side. She closed in on Nathan and delivered a powerful punch to his chest, momentarily stunning him.

Alina didn't let up; she continued her relentless assault with a flurry of kicks and punches, pushing Nathan back on his heels. Nathan tried to counter her attacks with fire-enhanced strikes, but Alina's agility and speed allowed her to evade and deflect most of them.

Realising that his fire magic wasn't going to be enough to overpower Alina, Nathan switched tactics and attempted to grapple with her himself. He lunged at her with both hands outstretched, trying to catch her off guard, but Alina was prepared as she had dealt with this very situation in training this very day. She sidestepped Nathan's advance and swiftly locked one of his arms into a painful armbar, putting a fair amount of pressure on the back of his elbow.

Nathan gritted his teeth in pain, but then couldn't help but howl in pain as his struggling caused the technique to pull at his arm harder and harder. His face contorted as he struggled to free himself from Alina's grip but it was no use.

Desperate, Nathan summoned a small burst of fire from his free hand, aiming it at Alina's face. Alina quickly released the armbar and narrowly ducked the flames, feeling the heat singe her hair.

Not wasting any time, Alina continued her offensive, this time landing a series of body blows that further weakened Nathan. She then executed a perfectly timed leg sweep, knocking him off his feet and onto the ground. Before Nathan could recover, Alina moved in and wrapped her arms around his neck to secure a chokehold, cutting off his airflow and preventing him from casting any more spells.

Nathan's face turned red as he struggled for breath, his hands desperately clawing at Alina's arm. Just as he was about to lose consciousness, Marcus' voice travelled through the walls of flame.

"You're not going to win that easily," Marcus snarled and looking up in surprise, Alina could see that Marcus had entered into their arena of battle, his eyes now burning with anger.

Marcus then launched a basketball-sized fireball at Alina, forcing her to release her grip and cover herself with a protective shell of fire just before the attack landed. The only positive was that the walls of fire that had segregated the sands had now fallen, with Marcus' attention transferred to Alina.

Before Marcus had been involved, Alina had skilfully combined her new hand-to-hand combat and grappling techniques to outmanoeuvre Nathan, proving that magic wasn't the only path to victory in a battle. But Marcus was there to remind her that a Master-ranked mage was a completely different story.

Kai, Lyra, and Elijah shouted their objections, but Marcus ignored them, focusing all of his rage on Alina. They realised now though that they had a chance to take on Marcus together, with Owen stepping back in shock at Marcus's unbridled fury.

The three friends charged at Marcus, their determination and teamwork surely giving them an unexpected advantage. However, Marcus was a Master-ranked mage, and his power was not to be taken lightly. He managed to fend off their attacks with superior speed and agility, but it was clear that he was struggling to maintain control over the situation. A four-way battle was never going to be easy, even for a Master.

Kai, Lyra, and Elijah fought with everything they had, using their various abilities, spells and newfound techniques to push Marcus back. With every strike and counter, they showed Marcus that they were not to be underestimated, but the Master seemed able to keep up with the three, shrugging off spells and dodging swipes whenever they came at him.

Despite the intense battle, Marcus's anger seemed to grow even stronger, fuelling his magical abilities. Owen watched from the side-lines, his face a mixture of shock and disbelief at the sheer force of Marcus's fury. But he simply watched and did nothing more.

Then Marcus had had enough, and with a roar, Kai felt the effect of his next spell before it was even cast; the heat that preluded the magic was enough to cause sweat to wet his face in an instant.

The air around Marcus shimmered with heat as he gathered his power, his anger fuelling the flames that now danced around him. Kai, Lyra, Elijah, and Alina braced themselves for the impending onslaught, but the look of sheer dread for what was coming was evident in all their faces.

With a deafening roar, Marcus raised his arms and from his body, he unleashed a torrent of fire that surged towards the group as though it was a wave of pure crimson. They desperately tried to shield themselves with their arms, and the Journeyman-ranked mages Elijah and Alina cast a weak protective shell around themselves. Kai and Lyra had no means of defence against this spell though.

The wave of fire approached and Kai felt the heat cascading towards him. Deep down he knew that he could feel the anger in the spell that would surely end his life, and in that moment he heard that tiny voice inside his soul saying: 'Pathetic. Weakness. Unworthy.'

Then at the last moment, Elijah and Alina stepped before the pair of Apprentices and stood in the wake of the spell.

The protective shell that Elijah and Alina had cast around themselves expanded, encompassing Kai and Lyra as well. It shimmered with a warm orange light, a stark contrast to the fiery red onslaught that was mere moments from reaching them and Kai immediately felt the shell pushing back against the heat that approached.

As the wave of fire crashed against the shield, the heat and pressure returned with a new intensity. The shield flickered, threatening to give way under the relentless assault. But Elijah and Alina stood strong, their faces contorted with concentration as they poured all of their remaining energy and mana into maintaining the barrier.

Kai and Lyra, feeling the intense heat and pressure from the spell, looked on in awe and gratitude as their friends risked everything to protect them.

The shield would not last long though. Marcus was far too powerful for his spell to be quashed by a pair of Journeyman-rankers. Surely only seconds remained and then, with a final, resounding boom, the torrent of fire dissipated, leaving the four friends standing in the midst of the training sands, surrounded by a thin layer of smoke and no sounds, only silence. The protective shield had held just long enough before it collapsed, a testament to the power and determination of Elijah and Alina.

As they all caught their breath, the friends exchanged looks of relief and gratitude. They knew that they had just faced a life-threatening situation, and they had come out victorious.

As the fire began to subside, the friends were still standing, their clothes singed and faces streaked with sweat and soot. Their resilience and teamwork had saved them from the worst of Marcus's fury, but something told them that this wasn't over yet.

Elijah, thinking quickly, looked at Marcus who was doubled over and he took advantage of the Master's momentary exhaustion, casting a blast of heat that pushed him back. The sudden blast caught Marcus off guard, causing him to stumble, yet again he showed just how powerful he was when he kept his balance and unfolded himself to his full height.

Seizing the opportunity, Lyra and Kai launched a synchronized attack, both charging at Marcus where he stood. As they ran though, Kai couldn't help but notice the look of delight on Marcus' face.

"What is going on here?" Boomed the unmistakable voice of Grandmaster Orthos and the sheer weight and tone almost made Kai fall over as he charged.

Grandmaster Orthos had appeared just in time, his commanding presence bringing an immediate halt to the ongoing chaos. Everyone on the training sands froze in place, their faces a mixture of fear, guilt, and surprise.

Marcus quickly composed himself, trying to hide the delight that had been so evident on his face moments before. He attempted to mask his expression with one of feigned innocence, as if he had not been the instigator of the entire situation.

"We were simply testing our skills, Grandmaster," Marcus replied smoothly, but the flicker of uncertainty in his eyes betrayed his truth.

Orthos' gaze swept over the group, taking in their battered appearances and the damage around the training sands. It must have been clear to him that this was no ordinary training session; the destruction and the intensity of the battle were far beyond what would be considered acceptable.

"I do not think that this has been a fair test of strength. There is no honour in harming others who have no business sharing the sands with you," the

Grandmaster said sternly, his voice echoing across the sands. " I am deeply disappointed."

He fixed his piercing gaze on Marcus, making it clear that he knew exactly who he was talking to. "Fighting amongst ourselves will only weaken our cause," he continued, his voice heavy with disapproval. "We should be united against our true enemy, not tearing each other apart."

Silence fell over the group as they all lowered their heads, ashamed of their actions. Even Marcus seemed momentarily chastened by the Grandmaster's words.

Orthos sighed, rubbing his temples. "I want all of you to clean up this mess and then report to my office immediately. We will discuss the consequences of your actions and how to prevent such incidents in the future."

The group all nodded, fully aware of the gravity of the situation. As they began to clean up the training sands, they couldn't help but feel a sense of relief that the battle was over and that they had been spared any further harm. But at the same time, they noticed that Nathan and Owen hadn't been on the sands when Orthos had arrived, and that Marcus himself had turned and left too, just after the Grandmaster. It seemed that being a Master-ranked mage had other perks too, and one of those was not answering for your misdeeds.

Chapter 7 – Snitch

The Grandmaster's office was a spacious, well-lit room, filled with shelves that held countless books and scrolls. An enormous wooden desk stood at the centre, covered in neat stacks of parchment and a variety of magical artifacts. The walls were adorned with tapestries depicting great battles and moments in mage history, while tall, arched windows let in beams of sunlight that illuminated the dust motes dancing in the air.

Kai, Lyra, Alina, and Elijah entered the office with a mix of trepidation and curiosity, unsure of what to expect in their meeting with the Grandmaster. As they stood before his desk, they couldn't help but glance around at the impressive collection of knowledge surrounding them.

Grandmaster Orthos sat behind the desk, his piercing eyes surveying them with an unreadable expression. After a moment, he spoke.

"First, I want you to tell me everything that happened that led you four to think that you would be able to stand against a Master-ranked mage. And one as skilled as Marcus. I want to know how all of this started, and what exactly happened to lead to the situation where I would find four mages below Master rank all seemingly happy to charge towards their deaths."

Kai, Lyra, Alina, and Elijah exchanged nervous glances, realising that it was time to come clean about the events that led to the confrontation. Kai, being the most composed of the group, took a deep breath and began to speak.

"Grandmaster Orthos, we were all training together on the sands when Marcus, Nathan, and Owen approached us. They suggested a friendly match to test our skills and to learn from one another. We agreed, believing that it would be a valuable learning experience for us all."

Kai continued, carefully choosing his words to avoid implicating Marcus in any wrongdoing. "The match began, and we all gave our best efforts. However, as the intensity of the battle grew, it seemed that we lost control of our emotions and magic. It was never our intention to harm one another, but things escalated quickly."

Lyra chimed in, reinforcing the story. "We did our best to defend ourselves, but Marcus's power was overwhelming. We are grateful that you arrived when you did, Grandmaster."

The Grandmaster peered back at the group and it looked to them all as though his eyes were searching for something more. After a short pause, he spoke again.

"Is there anything else that you have to tell me?"

The four friends exchanged nervous glances once more, each contemplating whether or not to reveal the full truth about Marcus's actions. They hesitated for a moment, unsure of what to say. Finally, Kai decided to address the Grandmaster's question.

"No, Grandmaster," he replied, his voice steady but holding a hint of uncertainty. "That is the whole story. We simply got carried away during the training match and we are grateful for your intervention."

Grandmaster Orthos studied their faces for a few more moments, searching for any signs of deceit. Eventually, he sighed and leaned back in his chair. Either he had been soundly fooled, or he simply didn't want to acknowledge the truth.

"Very well," he said, his tone serious but not unkind. "I will take your words at face value. However, I must remind you all that trust and honesty are essential components of our cause. We cannot afford to have secrets or hidden agendas amongst ourselves. If there is ever anything that needs to be brought to my attention, do not hesitate to do so."

The four friends nodded solemnly, understanding the gravity of the Grandmaster's words. They silently vowed to remain truthful and united in their mission, even though they knew they had just kept the truth about Marcus from him.

"Thank you, Grandmaster," Alina said, speaking for the group. "We will remember your words and strive to uphold the values of our order."

Orthos narrowed his eyes again as he contemplated Alina's words. Then he sighed again. "It is crucial to remember that we are all on the same side, and we must support each other in our mission to oppose King Roderick's oppressive regime." Then his gaze lingered on them for a moment longer before he dismissed them from his office.

As they left, each of them couldn't help but feel a mix of relief and unease about the situation they had just navigated. They knew that they had managed not to get Marcus into trouble with the Archmage – if they got a reputation as snitches then their lives would no doubt have been far worse - but they also couldn't shake the feeling that perhaps it wasn't the right decision. They understood that unity was essential in their fight against King Roderick, and they worried about the potential consequences of their actions.

Once outside the Grandmaster's office, the four friends huddled together, discussing their next steps. It was clear that they needed to be more cautious in their interactions with Marcus, as well as with Nathan and Owen.

"We have to be careful," Kai warned. "We were lucky this time. And we need to watch our backs around Nathan and Owen as well. They escaped at some point while we fought Marcus, but I don't think we've heard the last from any of them."

Lyra nodded. "We should focus on our training and our mission. We can't let these incidents distract us from getting as strong as we can."

Alina and Elijah shared determined looks. "You're right," Alina said. "We have a responsibility to uphold the values of our order and fight against King Roderick's tyranny. We must stay united and support one another, no matter what challenges we face."

Then at that moment, Marcus rounded a corner ahead of them and as he saw the group huddled there, his face twisted in a mixture of warring emotions, pure hatred for each and every one of the group, and a forced smile that gave Kai the chills.

Marcus reached the group and whispered to them all in a tone that was almost imperceptible.

"This isn't over. And if you've been stupid in there," he nodded towards the Grandmaster's office, "I'll get you. I don't care where you hide, how far you run, I'll get you, each and every one of you."

The four friends exchanged nervous glances as Marcus stalked away, his threat still hanging in the air. The gravity of the situation seemed to weigh heavily on them, but they knew that they couldn't let fear dictate their actions.

"We can't let him intimidate us," Elijah whispered, trying to muster some courage. "We need to stay strong and focused. It's the only way we'll make it through this."

Lyra clenched her fists, determination sparkling in her eyes. "He's right. We need to keep our heads up and stick together. We can overcome anything as long as we have each other."

Kai nodded, his resolve growing stronger with each of their reassuring words. "We'll continue training and improving ourselves. If Marcus or anyone else tries to stand in our way, we'll be prepared to face them."

Alina looked at her friends, her expression filled with pride and admiration, but also tinged with fear. "We've come this far together, and we'll continue to face whatever comes our way. As long as we remain united, there's nothing we can't overcome… but then… he was so strong wasn't he?"

The group remained silent for a moment as the question hung in the air until eventually, Lyra said: "I don't know about you guys, but I'm starving."

The group let out a collective sigh, grateful for the change in topic. "You're right," Kai said with a slight smile, "all that fighting and talking with the Grandmaster has worked up quite an appetite."

Elijah chuckled, the tension beginning to dissipate. "Come on, then. Let's head to the dining hall and refuel ourselves. We'll need the energy for our upcoming training sessions."

As they made their way to the dining hall, the conversation shifted to lighter topics, like their favourite foods and stories about previous feasts they had attended. Their laughter and camaraderie filled the air, temporarily overshadowing the looming threat of Marcus and the challenges that awaited them.

Upon reaching the dining hall, the four friends piled their plates high with steaming, fragrant dishes, eager to satisfy their hunger. They sat down at their usual table, surrounded by fellow mages who were also enjoying their meals and discussing the day's events.

As they ate and chatted, the group couldn't help but glance around the room, watching their fellow mages with a newfound sense of wariness. They knew that they needed to be cautious, both in their dealings with Marcus and in navigating the complex web of relationships within their order.

"So Lyra," Kai said with his mouth full of juicy steak. "You said your older brother taught you to fight? That must've been a wild ride?"

"Yeah, I don't buy it," Elijah chimed in. "No-one gets that good by training with their brother. It's like you're superhuman or something."

Lyra smiled warmly. "Yep, just me and him, day in day out for as long as I can remember. He was always patient, kind, and dedicated to helping me become the best fighter I could be. He saw potential in me and never gave up, even when I struggled or felt like I couldn't go on."

Alina looked at Lyra, admiration in her eyes. "That's amazing. It just goes to show the power of having someone believe in you and support you every step of the way."

Elijah nodded, his previous scepticism replaced by respect. "You're right, Lyra. Having someone who truly believes in you can make all the difference. I'm sorry I doubted you."

Lyra waved off his apology with a good-natured laugh. "Don't worry about it, Elijah. We all have our own paths to becoming the best version of ourselves. For me, it was my brother's unwavering support. For others, it might be something completely different. Like who knows what Marcus' deal is."

Kai smiled. "So is your brother here in the Brotherhood of the Flame?" but he immediately regretted his words when he saw Lyra's face fall and tears begin to well in her eyes.

"My family… all of them… Roderick…" she started to say, then composed herself.

Kai immediately realised his mistake and reached out to place a reassuring hand on Lyra's shoulder. "I'm so sorry, Lyra. I didn't mean to bring up painful memories."

Lyra gave a small, sad smile and wiped her tears away. "It's okay, Kai. You didn't know. My entire family were taken by King Roderick's forces and executed. They're all gone. But I'm still here and I'll never stop fighting for what's right."

The table fell silent, each of the friends processing the heavy news. Alina reached out and grasped Lyra's hand, offering a silent show of support.

"I'm so sorry, Lyra," Elijah murmured, his eyes filled with empathy. "We're here for you, and we'll do everything we can to make sure their sacrifices weren't in vain."

Lyra nodded, her eyes filled with determination. "Thank you, all of you. I know we're fighting for a just cause, and I'll do everything I can to honour their memories and carry on their legacy."

"What about the rest of you?" Lyra said in an attempt to change the subject.

Kai took a deep breath before speaking, "My parents are still alive, thankfully. And they're right here in The Pit. They both have mana… but they're Apprentices and never learned how to cast any spells. They work here now and really, I'm thankful that they're safe…"

Alina chimed in, "My family was part of a community of mages that lived in hiding, trying to escape persecution from the King's forces. When the Brotherhood found us, they offered us protection and a chance to join their cause. My parents stayed behind to help safeguard the hidden community, but I chose to fight. I want to create a world where we don't have to live in fear."

Elijah hesitated, then sighed. "My story is... different. I was an orphan, found and raised by a kind, old mage who taught me everything about magic. He was like a father to me. But King Roderick's soldiers discovered our home and killed him. I barely escaped with my life. I joined the Brotherhood to avenge his death and ensure no one else suffers like I did."

The rest of the meal passed with lighter conversation, as the friends did their best to focus on the present and the camaraderie they shared. When they finally finished eating, they decided to head back to their rooms to rest and prepare for the next day's training.

That night, as they lay in their beds, each of them couldn't help but reflect on the events of the day and the bonds they had formed with one another. The threat of Marcus and the challenges that awaited them were ever-present, but they also found strength and solace in the knowledge that they weren't alone.

Chapter 8 – Living Arrangements

The four friends met early the next morning at the training grounds, their breath visible in the chilly air that descended in through the open roof – which would no doubt be a good thing when some of the larger spells would erupt within the battles.

The group had prepared themselves for a rigorous session, as today was another day of 'Shark Tank,' the unique training exercise introduced by Lyra to test their magical abilities and combat skills in a high-pressure environment, with little rest between.

The Shark Tank worked like this: each participant would face off against a series of opponents, one after another, with only brief pauses between bouts. The goal was to see how long they could last and how well they could adapt to different fighting styles and strategies. It was both physically and mentally demanding, pushing mages to their limits and forcing them to dig deep to find the strength and resilience needed to succeed whilst fighting against fatigue from fighting new and fresh opponents over and over.

As the exercise began, Elijah and Lyra were the first to step into the ring, squaring off against each other. Their fellow mages gathered around the edges of the training area, eager to watch the match unfold.

Kai and Alina stood together, their eyes locked on the fight as they exchanged observations and encouragement. As the battle between Elijah and Lyra began, Alina leaned in and spoke to Kai in a low voice.

"Hey, Kai, I've got some good news," she said, a hint of excitement in her tone. "I've made arrangements for the four of us to share a dorm... if that's something you'd want. The Pit has plenty of space, and being a Journeyman-ranked mage has its perks. If we all want to, we can move in today."

Kai's eyes widened with surprise, but he quickly smiled at the idea. "That sounds great, Alina. Living together could definitely help us build stronger bonds and support each other even more. I'm in, and I'm sure Elijah and Lyra will be too. I think it'd be a good idea for us to stick close together too, just in case Marcus and his gang decide to go at us again."

Alina grinned, pleased with his response. "I thought you'd like the idea. We can talk to them after the Shark Tank and start moving in this afternoon."

Their attention returned to the fight, where Lyra was unleashing a flurry of powerful spells and Elijah expertly dodged and countered her attacks. The two friends were a whirlwind of motion, their magic crackling in the air as they pushed each other to new heights. Smoke and fire billowing out of their makeshift ring.

The Shark Tank exercise went on for hours, with each participant testing their limits and learning valuable lessons from their successes and failures. When it was finally over, Kai, Alina, Elijah, and Lyra regrouped, sweaty and exhausted but filled with a renewed sense of purpose. Once again, Kai was the only member of the group who had not won a single bout.

"You want some good news?" Kai asked, panting.

Elijah, still catching his breath, raised an eyebrow. "I could use some. What's up?"

Kai grinned, trying to hide his own exhaustion. "Alina's managed to arrange for us to share a dorm. She figured we could use the extra support, and it'll help us stick together in case Marcus or anyone else tries anything. We can move in today if we're all on board. I don't know how she did it, but it sounds great to me!"

Lyra's eyes lit up at the idea, and she nodded enthusiastically. "I think that's a fantastic idea. It'll definitely help us grow closer as a team and watch each other's backs."

Elijah smiled, his weariness momentarily forgotten. "I'm in. It'll be nice to have a place we can call our own, where we can trust the people around us."

Alina beamed at their positive reactions. "Great! Once we're cleaned up, we can start moving our stuff to the new dorm. And it wasn't anything too difficult, I just asked, and the Grandmaster agreed!"

After showering and changing into fresh robes, the four friends gathered their belongings and made their way to their new shared living space. Upon entering the new dorm, they found a large, comfortable common area with a few chairs. A large, comfortable looking sofa, a small kitchenette, four private bedrooms, and a shared bathroom.

Kai's eyes bulged at the absolute upgrade they had managed to bag.

"How…" he started, then tried again. "How did you do this?" he asked in total awe. "It's like a five-star hotel compared to where we were before!"

"Oh I don't know," Elijah said. "The windows in the other dorm were bigger so they let more light in, this one's a bit dark if you ask me."

Kai turned to look at Elijah incredulously, and when he did so he could see from the smile in his friend's face that he was joking.

Alina laughed at their exchange, clearly pleased by their reactions. "Well, I had to pull a few strings and call in a couple of favours," she mocked, "but I thought it would be worth it for us. Plus, having Journeyman-ranked mage status has its advantages too you know."

Lyra grinned and playfully nudged Alina. "You never cease to amaze us, Alina. Thanks for setting this up. It's going to make a huge difference in our lives."

Elijah nodded enthusiastically, his earlier teasing giving way to genuine appreciation. "Yeah, seriously, Alina. This is incredible. We owe you big time."

Alina waved off their thanks with a modest smile. "Don't mention it. We're in this together, and I wanted to make sure we had the best possible environment to support each other and grow as a team."

As they began unpacking and settling into their new home, a sense of camaraderie filled the air. They laughed and chatted, sharing stories and inside jokes as they set up their personal spaces. By the end of the day, the once-empty dorm had been transformed into a cosy, inviting space that radiated warmth and friendship.

The four friends quickly grew accustomed to their new living arrangements, finding comfort and safety in their shared space.

Kai's room was much smaller than the dorm he had slept in the night before – but it was his own. He had his own door! For the first time since joining the Brotherhood of the Flame, he felt like he truly had a place of his own, a sanctuary where he could escape the chaos of the world outside and find solace. He still couldn't believe that Alina had managed to swing this. Perhaps the Grandmaster felt sorry for them?

There was a small bed, a wooden table and a wardrobe in his room and nothing else, but he knew that as he collected more and more personal items as time went by, he now had a place to keep them and maybe even display them!

It may have seemed like he was taking way too much from having a simple room, but for Kai, he hadn't had a place of his own in so so long, and the feeling of personal space was incredible.

In honour of their first day in their own place, the group decided to bring their dinner back to the communal part of their dorm and eat together, away from the other mages and the hustle and bustle of The Pit.

Each sat behind their plate, filled with a hearty meal and as they ate, the conversation turned to the history of The Pit, the ancient fort they now called home.

"You know," Lyra began thoughtfully, "I've heard that The Pit was once a fortress used by a powerful desert kingdom, long before it was abandoned and then claimed by the Brotherhood of the Flame. It's incredible to think about the history these walls have seen."

Kai nodded, his curiosity piqued. "Yeah, I've heard similar stories. They say that the fort was built on a strategic location, making it difficult for enemies to approach and giving its occupants a prime vantage point for spotting intruders. Over time, the kingdom eventually fell, and the fortress was left to the sands of the desert. When The Brotherhood took it over, it must've taken so long to clear all that sand out."

Elijah chimed in, "I wonder if there are still hidden chambers or passages beneath the fortress, lost to time and waiting to be discovered. Who knows what kind of treasures or artifacts could still be buried deep within the basement?"

Alina's eyes sparkled with excitement at the thought. "That would be amazing. Imagine finding ancient scrolls, powerful artifacts, or even long-lost magical knowledge. The possibilities are almost endless!"

Lyra grinned. "We should explore the basements and see what we can find. It could be a fun way to spend a day off, and who knows? Maybe we'll make some incredible discoveries that could aid us in our fight against King Roderick."

Kai agreed enthusiastically. "Count me in! It would be like a treasure hunt, and it's not every day you get the chance to uncover the secrets of a long-lost civilisation. Though I have to say, if there was anything down there I think that the Archmages and the Grandmaster would've found it by now."

Elijah and Alina both nodded, sharing their friends' excitement and ignoring Kai's last statement. "Let's do it," Alina said with determination. "We'll gather some supplies, make a plan, and set out to uncover the hidden mysteries of The Pit!"

Kai smiled. It was funny that they could make these plans to go exploring and to uncover some hidden secrets deep below the place they now called home, but somewhere deep inside, he knew that they would probably never actually go through with it.

But the idea brought a sense of adventure and excitement that filled the dorm with an infectious energy, and as they continued to discuss their theoretical expedition, their conversation turned to their own personal goals and ambitions within the Brotherhood of the Flame.

Alina spoke up first. "I want to become a Master-ranked mage and make a difference in this world. I want to use my magic to help protect those who can't protect themselves and fight for justice."

Elijah nodded, sharing Alina's resolve. "I want to learn all there is to learn about magic, and maybe even make my own discoveries that could change how we understand the world. I also want to use my knowledge to make a difference and help those in need."

Lyra's eyes gleamed with determination. "I want to become the best fighter I can be, not just with magic, but with martial arts and strategy as well. I want to be able to hold my own against any opponent and be a force for good in the world."

Kai hesitated for a moment, considering his own goals. "I want to find my place in this world, and I think being here at The Pit is the first step towards that. I want to grow stronger, learn how to fight, and become someone who can make a real difference, even if I can't access my mana like the rest of you."

Elijah slapped Kai on the shoulder with a smile. "Don't you worry, it takes time to become as awesome as us, but if you keep trying… actually no scratch that, you're never going to be as awesome as us, but you can keep trying?"

Kai peered at Elijah for a moment before he burst out laughing. He still felt bad that he was very clearly the weak link in their group, but at least he could laugh at himself if nothing else.

As they laughed together, the atmosphere in the room lightened, and any lingering insecurities amongst the group seemed to fade away. They knew that each of them had their own unique abilities and strengths, and together, they formed a team that complemented and supported one another.

Lyra chimed in, still chuckling. "Hey, we're all learning and growing here. No one expects any of us to be perfect. We're in this together, and we'll help each other become better, stronger mages – and fighters, in your case, Kai."

Alina nodded with a wide smile. "That's right. We're a team, and we'll face every challenge together. And who knows, maybe one day you'll unlock your mana and surprise us all, Kai."

Kai couldn't help but smile at his friends' encouragement. Their unwavering belief in him, despite his limitations, gave him hope and motivation to keep pushing forward. It made him feel warm, loved even.

"Thanks, guys," Kai said, his voice full of gratitude. "I'll do my best not to disappoint you. And who knows, maybe I will unlock my mana one day."

Then as though Kai hadn't said anything at all, Alina turned and leaned in towards Lyra, whispering in her ear. Kai couldn't hear what she had said, but whatever it was, it seemed like Lyra was on board; her eyes had widened and a huge grin covered her face.

"We're going to… uh… do girl things," Alina announced a moment later and she and Lyra both stood up from the soft couch and walked out of the room.

Kai raised an eyebrow, a little confused by their sudden exit. He glanced over at Elijah, who just shrugged, equally puzzled.

"I guess we have the place to ourselves for a bit," Elijah said, trying to sound nonchalant. "We could use the time to practice some spells or work on our combat techniques."

"Nah," Kai said. "That's what the arena's for. Plus we just moved into this place, I don't want to start messing it up already."

Elijah nodded, realising that Kai had a point. "You're right. We should probably find something else to do that doesn't involve throwing spells around in our new home."

Kai thought for a moment, then suggested, "How about we explore the rest of the dorm? We've only really seen our rooms and this common area so far. Maybe there's something interesting hidden away that we haven't found yet."

So that's what the pair did. In truth they found nothing but both of them were pleased regardless; the place was their own and the more they knew about it, the more comfortable it would be.

A short while passed and eventually the hunt got less exciting. Kai had his ear against a wall as he tapped it, searching for the tell-tale hollow thud of a secret compartment, and Elijah was lying on the ground with his arm under the sofa.

That was when Alina and Lyra returned to the room.

"Well?" Alina said, drawing the attention of Kai and Elijah.

When Kai looked at the two girls, his jaw fell and he stood with his mouth hanging open for longer than he'd care to admit.

Alina had cut her hair to shoulder length, and it was now so jet-black that it practically shone in stark contrast to her bright red eyes. Lyra though, Kai had no idea how they had managed it, but her hair was also now completely jet black except for a streak of red that hung down in a tight curl.

"Wow," Kai finally managed to voice, still staring at the girls' new hairstyles. "You two look… incredible."

Elijah scrambled to his feet, his eyes wide with surprise. "Yeah, I didn't expect you guys to come back looking so different. It suits both of you, though."

Alina and Lyra exchanged amused glances before Alina spoke up. "Thanks! We wanted to try something new, and we thought, why not make a change to mark our new beginning here at The Pit? Plus, it's fun to experiment with our looks every now and then."

Lyra nodded, her red streak of hair catching the light as she moved. "I know it's a bit of a shock at first, but we really like how it turned out. And it's a nice reminder that we're all in this together, forging our own path."

Kai and Elijah couldn't help but smile at their friends' enthusiasm and the pair looked at each other for a moment before Elijah spoke.

"Don't even think about it."

"No idea what you're talking about," Kai replied with a grin.

Chapter 9 – An Unexpected Victory

The sun had barely risen the next morning when the group of friends found themselves back on the training sands, ready for another day of rigorous training. Today, however, they wouldn't be participating in the usual Shark Tank exercise. Instead, Lyra had taken the lead, eager to share a specific combat technique with her friends.

Gathered around Lyra, the group listened intently as she explained the move she wanted to teach them – it was a combination: a double-leg takedown followed by a transition into a full mount, and then falling to the side into an armbar. The technique combined elements of grappling and ground fighting, skills that would prove valuable in close-quarter combat situations.

With the others watching, Lyra demonstrated the move with precision and fluidity. She crouched low, shooting in to grab her imaginary opponent's legs, then drove forward with her shoulder, taking them down. In a swift, seamless motion, she transitioned into a full mount, pinning her opponent to the ground. Finally, she fell to her side, trapping the opponent's arm and applying pressure in a textbook-perfect armbar.

The group clapped and cheered as Lyra finished her demonstration, impressed by her skill and eager to learn the technique for themselves. They paired off – Alina with Lyra, and Kai with Elijah – and began practicing the move under Lyra's watchful eye.

At first, their attempts were clumsy and uncoordinated, but with each repetition, they clearly grew more comfortable with the movements. Lyra offered guidance and encouragement, patiently correcting their mistakes and helping them refine their technique.

As they practiced, the friends found themselves growing more and more excited about the move. The takedown was powerful and effective, the full mount was a dominant position that offered numerous opportunities for attack, and the armbar was a painful and potentially fight-ending submission. Together, these elements formed a devastating combination that could easily catch an opponent off guard and turn the tide of battle in their favour.

After an hour of drilling the technique, Lyra called a break. The group collapsed onto the training sands, a little tired, but exhilarated by their progress and the effectiveness of the move.

Once they had rested for a moment and all caught their breath, Lyra spoke.

"So you think you're all ready to try this out in a real fight?" she asked and Kai was the first to nod his head.

"Let's do it," he said enthusiastically and the pair entered the makeshift ring a moment later to begin the fight, Elijah and Alina watching in anticipation.

The two circled each other warily, both aware of the other's plans to shoot in for the takedown, but neither wanting to telegraph their first move. Kai, despite his inability to access his mana and the fact that he had still not won a fight, had improved significantly under the guidance of his friends, or more specifically, Lyra. Lyra, ever the skilled fighter, was determined to put up a good fight, but knew that ultimately this one was weighted heavily in her favour.

Kai suddenly saw an opportunity as Lyra's gaze flashed away from him for just a moment and in a surprising turn of events, he managed to shoot in as quickly as he had ever moved and caught Lyra with the double-leg takedown they had been practising. It was more luck than skill, but he swiftly moved into a full mount just like he had been shown, and then, with a burst of adrenaline, he fell to the side and locked in the armbar.

Lyra had of course for the most part, let all of this happen. Not so much the technique itself, she had simply let her attention wander for a moment to give Kai an opening that she wasn't sure he would take. When he had hit her with the takedown, she had been genuinely surprised at just how effective it had been.

Then something happened.

Lyra's eyes widened in surprise and pain as she found herself trapped in the submission hold.

She winced and tapped Kai's shoulder with her free hand and made to move, but for whatever reason, Kai wasn't letting her go.

"Kai, let go!" she gasped, trying to tap out again. But something was wrong – Kai's grip remained unyielding, and when she saw his eyes, his expression seemed distant, as if he were lost in a trance.

As Kai held the submission, a whispering voice inside his very soul was speaking softly to him, urging him to break Lyra's arm, to prove his strength and dominance. The voice was intoxicating, and Kai found himself unable to break free from its hold as he kept Lyra at his mercy.

Alina and Elijah quickly realised something was amiss and rushed to intervene.

"Kai, snap out of it!" Alina shouted, but her words seemed to fall on deaf ears.

Finally, Elijah managed to pry Kai's grip from Lyra's arm, pulling him off her and throwing him to the sand. Then Kai's eyes cleared, and the dark voice in him vanished, but not before it once again muttered a quiet 'pathetic'.

Horrified by his own actions, Kai immediately began to apologise profusely. "Lyra, I'm so sorry! I don't know what happened… I didn't mean to hurt you!"

Lyra, still recovering from the shock and pain, nodded her understanding. "It's okay, Kai. I know you didn't mean it. But… what happened? and why. Why wouldn't you let me go? Did you *want* to hurt me?"

Kai, still in shock and disbelief, tried to explain. "No, I… I don't know what happened, Lyra. There was this voice inside my head, whispering to me, telling me to break your arm. It was like I was under some kind of spell, and I couldn't control my actions. I didn't want to hurt you, I swear!"

Elijah, who was still standing close by, furrowed his brow in concern. "That's not normal, Kai."

Alina, always the supportive friend, placed a hand on Kai's shoulder. "We'll figure this out together, Kai. Don't worry, we won't let whatever this is hurt you or anyone else." Her smile was warm, but it looked far from comfortable.

Lyra, now sitting up and flexing her arm gingerly, managed a weak smile. "Let's just be more cautious during our training sessions, at least until we know what's going on. And maybe we should bring this up with the Grandmaster ? It's better to be safe isn't it?"

Kai still felt the weight of guilt on his shoulders, but the last thing he wanted to do was tell anyone else about this. " I'm so sorry, Lyra. I think I'll be OK though, plus I don't want to cause an issue with the Grandmaster – I mean I've already been demoted, what's next? I get kicked out of The Pit altogether?"

Lyra smiled. "I don't think so... I mean not now that you've actually won a round after all!" Her smile though did not reach her eyes. If anything, she looked worried at her own words.

Kai forced a weak laugh, trying to keep the mood light despite the gravity of the situation. "You're right, Lyra. Maybe it was just a fluke or something. Maybe I just got overwhelmed. I'll be more careful in the future, I promise."

Elijah chimed in, trying to ease the tension in the room. "Let's not jump to conclusions. It's possible that this was just a one-time thing. We should keep an eye on it, but there's no need to panic yet."

Alina nodded in agreement. "We'll be here to support you, Kai, no matter what. Just make sure to let us know if anything like this happens again, alright?"

Kai took a deep breath, appreciating the support of his friends. "Thank you, all of you. I'll definitely let you know if anything happens again. And I promise to be more careful."

The group, still shaken by the recent incident, decided it was best to continue with their training. After all, the purpose of their sessions was to learn and grow stronger, and they couldn't let their fears hold them back. So, with renewed determination, they resumed their training.

"So Kai," Elijah said mockingly. "You won a round... so up against Alina you go!"

Kai, still feeling guilty about what had happened to Lyra, stepped up to face Alina who had already entered the ring. He couldn't help but feel a mixture of pride and apprehension at Elijah's words, having won his first-ever battle, and against Lyra. It was a small victory, but Kai couldn't shake the worry that he might lose control again.

As they squared off, Alina gave Kai a reassuring smile. "Just take it one step at a time," she said soothingly. "Focus on the technique, and let's both learn from this experience."

Kai nodded, taking a deep breath as he prepared to face her. They began to circle one another, each carefully watching the other's movements, searching for an opening.

After a few moments of sizing each other up, Kai lunged forward, attempting to catch Alina off guard. However, she was too quick for him and grabbed a hold of his head as he attempted the takedown. Kai had no option but to fall to the ground – exactly where he didn't want to be.

Kai then found himself flat on his back, with Alina swiftly transitioning into a full mount position. As she fell to the side and locked in the armbar that he was going to try to use himself, Kai felt a brief moment of panic. He quickly tapped out, hoping that Alina would release him without hesitation.

Thankfully, she did, and the two friends disentangled themselves with good-natured smiles. Kai laughed nervously, trying to play off the loss. "Well, that was definitely a fluke earlier, then," he joked, referring to his win against Lyra. "You really got me there, Alina."

Alina chuckled as she helped Kai back to his feet. "We're all learning, Kai. You'll get the hang of it soon enough. Just keep practising.'

As Elijah entered the ring in Kai's place and began his bout with Alina, Kai couldn't help but feel a lingering worry deep within him. He was relieved that he had managed to avoid losing control again, but he couldn't shake the memory of the voice that had urged him to hurt Lyra.

He knew that he had to stay vigilant and not let himself be consumed by his fears, but the uncertainty of what the voice represented weighed heavily on him. Was it a manifestation of some hidden darkness within him, or an external force trying to manipulate him for some unknown purpose?

Despite his concerns, Kai forced himself to focus on the training session. He couldn't afford to let his fears distract him from the task at hand and as he practised with his friends, he began to regain a sense of control. That though, unfortunately meant that as the day went on, he wouldn't even come close to winning a second round.

The rest of the day's training session continued with Kai pushing himself harder, attempting to improve and learn from his friends. He watched as Elijah and Alina sparred, taking note of their techniques and the fluidity of their movements. Though he couldn't replicate their success in the ring, he was determined not to let that discourage him.

As the hours passed and the sun began to set, the group decided to call it a day. They were all exhausted but satisfied with the progress they had made. Lyra, despite the earlier incident, still encouraged Kai with a gentle smile, letting him know that there were no hard feelings.

As they left the training area and returned to their dorm, the group discussed the day's events and the various techniques they had learned. They shared their thoughts and insights, helping each other understand the finer points of the moves and how to apply them effectively.

Kai, however, couldn't help but feel a sense of disappointment in himself. Despite his best efforts, he hadn't been able to achieve another victory, and the memory of the voice still haunted him. He tried to keep his concerns hidden from his friends, not wanting to dampen their spirits or make them worry about him.

As they ate, Elijah hesitated for a moment before finally mustering the courage to bring up the topic. "Kai," he began, nervously scratching the back of his head, "I don't want to make a big deal out of it, but I think we should talk about what happened during your fight with Lyra."

The room went silent, the laughter dying down as everyone's attention shifted to the matter at hand. Kai's face flushed with embarrassment and guilt as he glanced at Lyra, who gave him a reassuring nod and half-smile.

"I'm really sorry, Lyra," Kai said, his voice filled with remorse. "I still don't know what happened. It was like I was under a spell or something, and I couldn't control myself."

Lyra offered him a kind smile, her eyes understanding. "Kai, it's okay. I know you didn't mean to hurt me. We just need to figure out what's going on and make sure it doesn't happen again."

Alina chimed in, her voice gentle and supportive. "It's important that we stick together and help each other through this. We're a team, and we'll find a way to overcome whatever challenges come our way, together."

Kai nodded, grateful for his friends' unwavering support. "Thank you, guys. I promise I'll do everything I can to make sure it doesn't happen again. I don't want to be a danger to any of you."

Elijah, trying to lighten the mood, playfully punched Kai's arm. "Hey, we all have our off days, right? Just make sure you don't try to break any more arms, and we'll call it even. But if I find out that Marcus is somehow behind this…" he trailed off and Kai wasn't exactly sure how the Master mage would have anything to do with it, but he thought that perhaps anything was possible.

The group chuckled, the tension in the room dissipating as they returned to their meal.

Alina, sensing that Kai was still feeling down, made a suggestion. "Hey, how about we all take little break from training tomorrow? Maybe explore more of The Pit or check out some of those mysterious basement levels? It could be a good way for us to relax and take our minds off things for a while."

The others agreed, excited by the prospect of a day off and the chance to do something different together. Even Kai, who couldn't shake the lingering concern about the mysterious voice, felt a spark of excitement at the idea.

"Yeah, that sounds great," Kai said, managing a genuine smile. "I think we all could use a little break."

The group spent the rest of the evening discussing their plans for the following day, eagerly anticipating their outing. It would be good to do something different, and to do anything that would take his mind off what had happened during the day.

Chapter 10 – Spelunking

As soon as the sun had risen and awoken the group the next morning, Kai leapt out of his bed, threw his robes on and ran into the common area.

"Guys, are you ready for our day of exploration?" Kai asked, his enthusiasm palpable. It was nice to be able to do something that wouldn't involve him being beaten over and over again by his friends.

One by one, his friends emerged from their rooms, rubbing the sleep from their eyes but eventually sharing Kai's excitement for the day ahead.

"It's too early to be this happy," Elijah announced first in a gruff tone.

"Don't be like that," Kai replied chirpily. "Lets get some food in us and we'll all be raring to go in no time!"

As the group finished getting ready, some a little more reluctant than others, they decided to head to the main hall for breakfast before embarking on their exploration. The atmosphere in the hall was lively, with mages of all ranks discussing their plans for the day or sharing stories from their recent training sessions.

As they enjoyed their meal, the conversation naturally turned to what they might find in the basement levels of The Pit.

"I've heard rumours about hidden chambers filled with ancient relics and powerful artifacts," Lyra said, her eyes gleaming with excitement.

Alina nodded, adding, "Some say there are enchanted scrolls and tomes containing forgotten spells and techniques down there that could make us even stronger."

Elijah chimed in with a grin, "Or maybe we'll find a treasure trove of magical items that will make us rich beyond our wildest dreams!"

Kai chuckled at Elijah's enthusiasm, but he couldn't help but feel a spark of excitement at the thought of what they might discover. "Whatever we find, I'm sure it'll be a great adventure. And who knows, maybe we'll even uncover something that can help us get strong enough to beat Marcus next time he decides to be an ass?"

After finishing their breakfast, the group set off in their search of a staircase that would lead them down into the basement levels because, well they'd never actually seen one before.

They wandered through the corridors of The Pit, their eyes scanning the walls and floors for any signs of a hidden passage or secret entrance and after what felt like hours of searching, Kai finally spotted a worn and almost imperceptible symbol etched into the stone floor. He called his friends over, pointing to the faint outline of a spiral staircase.

"Great find, Kai!" Alina exclaimed as they gathered around the symbol and she brushed the undisturbed dust away from it. "Now, how do we open it?"

They carefully examined the area, looking for any hidden mechanisms or triggers that would reveal the entrance to the basement levels. Elijah was eventually the one to discover a loose stone in the wall, which, when pressed, caused the floor to rumble and shift. The stone around the symbol sank, revealing a narrow staircase spiralling downward into darkness.

The group exchanged excited glances before carefully descending the staircase, their excitement growing with each step. The air grew colder, and the atmosphere more foreboding, but they were undeterred by the darkness that enveloped them.

As they continued to descend, their steps echoing through the narrow passageway, the Alina and Elijah cast small flames in their hands so that they could see where they were going. They marvelled at the ancient architecture and the mysterious symbols that adorned the walls. They could sense the history and power that lay hidden beneath The Pit, and they couldn't wait to uncover its secrets.

Finally, the staircase opened into a vast, already dimly lit chamber, its walls lined with countless doors, each one marked with a unique emblem. The group hesitated for a moment, overwhelmed by the sheer number of choices before them.

"Where should we start?" Lyra asked, her voice hushed in the cavernous space.

Elijah shrugged, "Maybe we should just pick a door and see where it leads? We can always come back and try another one if it doesn't go anywhere interesting."

Kai nodded in agreement. "Sounds like a plan. Let's start with that door over there." He pointed to a door marked with an emblem resembling a stylised flame.

They carefully approached the door, their hearts pounding with anticipation. Kai reached out and pushed it open, revealing a long, narrow corridor lined with unlit torches. Elijah and Alina took the lead and began to light torches as they passed them to illuminate the dark hallway.

As they made their way through the passageway, they noticed that the walls were adorned with intricate carvings depicting scenes of powerful mages and legendary battles. They marvelled at the craftsmanship and the sense of history that seemed to radiate from every surface.

At the end of the corridor, the group found themselves in a large chamber filled with shelves upon shelves of ancient scrolls and dusty tomes. They gasped in awe at the sight, their eyes widening as they took in the sheer volume of knowledge that surrounded them.

"Can you imagine what secrets these scrolls might hold?" Alina whispered, her voice barely audible in the hushed chamber.

Lyra gently picked up one of the scrolls, her fingers trembling with excitement. Then she carefully unrolled it, her eyes scanning the paper within.

Kai watched Lyra as her eyes widened in awe and he couldn't help but ask: "What is it?"

Lyra slowly turned to face the group with wonder in her eyes.

"This will change everything you know about fire magic… the difference this is going to make…"

Alina stepped forward, closer to Lyra. "Really?" She asked.

"Nope," Lyra said with a smile as she turned the parchment around so that the rest of the group could see that it was empty.

Kai moved towards the rest of the books and scrolls and found that as he opened them, they too, were all entirely empty.

"Looks like we found an old storeroom then," Elijah said. "Jackpot."

"Shut up Elijah," Alina said with a smile. "At least we found the place. And a hidden staircase? There's bound to be something good down here, right?"

Once they were sure that there was nothing of note in the room, the group turned to backtrack to where the other doors were. As they left the room, though, the hairs on the back of Kai's neck stood up, as though someone was watching him. The still air seemed like it had been disturbed, but when he peered down the flickering corridor, there was nobody there.

"What's up Kai?" Elijah asked as he passed Kai.

"Nothing… it's… nothing," he decided to keep his thoughts to himself. It was probably nothing anyway.

The group continued back to the chamber with the numerous doors, each feeling a renewed sense of determination. They knew there had to be something of value hidden within these mysterious depths and as they scanned the walls again, a particular door caught their eye. It stood apart from the others, made of a strange metal and lacking the intricate carvings found on the other doors.

"What do you think is behind this one?" Lyra asked, her curiosity piqued.

Kai approached the door, tentatively placing his hand on the cold metal surface. "I don't know, but it's definitely different from the others. Let's see what's inside."

With a deep breath, he pushed the metal door open, revealing a small, dark room that held torches around its perimeter. Elijah and Alina quickly lit the torches so that they could see what they were dealing with.

Once they could see inside the room properly, they saw that in the centre stood a single, ominous-looking chair surrounded by chains and restraints coming from an open grating on the ground. The group hesitated at the sight, feeling a wave of unease wash over them.

"What is this place?" Alina whispered, her voice tinged with fear.

Elijah took a step forward, examining the chair and the chains more closely. "It looks like some sort of restraint or torture device. Maybe this was a place where they kept dangerous mages under control?"

Kai shook his head, trying to shake off the disturbing imagery that filled his mind. "I don't like this place. It feels… wrong." His words weren't simply an observation though, because deep down inside his soul, in the place where the voice had come from before, he could feel something. Something he hadn't felt from that place before: fear.

Lyra nodded in agreement. "I don't think we'll find anything helpful here. We should try another door."

But as they all turned to leave, the metal door suddenly slammed shut behind them, all but one of the torches extinguishing and plunging the room into a new dim light. The sound of footsteps echoed through the small space, and as their eyes adjusted to the dim light, they saw the imposing figure of Marcus standing before the door.

"Ah, I see you've found one of the more interesting rooms in this place," Marcus said with a sly grin. "I'm curious to know what you think you'll find down here. Or perhaps you're just looking for a way to get the upper hand on me?"

The group exchanged nervous glances, their hearts pounding in their chests. They knew they were cornered, and they had no choice but to face whatever Marcus had in store for them.

Marcus paced slowly around the room, his eyes flicking between the stunned group and the ominous chair in the centre. He took a deep breath and began to speak, his voice low and steady.

"This chair," he began, gesturing to the intimidating contraption, "was used by powerful fire mages of the past who believed that the best way to increase their affinity with fire mana was to endure intense pain caused by fire itself."

The group exchanged disbelieving looks, unable to figure out why Marcus was even taking the time to explain this to them. He continued, his eyes narrowing as he studied the chair and its intricate restraints.

"They believed that by subjecting themselves to unbearable pain, they could gain a deeper understanding of their element and, in turn, unlock the true potential of their powers. They would sit in this chair, bound by these chains, and allow themselves to be consumed by the very flames they sought to control."

As Marcus spoke, the group felt a chill run down their spines. The idea that such powerful mages would willingly subject themselves to such torture was both horrifying and fascinating. They couldn't help but wonder what would drive someone to take such extreme measures.

Marcus paused, a dark grin spreading across his face. "There's even a rumour that the Grandmaster himself tried this technique but couldn't withstand the pain. That's why this chair hasn't been used since and had been condemned to storage."

Elijah raised an eyebrow, his scepticism evident.

"You're telling us that the Grandmaster of the academy was so desperate to increase his power that he subjected himself to torture? That seems a bit far-fetched, don't you think?"

Marcus' head snapped about, his expression turning serious. "Desperation can drive people to do unimaginable things. And when you're at the top, the pressure to maintain your position can be crushing. The Grandmaster was no exception. He sought to push the boundaries of his power, to explore the depths of his connection to fire mana. And in doing so, he learned a valuable lesson."

Alina couldn't help but ask, her voice barely audible, "What lesson was that?"

Marcus locked eyes with her, his voice grave. "That there are limits to what the human body and mind can endure. That power comes at a cost, and sometimes, that cost is too great for a person to bare."

The group fell silent, the weight of Marcus's words settling heavily on their shoulders. They couldn't help but consider their own limits and the lengths they were willing to go to achieve their goals. Would they, too, be willing to endure such suffering in pursuit of power?

Lyra, her eyes filled with a mixture of curiosity and fear, posed a question. "If this chair hasn't been used since the Grandmaster's time, why is it still here?"

Marcus glanced at the chair, his expression unreadable. "I suppose it serves as a reminder of the lengths people will go to in their quest for power. A cautionary tale, if you will. And perhaps, for some, it's a symbol of the sacrifices one must be willing to make to achieve greatness."

He turned back to the group, his eyes scanning their faces as if searching for something. "But enough about the past. What I want to know is why you're all so interested in these hidden chambers. Are you, too, searching for a way to increase your power?"

The group exchanged wary glances, unsure of how to respond. They knew Marcus was a formidable opponent, and they didn't want to reveal their true intentions. It was Kai who finally broke the silence.

"We're just exploring," he said cautiously, trying to keep his voice steady. "We thought we might find something interesting down here. That's all."

Marcus studied Kai for a moment, his gaze piercing, before slowly nodding. "Very well," he said, his voice taking on a slightly sinister tone. "In that case, I have a proposition for you, Kai."

The group tensed, sensing that something was amiss. Marcus walked over to the chair, running his fingers along the cold metal chains.

"Since you can't use your mana, you're at a severe disadvantage compared to the rest of your peers. But what if I told you that this chair could unlock your true potential as a fire mage? All you have to do is sit in it and experience the pain, just for a moment. Who knows, you might even learn something about yourself."

Kai hesitated, his eyes darting between the chair and Marcus. The idea of willingly subjecting himself to such pain was terrifying, but the thought of finally becoming a true fire mage was undeniably tempting. It had been so long since he actually felt like he fit in.

Of course, he knew that now he had friends, and by all accounts, things were getting better, and he *was* getting stronger under Lyra's tutelage, but he knew that deep down, he was behind. And if nothing changed, that was always going to be the case.

The others immediately objected, their voices filled with concern. "Kai, don't even think about it," Lyra exclaimed. "I know you feel down about your mana, but there has to be another way!"

Elijah stepped forward, his eyes locked on Marcus. "You just told us that the Grandmaster himself couldn't handle the pain. What makes you think Kai can?"

Alina chimed in, her voice shaking with emotion. "You don't have to do this, Kai. We'll find another way to help you with your mana, I promise."

Kai looked around at his friends, their faces etched with worry and fear. But there was something in Marcus's words that resonated with him, a desperate hope that he might finally unlock his true potential. With a deep breath, he shut out all of the noise and made his decision.

"I'll do it," he said quietly, his voice wavering slightly. "If this is what it takes to become a real fire mage, then I'm willing to try."

He didn't have to look twice to see the smile that grew on Marcus' face.

The others protested loudly and even tried to pull him away, but Kai was resolute. He walked slowly over to the chair, his heart pounding in his chest. As he sat down, he could feel the cold metal biting into his skin, the chains heavy and unforgiving. He looked up at his friends, their faces a mix of shock, fear, and disbelief.

The room seemed to hold its breath as Kai settled into the chair, his fate now uncertain. The air was thick with tension, and the group could only watch in stunned silence as Marcus began to close the metal restraints, trapping him in place.

Kai ignored his friends begging to reconsider; it had already gone too far, and he couldn't shake the thought of awakening his mana.

Chapter 11 – Pain and Suffering

The cold metal of the chair bit into Kai's skin as the restraints closed around him. He closed his eyes, trying to prepare himself for the pain he knew was coming. But nothing could have prepared him for the searing agony that suddenly engulfed him as soon as Marcus had done whatever he had to begin the process. The Master-ranked mage must've lit a fire beneath the chair because Kai could hear the telltale crackling of a fire, and the gasps of his friends.

Within a few moments, it felt as if his very soul was on fire, the heat so intense that it threatened to consume him entirely. Without realising it, he opened his mouth and began to scream, his voice echoing throughout the chamber, but the pain only seemed to grow stronger. His friends watched in horror, unable to tear their eyes away from the terrible scene though they knew there was nothing they could do to help.

"Make it stop!" Lyra begged, but Marcus simply watched motionless and wide-eyed.

Elijah moved to try to free him, but the chair had become too hot to touch, as if it was feeding off Kai's suffering. Every time any of the group tried to get close, the heat forced them back, their skin blistering from the scorching air. Desperate, they searched for a way to break the spell, but it seemed as if the device was beyond their understanding.

The pain continued to build, pushing Kai to the edge of his endurance. He could feel his consciousness slipping away, the world around him fading into darkness. Just when he thought he couldn't take any more, a vision filled his mind, transporting him to a time and place that was not his own.

He found himself in the midst of a great battle, the sky above him filled with fire and smoke. He was no longer in his own body, but rather inhabiting the mind and body of a powerful fire mage, commanding the flames with a skill and precision he had never known. The mage's every movement was a dance of destruction, a deadly symphony of fire and death.

Kai could feel the mage's emotions as if they were his own, the thrill of the battle and the burning desire for victory as flames erupted from his hands, engulfing all of the enemies before him. But beneath it all, there was something else, a dark secret that threatened to tear the mage apart. As the vision continued, Kai was drawn deeper into the fire mage's memories, experiencing the pain and suffering that had shaped his life.

He witnessed the mage's childhood, marked by tragedy and loss, and the long, lonely years of training that followed. He felt the mage's struggle to control the raging flames within him, the constant battle against his own destructive nature. And he saw the moment when the mage had first discovered the ancient chair, the promise of power that had led him down a path of darkness and despair.

As the vision reached its climax, Kai could feel the mage's final, desperate attempt to harness the full power of the flames. The pain was unimaginable, a thousand times greater than anything he had ever experienced, and it threatened to shatter his very being. But in that moment, something within him changed, a spark of defiance that refused to be extinguished.

With a final, Herculean effort, Kai forced the flames to recede, breaking free of the terrible vision that had consumed him. The chair, no longer able to contain the power that he had unleashed, shattered into a thousand pieces, the ancient metal melting away as if it had never existed and Kai rose to his feet, covered in white-hot flames that turned the entire room into a furnace. He stood, screaming through the pain for a long moment before crumpling to the ground in a heap, his vision fading to darkness.

Eventually, once the noise and the heat dissipated, Kai felt himself being lifted from the wreckage, voices faint and distant as they carried him to safety. His body felt numb, as if the pain had burned away all sensation, and he was unable to move or even open his eyes. But even as he drifted in and out of consciousness, he knew that something within him had changed forever.

The next time he awoke, the world around him was silent and dark. He tried to open his eyes, but nothing happened, the darkness as complete and unyielding as the void itself. Panic began to set in as he realised the terrible truth: the ordeal with the chair must've left him blind.

He could hear his friends talking in hushed tones around him, their voices filled with worry and guilt. They had tried to stop him from sitting in the chair, and now they were left to deal with the consequences of his actions. He wanted to reassure them, to tell them that he didn't blame them, but he couldn't form the words, his throat dry and raw from his screams.

As they continued to care for him, Kai's thoughts turned to the vision he had experienced, the life and suffering of the fire mage that had somehow become intertwined with his own. He couldn't understand why he had been granted this glimpse into the past, but he felt an undeniable connection to the mage, as if their fates were somehow linked. He didn't know what this war was that he had seen, but he knew it had long passed.

In his mind's eye, he replayed the memories of the mage's life, searching for clues or answers that would help him make sense of his own situation. As he delved deeper into the past, he began to notice subtle patterns and similarities, echoes of his own life that seemed to be reflected in the mage's experiences.

He thought about the mage's struggle to control the flames, and the constant battle against his own destructive nature. It reminded him of his own difficulties with fire magic, the fear that had always held him back and kept him from reaching his full potential. And he remembered the mage's discovery of the ancient chair, the temptation of power that had led him down a dark and dangerous path.

Kai realised that he had been given a unique opportunity, a chance to learn from whoever this was and forge a new path for himself. He vowed that he would not succumb to the darkness, that he would find a way to overcome his newfound blindness – which he hoped beyond anything that was temporary - and become the fire mage he was always meant to be.

As Kai lay there, trying to make sense of his new reality, he could hear gentle footsteps approaching. Someone sat down beside him, their voice soft and soothing as she spoke.

"Kai, we're all here for you," Lyra reassured him. "I know you must be scared, but we're going to help you through this, I promise."

Kai wanted to respond, to thank her for her kindness and support, but his voice still wouldn't come. Instead, he simply lay there, listening to the soothing sound of her voice as she continued.

"We'll be by your side every step of the way, making sure you get the care you need to recover. We'll help you learn how to adapt and cope with whatever changes need to happen."

Kai could hear the optimism and hope in Lyra's words, and it made his heart swell with gratitude. He wished he could tell her how much her words meant to him, but all he could do was listen.

"You're strong, Kai. And you're not alone," Lyra continued. "We're all here, and we'll face this together, as a team."

As she spoke, Kai could feel the warmth of her hand gently clasping his own, a comforting presence that anchored him in the darkness. The reassuring touch helped ease the fear and panic that had threatened to overwhelm him.

But exhaustion began to settle in, and Kai could feel himself drifting off to sleep. As he slipped back into unconsciousness, he held onto the promise of the support and love of his friends, and the hope that they would find a way to overcome the challenges that lay ahead.

Later that night, when the room was quiet and the others had left to get some rest, Marcus entered into Kai's roon. He approached Kai's bedside, his footsteps barely making a sound. He stood there for a moment, as if unsure of what to say.

"Kai... I'm... sorry," Marcus began hesitantly, his voice lacking its usual arrogance. "I never thought that chair would do this to you. I mean, I knew it was dangerous and I knew it was going to hurt, but... I didn't think it'd do all this."

Kai could hear the uncertainty in Marcus's voice, but also the lack of genuine remorse. It was clear that Marcus was still struggling to come to terms with his own role in what had happened.

"But," Marcus continued, his voice regaining some of its usual confidence, "this might be a turning point for you. You have a choice, Kai, to fight or just to give up. Use it to your advantage, learn from it, and come back stronger."

With those final words, Marcus turned and left the room, the sound of his footsteps fading into the distance and Kai once again succumbed to unconsciousness.

A few hours later, the door opened again, and this time the heavy, purposeful footsteps of Grandmaster Orthos filled the room. He made his way to Kai's side and stood there in silence for a long moment.

"Kai, I wanted to explain a few things to you," Orthos began, his deep voice filled with concern. "You should know that the chair was never meant to be used again. It's a relic of our past, a reminder of the lengths some mages were willing to go to in their pursuit of power."

Orthos paused for a moment before continuing, "I, too, once sat in that chair, many years ago. I was young and foolish, believing that the pain and suffering it inflicted would make me stronger. I was wrong. The chair only brought me pain and nearly cost me my life. I was a Master-ranked mage back then and even as powerful as I was, I understand the suffering you have experienced. Oh, and don't worry about your parents. They are out gathering supplies and won't be back for a few weeks, but we have sent them a message so they know what happened."

Kai felt a very real sense of guilt, knowing that his parents would worry for him, but still he couldn't respond.

The Grandmaster sighed, the weight of the memory heavy on his shoulders. "I kept the chair as a reminder of that mistake and a warning to others. But I never expected an Apprentice to find it, let alone use it again. I'm truly sorry, Kai."

Kai listened to Orthos' words, taking comfort in the knowledge that even the Grandmaster had once made a similar mistake.

Orthos placed a reassuring hand on Kai's shoulder. "You have a strong spirit, Kai. With the support of your friends and your own determination, I have no doubt that you will rise above this challenge."

With that, Grandmaster Orthos left the room, leaving Kai to contemplate the path that lay ahead of him.

As he listened to the gentle sound of silence in the room, he felt an odd sense of comfort despite the darkness that surrounded him and it dawned on him that he wouldn't rather be anywhere else but here.

But then he felt somewhere deep down inside that although he was alone in the room physically, there was another presence there with him. He tried to listen as best he could to try to figure out what it was that was causing him to feel this way, but as he listened there was simply silence.

Kai then turned his attention inwards and to the only thing that he had in the quiet and still darkness: his thoughts.

"How could I have been so stupid?" he thought to himself.

"Why did I think that sitting in that chair would be a good idea? What drove me to seek such power, even if it meant risking everything?"

Then he felt something deep down inside of him stir. It wasn't an obvious feeling, rather more like something had heard him and had moved almost imperceptibly.

Then as he focused on this subtle sensation, Kai realised that whatever it was, it was different from anything he had experienced before. It felt like a dormant force within him that had been somehow awakened, or at least shaken up. Perhaps it was by the chair or the shared vision of the past.

Kai pushed his mind down into himself to explore this newfound connection, attempting to communicate with whatever this was through his thoughts. "Is there something there? Can you hear me?" he asked inwardly, hoping for a response or a sign.

To his surprise, he felt the presence within him respond, not with words, but with another feeling of movement, or at least a subtle shifting. To Kai's mind, it was as though this thing within him could hear him, but was choosing not to listen… just like his mana did whenever he had tried to use it.

"I know you can hear me," Kai tried. But this time there was no movement or response.

Frustrated but still curious, Kai continued to focus on the presence within him. He wondered if it was related to his inability to control his mana or if it was something entirely different. Either way, he felt an inexplicable connection to it, and he was determined to understand it better.

As he concentrated on the presence, he tried a different approach, speaking to it with warmth and sincerity. "I don't understand what you are or why you're here, but I know we're connected somehow. I need your help. I'm lost, blind, and I want to become the fire mage I was meant to be. Please, can we work together?"

This time, he felt a slight change in the presence, as if it were considering his request.

A long moment passed, and then Kai felt a surge of pain encompass his entire body. It was like he burnt with a terrible heat from within, but through the pain that inevitably caused him to lose consciousness once again, he heard the one single word ringing throughout all of his being.

"Weakness."

Chapter 12 – A Terrible Secret

Kai awoke some time later, his body still aching from the surge of pain he had experienced. The word "weakness" echoed in his mind, and he couldn't help but feel a mixture of anger and disappointment. It seemed that the presence within him had rejected his plea for help and cooperation, deeming him unworthy. It really was no surprise, he'd never been worthy of, well anything as far as he could remember.

"I know you think I'm weak, but I'm not," he said internally. "I may be blind, but I'm learning and growing every day. I'm becoming the fire mage I was meant to be, with or without your help. But I still believe we can work together, and that we can be stronger as one. So, I ask you again, please, let's join forces and become something greater."

For a long moment, there was only silence, and Kai braced himself for another wave of pain or rejection. But then, to his surprise, he felt nothing more than a subtle shift within him. The presence seemed to stir, and though it did not speak, the only thing that Kai could think, was that the presence had accepted his words and would either help him somehow, or it would stay out of his way.

Over the next two days, Kai focused on his recovery and the connection he had formed with the mysterious presence within him, though the latter saw no progress. He began to notice small improvements in his physical state though, such as a tingling sensation in his fingers and toes where before there was nothing to note. It was as if his body was slowly awakening from a deep slumber. This progress filled him with hope, and he eagerly awaited the day when he would be able to move more freely and regain some semblance of control over his body.

During this time, Kai's friends visited him often, providing him with much-needed comfort and support. They spoke to him about their daily lives, sharing stories and laughter despite Kai's inability to respond in any meaningful way. Their visits were a bright spot in his otherwise dark world, and he cherished each moment spent with them.

On the second day, as Lyra and Elijah sat by his bedside, Kai mustered all his strength to let them know that he was still fighting, still present. With great effort, he managed to force out a faint grunt, which surprised his friends.

"Kai?" Lyra asked, her voice filled with hope and astonishment. "Was that you?"

Elijah leaned in closer, and Kai could imagine his friend's face, his eyes wide with disbelief. "Kai, if that was you, try to make the sound again."

Kai focused on his throat, willing the muscles to contract and produce the sound once more. He managed another soft grunt, proving to his friends that he was indeed still with them. It was weaker this time though, it had been so difficult to muster what he could the first time.

Tears of joy filled Lyra's eyes as she clasped Kai's hand. "I knew you were still in there, Kai. I knew you wouldn't give up."

Elijah smiled, patting Kai's shoulder gently. "You're one tough guy, Kai. We're all here for you, and we'll help you get through this, no matter what it takes."

As the days went by, Kai continued to regain feeling and limited movement in his extremities. The sensation of returning strength in his limbs brought with it an overwhelming sense of gratitude and determination. With each small victory, he felt more and more certain that he would eventually overcome his current limitations.

In the quiet moments when his friends were not with him, Kai focused on his connection to the presence within. Though it had not communicated with him since their last interaction, he couldn't shake the feeling that it was still observing him, perhaps waiting for the right moment to reveal itself again. Kai hoped that when the time came, they would be able to work together to achieve greatness. Maybe as he became a little stronger, the presence would be more willing to deal with him. At the very least, he sensed that this thing inside of him was his ticket to harnessing the flames within.

During his friends' visits, Kai listened intently to their conversations, his newly heightened senses allowing him to pick up on the subtle nuances of their voices and emotions. He felt grateful for their unwavering support and knew that their bond would only grow stronger through this shared experience.

On the third day, as Kai lay in bed, a sudden surge of warmth filled his chest, emanating from deep within and it felt very much to Kai as though the presence inside him was acknowledging his progress, giving him a small nod of approval somehow. That it could see that he was a fighter, and was becoming stronger each and every day. Though the voice remained silent, the warmth was enough to bring a flicker of hope to Kai.

A particular highlight was a second visit from Grandmaster Orthos.

"Your friends tell me you've been making progress, Kai," he said, his voice gentle yet authoritative. "I'm glad to see that you're fighting, that you're not giving up. I believe you have the strength and determination to overcome this."

Kai grunted softly in response, and Orthos' seemed surprised. "So, it's true. You're finding your voice again. That's excellent news, Kai. Keep pushing yourself, keep fighting. I have faith in you."

As Orthos left the room, Kai's thoughts had returned to the presence within him. With every passing day, his curiosity about the entity grew stronger. He wondered what its true nature was and how it might play a role in his journey to become a powerful fire mage. Although the voice remained silent, Kai took comfort in the feeling that he was not alone in his struggles.

His friends continued to visit and support him, sharing their own experiences with magic and the trials they had faced. Kai absorbed their stories, internalising the lessons and wisdom they offered. He began to understand that everyone had their own struggles, and that perseverance and determination were key to overcoming any and all obstacles that they each faced.

As Kai's strength gradually returned, he eventually found himself able to move his fingers and toes with more control. This progress was both exciting and encouraging, and he eagerly shared the news with his friends by way of short show and, well, not tell sessions, but their faces lit up with joy and pride each time he could do something new, knowing that their friend was on the path to recovery.

One evening, as the day was drawing to its conclusion, Kai lay in his bed, reflecting on his journey so far. He thought about the presence within him, and how it had been with him all along, even if it had chosen not to reveal itself. He realised that perhaps it was just waiting for him to prove himself, to demonstrate that he was worthy of its assistance and guidance.

With renewed determination, Kai made a silent vow to the presence within. He would continue to push himself, to grow and learn and he would not give up, no matter the challenges he faced.

"What was that battle?" Kai asked inwardly to the entity all of a sudden. He had spoken in one-way conversations like this to the entity before, but it had never garnered a response. He had also tried to beg, plead and bargain with whatever it was inside of him, but at this point he felt that he had nothing to lose in just asking questions, and this one in particular was about the visions he'd seen whilst he was in the chair.

To his surprise, Kai felt the presence within him stir, as if it were considering whether or not to respond. For a long moment, there was silence, and Kai thought that perhaps his question would go unanswered as usual. However, just as he was about to give up hope, he sensed a faint shift in the presence, and a series of images and emotions flooded his mind.

The battle he had seen while in the chair was an ancient conflict, one that had shaped the history of the magical world. It was a time when mages fought each other for power and control, and the thirst for knowledge and mastery over their abilities led many down dark paths. The presence seemed to convey a sense of regret and sorrow, as if it too had been a part of that tumultuous period and had witnessed the destruction it had caused.

One of the prevailing themes that Kai could feel within their link though, was a deep understanding that mages of the water affinity were not to be trusted. Somehow he could sense that the great wars that occurred in the past, were between the fire and water schools.

Eventually, the images faded, and Kai felt the presence withdraw, returning to be the silent observer within him. Though it had chosen to share this information with him, Kai knew that he had only been given a glimpse of a much larger story. It seemed that the presence was still hesitant to fully reveal itself,

Then a single word came from the presence. This time though, it was not filled with enough power to cause him to pass out. It sounded as though it was a whisper from a mile away. Like if he hadn't been focussed on hearing it, then he wouldn't have. It was like the entity was suppressing all of its power in order for Kai to be able to hear it without discomfort.

"War," it said.

"You can understand me?" Kai tried and he felt the presence recede into almost nothingness again before pain erupted from within, filling every moment of his existence with a pain that he could do nothing to combat; it was from within him and nothing he tried would make it stop.

"Yes," the single word reply came.

Kai felt his entire body cover in a cold sweat and his heart rate was beating so fast and hard that caused him to worry. But after a few moments, the pain disappeared and his broken body returned to normal.

Kai lay in his bed, focusing on the memory of the pain that seemed a little too difficult to shake. He knew that if he wanted to establish some connection with the entity, he needed to find a way to communicate without causing himself unbearable pain. So he decided to approach the presence with a proposal.

"I know that communicating with me is difficult for both of us," he thought, directing his words towards the presence. "But I believe that we can work together, to help each other. If we can find a way to communicate without causing me so much pain, I think we can achieve great things."

Kai waited anxiously for a response, hoping the presence would be open to his suggestion. The entity stirred within him, and he felt a sense of curiosity emanating from it.

"Try," the presence replied hesitantly, the words barely audible in Kai's mind. Though this time as the words sounded even further away, the pain he felt accompanying them paled in comparison to the last time.

Feeling a surge of hope, Kai suggested they begin a trial-and-error process to find a method of communication that wouldn't harm him. Over the next several hours, they experimented with different techniques. They started by trying to lower the intensity of the presence's responses, but even the faintest whispers caused Kai pain. Less pain admittedly, but it was still there.

Frustrated but undeterred, they tried a different approach. Kai focused on building a mental barrier, attempting to shield himself from the brunt of the pain. The presence then attempted to communicate, but the barrier was not strong enough, and Kai still experienced a sharp, piercing pain from the entity's words.

Determined, they continued their efforts. Kai wondered if they could communicate through emotions or sensations instead of words. The presence agreed to try, and they spent the next hour experimenting with this method.

To Kai's surprise, this approach showed promise. The presence could convey emotions like curiosity, agreement, or confusion without causing Kai pain. While this method was limited, it was a start and Kai couldn't help but feel a sense of achievement. Something told him that if he just kept going, kept trying that this was going to be the answer to so many of his problems.

Kai and the entity kept working together, refining their new method of communication. Eventually, they discovered that by combining simple emotions with faint whispers, they could convey more complex ideas without overwhelming Kai or causing him too much pain.

As they continued to practice, their communication became smoother and more efficient. Though not perfect, it was a significant improvement from the unbearable pain Kai had experienced before.

Eventually, Kai thanked the presence for its cooperation and patience. The entity responded with a feeling of warmth and reassurance, a sign that it too was satisfied with their progress.

The result of Kai's trial-and-error was that the entity within him could respond in a tiny, almost imperceptible single-word whisper to anything Kai wished to ask. But along with the whisper, and something that was far more useful, was the ability for the entity to convey emotion with its word. As much as that may not sound like it was very helpful, Kai was amazed at the wealth of information that could be communicated by the pairing. For example, an angry 'no' and a sad 'no' are two very different things.

"Do you think anyone can help us?" Kai asked inwardly to the entity, but before he had even finished his sentence, he felt the overwhelming feeling that the entity did not like this idea.

"OK… so we won't tell anyone about you?" he tried.

The feeling of acceptance and agreement returned. This was essentially how they had managed to learn how to communicate and although not perfect, it was at least progress.

"So I can't just keep calling you 'the entity'," Kai thought. "Do you have a name?"

There was a moment of silence before the entity responded with a barely perceptible whisper. "Forgotten." The words were accompanied by an emotion of deep sadness and loss, as if remembering a time when it had a name and a purpose.

Kai hesitated, not wanting to cause the presence any further distress. "Well, if you don't mind, I'd like to give you a name. Something to call you by so that it feels more personal when we communicate."

The entity seemed to consider this for a moment, then sent a feeling of curiosity and tentative acceptance.

"How about… Azar?" Kai suggested. The name had come to him suddenly, as if it had been whispered by the wind. He didn't know where it came from, but it felt right.

The entity seemed to mull over the name, and then Kai felt a gentle warmth and agreement. "Acceptable."

With a name for the entity, now called Azar, their connection felt more profound, and Kai felt a growing sense of companionship. He couldn't help but feel a small sense of joy at the progress they had made together.

"So, Azar," Kai began, "Now that we can communicate, what should we do next? How can we work together to help me regain control over my body and master my abilities as a fire mage?"

Azar seemed to ponder this question, and then Kai felt a mix of determination and caution. "Practise," came the faint response.

"You think I can practise? I can't even move my own body and you think I can practise?"

A feeling of patience and reassurance emanated from Azar. "Mind."

Kai was intrigued by this idea. He realised that Azar was suggesting they could work together mentally to help him regain control over his body and enhance his abilities as a fire mage. It made sense; after all, Kai knew that magic was deeply intertwined with the mind, body and soul, and he had already made progress in communicating with Azar.

"Alright, let's try it. I'm willing to try anything," Kai agreed, filled with determination and hope. "But where should we start?"

"Secret…" Azar said with a wash of patience aimed towards Kai, and he understood right away that Azar was asking Kai to keep their practise a secret.

"OK, I won't tell anyone… not that I could anyway," he mumbled and he felt Azar send him back the sensation of belief in his words.

Kai took a deep breath and focused his thoughts inward, ready to begin their secret practice. "So, how do we practice like this, Azar?"

"Visualise," came the soft response, accompanied by a feeling of concentration.

Kai understood. He cleared his mind of any and all thoughts and sounds, and began to visualise. He tried to envision a space within his mind where he and Azar could work together. Slowly, the image of a sea of darkness faded into his mind's eye, illuminated in the centre by one small candle, with an orange flame flickering about its top.

"Is this what you mean, Azar?"

A sensation of approval washed over him.

"But what do I do with it?" Kai asked.

"Me," Azar replied and as Kai watched, the candle began to burn brighter and brighter until the entire world inside Kai's mind turned into a sea of orange light. And then it began to hurt. A lot. The pain grew and grew and Kai began to scream through the blinding brightness and heat. He could hear his physical body screaming too and before the pain grew too much to bear, his mind shut down and the pain was gone. All that was left was darkness.

Chapter 13 – History

"Kai?" Lyra's voice came from beside Kai and it caused him to return to his senses. He didn't know how long he had been unconscious for, but if he had to guess, it would have been days rather than hours.

Immediately Kai turned his attention to Azar, though before he reached out, he hesitated. Azar had done something that had caused him so much pain that he'd blacked out and he wasn't sure if he could handle it again.

But Kai knew that they had to continue their practice, that the progress they had made was crucial to regaining control over his body and mastering his magical abilities. With a deep breath, he tentatively reached out to Azar.

"Are you there, Azar?" Kai asked cautiously, bracing himself for any potential pain.

A wave of concern and regret washed over Kai. "Sorry," Azar whispered softly, clearly remorseful for the pain he had caused.

Kai let out a small sigh of relief, grateful that their connection hadn't been severed. "It's alright, Azar. We're both learning, and I know you didn't mean to hurt me. But we need to be more careful. Can you tell me what went wrong?"

"Power," Azar replied, the word accompanied by a feeling of caution. "Weakness."

Kai could only assume that what he was being told, was that Azar was far too powerful for him, and that Kai was simply too weak to deal with the being's might, no matter how much he tried to tamp down on it. He needed to know so much more, but for now he knew there was simply no way of knowing what he was supposed to do.

"I'm so sorry you're in so much pain, Kai," Lyra said. "If only we hadn't gone exploring. If only you hadn't sat in that chair…"

Kai could hear the sorrow in Lyra's voice, the tears welling in her eyes and as he listened, unable to make any move to comfort his friend, he too wished that he could cry.

"It's like you're just an empty vessel, you know?" Lyra choked out almost sounding angry. "Like if I could just pull apart a piece of my own strength, or my mana and give it to you… you know I would, right?"

That statement made Kai think. Had Lyra just said something that could work?

"Azar, are you hearing this?" Kai asked inwardly, to which Azar replied with the sense that he had heard.

"Then maybe we are doing this all wrong," Kai said to Azar. "If the problem is that you are way too powerful for your mana to help me, to be controlled by me, then why not…"

Then his train of thought was taken by Elijah's voice comforting Lyra. "It's not your fault, Lyra," he said.

"Why not, instead of trying to make your power smaller, just cut away a tiny piece of it and use my body, this empty, broken vessel to house it?"

Azar was silent for a long time and while Kai awaited an answer, he listened to Lyra and Elijah.

"Did you hear that Marcus isn't even being punished for this?" Lyra said. "He told the Grandmaster that it was Kai's choice to sit in the chair, that he had nothing to do with it!"

"It's a half-truth though, isn't it?" Elijah said calmly. "Kai did sit in the chair willingly and…"

"You think that he would've done it if Marcus hadn't filled his head with all that 'unlocking your power' crap? This is Marcus' fault, no matter how you try to rationalise it. And I swear, I'll get him back. I'll show him the meaning of pain…"

Kai let out a grunt. He wanted to tell Lyra not to worry about him or fighting Marcus. He wanted her to simply forget about the hatred she was harbouring and to get back to training with the others, but all he could do was grunt, so that's what he did.

"Kai?" Are you OK?" Lyra asked with concern in her voice. But Kai didn't respond, because Azar had finally answered Kai's earlier question, sending a feeling of cautious optimism along with the word: " Risk."

"I know it's a risk, Azar," Kai thought, "But at this point, I'm willing to try anything. I can't lay here forever, can I?"

A sense of agreement flowed through their connection. "Wait."

Kai turned his attention back to Lyra and Elijah who seemed to be talking a little easier after Kai's interruption as the pair had correctly guessed that he was not too interested in hearing a discussion about Marcus.

Then Kai felt the sense of something beginning to surge within him. It was painful again, but not like he'd experienced when dealing with Azar's suppressed power previously; this was more like a sliver of what Azar could do – as though he had cut a tiny portion of his power away and had given it to Kai.

Kai felt the power overwhelm him. It was as though he was a deflated balloon and this power had pushed him to the point of bursting. His insides felt like they were pressing against his skin and as they inflated, growing larger and larger he began to panic. This needed to stop before it killed him.

"Azar!" Kai shouted internally, his thoughts laced with urgency. "Stop! It's too much!"

"Too late," Azar whispered, conveying genuine concern and guilt and as he replied, Kai felt his skin stretching to the point that it was thin enough to tear by itself.

Then suddenly, it stopped.

The pain simply vanished and the sensation of inflation disappeared into nothingness and Kai felt just like he had before.

But it wasn't just like before. Something was different and as Kai checked all his mental faculties, he realised that the change was physical, not mental. He was clenching his fists.

Kai's internal eyes widened in disbelief. His hands were clenching and unclenching, and he could feel the sensation of touch, the texture of the sheets beneath his fingers. It was as if a miracle had occurred, and he had gained some new control over his body.

He tried to move something else, anything else but the rest of his body refused. The strength that Azar had given him had almost killed him in its transfer, clearly, but still it had only given him a tiny amount of control over his broken body. What it did though, was give him hope.

"Kai?!" Lyra cried as she realised that he was moving his hands. "Are you there? Can you move now?"

Kai focused on his connection with Azar, feeling a renewed sense of determination. "Azar, we've done it. My hands... I can move them! We need to do this again, but more carefully this time. I want to regain control of my entire body."

A sense of caution and agreement radiated from Azar. "Slowly," he whispered.

Kai took a deep breath and nodded internally. "Yes, slowly."

Then he turned his attention back to Lyra and tried to speak again, but all that came out once again was the low grunt.

"Can you move your hands whenever you want?" Lyra asked.

Kai didn't know what to do, there was no way he could communicate with his friends without some kind of system in place, so he was more than happy when Elijah spoke.

"Squeeze my hand three times if you have control," he ordered.

Kai squeezed his friend's hand three times.

Lyra's squeal of delight almost deafened Kai – which would've been an ironic twist of fate – but one that he definitely didn't need.

"Kai, that's amazing!" Lyra exclaimed, her eyes shining with tears of happiness. "We'll figure out a way to communicate better. I promise."

Elijah nodded, his expression filled with admiration and relief. "We'll come up with a system, Kai. For now, just focus on regaining more control over your body."

Over the next several days, Kai and Azar continued their careful practice, slowly transferring small portions of Azar's power into Kai's body. It was difficult to gauge how much could be transferred without Kai feeling as though he was going to be ripped apart from within, but with some trial and a few errors, and with each successful transfer, Kai gained more and more control over his limbs, and soon, he was able to move his arms and legs as well.

A big change that came alongside the transference and newfound control over his broken body though, was the fact that Kai and Azar could now communicate internally, freely. As though the usage of Azar's own power meant that this kind of talking didn't cause Kai any pain.

Kai had decided to keep his progress a secret from his friends. It wasn't because he felt ashamed or weak, rather he wanted to be sure that his progress would last and he knew that one day they would come to visit him, and he would be standing there under his own power, smiling at them.

As the days passed, Kai and Azar continued their transfers, slowly improving Kai's control and strengthening their bond. The progress was slow but steady, and with each passing day, Kai felt a bit more hope that he might regain control of his body and learn to master his powers as a fire mage. Because as more of Azar's power entered into his control, the more he knew that Azar could teach him everything that he ever needed to know and more about fire magic.

"Azar, were you a person before?" Kai asked. "I mean I know that I saw you in a great battle, but I don't understand how you're inside me somehow, and if so, what was your life like before you became trapped inside me? I know you were a powerful mage... a Grandmaster perhaps, even. Can you tell me more about you?"

Azar hesitated for a moment, as if sifting through ancient memories. Then, a flood of emotions and images poured into Kai's mind. He saw grand halls and libraries filled with tomes of knowledge, a bustling city with mages of all ranks working together, and he watched through the eyes of a younger version of Azar standing proudly among them all.

"I did once rise to the rank of Grandmaster," Azar whispered, his voice filled with both pride and sorrow. "I had mastered the Eternal Flame and I was respected, admired and I worked tirelessly to protect our people and uphold the principles of our order."

Kai was in awe of the images and memories he was receiving, but he didn't recognise any of them at all. He felt a deep sense of respect for the being that had once been a powerful and wise mage. "What happened, Azar? How did you end up trapped inside me?"

Azar's response was tinged with sadness. "During my time as a Grandmaster, I sought to deepen my understanding of the Eternal Flame. Do you understand the Eternal Flame? Do you know what it is?"

Kai nodded mentally before he realised he would actually have to respond. "I do," he said. "It is the flame inside all fire mages that we manipulate and use to cast our spells. It's how we're chosen as fire mages and why our eyes glow red."

Azar remained silent for a long time before he responded. Then he sighed. "This is not the truth of the Eternal Flame. But I will set the record straight for you. The Eternal Flame is present in all living beings, not just fire mages. It is the reason that people are warm to the touch, it is the reason we are alive, the reason our bodies maintain a constant temperature. Some individuals, like you and me, possess the ability to harness and control this flame, to bend it to our will and perform incredible feats of magic."

Kai listened intently, fascinated by this new concept of the Eternal Flame. "So, the fire magic that I wield... it's a part of this Eternal Flame?" He chose not to remind Azar that he couldn't actually perform any spells.

Azar confirmed. "Yes, it is one aspect of the greater force that exists within all living beings. You have a natural affinity for fire, which allows you to tap into and control this aspect of the Eternal Flame more easily than others. However, your control over this power is still underdeveloped, and that is why you struggle."

As Kai absorbed this information, he couldn't help but feel a sense of awe at the complexity and beauty of the magic that existed within him. He was eager to learn more about the Eternal Flame and how he could better harness its power.

"But, Azar, how did you become trapped inside me?' Kai asked again, bringing the conversation back to the mysterious circumstances that had led to their current predicament.

Azar sighed, a hint of remorse in his voice. "In my pursuit of knowledge, I performed a ritual to commune directly with the Eternal Flame, hoping to unlock secrets that had been lost to time. The ritual was powerful and dangerous, but I believed that the risk was worth the potential rewards."

"Unfortunately, the ritual did not go as planned,' Azar continued. "Instead of communing with the Eternal Flame, I became consumed by it. My spirit was ripped from my body and flung across the planes of existence. I ascended into a greater plane where I would reside for all eternity as pure energy. But that energy was then used by the universe to ignite the Eternal Flame inside of another. You, Kai."

"What?" Kai responded with total confusion evident in his tone. "Is that how everyone's Eternal Flame is ignited? By a previously powerful mage getting trapped inside of them? It doesn't make any sense."

"No, not all," Azar replied quietly. I believe that as I existed as pure energy within the universal sea of power, I was just… unlucky… to have been allocated to your flame. I was upset, angry perhaps even that I had been paired with one so weak, but now I can see in you potential, power, a stubbornness that could possibly have rivalled even my own…"

Kai felt a pang of sympathy for Azar, who had lost everything in his pursuit of knowledge. "I'm sorry, Azar. That must've been a terrible experience. And now you're stuck here, with me, unable to return to your world and your life." Then he added: "But you're right. I know I have the drive to become powerful. Just before I never knew how to do it properly, but with your guidance, I think I may have a chance."

Azar's voice softened. "It has been a difficult journey, but it could also be true that perhaps our meeting was not an accident. Our fates may be intertwined, Kai, and if you listen to my teachings well, we have the potential to achieve great things."

Kai felt a surge of determination. "Then let's work together, Azar. Let's see if we can find a way for you to regain your freedom, and for me to master this magic that flows through me."

Azar's agreement was accompanied by a sense of shared purpose. "Yes, together we will find a way."

Chapter 14 – Blind

Lyra, Elijah and Alina all spoke in hushed tones as they walked down the stone corridor to where they had come to visit Kai each and every day just before dinner. Elijah always seemed to take the 'manly' bravado when talking to Kai, as though it was all going to be OK at some point. Lyra always seemed emotional, worried that this was to be Kai's 'forever', and Alina had almost never uttered a word.

As the three entered into the medical room this evening though, the first thing they noticed was that Kai's bed was empty, and the prevailing noise in the room was the whimper that Lyra let out as she immediately jumped to a terrible conclusion.

But before any of them could voice their concerns, they heard a familiar voice coming from the corner of the room to the right of the doorway.

"Hey, guys," Kai said, a weak smile on his face as he stood there, using the wall for support. "Surprise."

Lyra, Elijah, and Alina stared at him in shock, their eyes wide and mouths hanging open. Kai could not see their reactions, but he could at least sense their astonishment.

"What... How?" Lyra stammered, her voice filled with a mixture of joy and disbelief.

Kai chuckled softly. "I've been working on it, with a little help from my... uh, internal flame. It's been a slow process, but I can now stand and walk, even if I'm still blind."

As his friends approached him, their expressions quickly changed from delight to concern. They were all staring at his eyes, which had taken on a pure, deep red hue with no iris or pupil in sight.

"Your eyes, Kai," Elijah said hesitantly. "They're... red."

Kai frowned, feeling a bit self-conscious. "Really? I can't see them myself, but I can feel that something is different. Weren't they always red though?"

Lyra stepped forward and quickly removed a cloth from her pocket. "Here," she said, gently tying it around Kai's head, covering his eyes. "Now you don't have to worry about people getting freaked out by your eyes."

Kai smiled gratefully at her. "Thanks, Lyra. But are they really that bad?"

Elijah answered before either of the girls could. "Like looking at a demon, mate," he said. "Totally freaky… but I'm glad you're up and about. You have a fight coming up in this week's tournament!"

"Shut up Elijah," Kai heard Lyra say, followed by a light thud as she must've hit him. "Don't worry about any of that Kai, you don't have any matches coming up."

Kai breathed a sigh of relief. He knew that one day he'd take to the sands again, but for now, all he wanted was to get strong enough to walk properly.

With Kai's new appearance concealed, the group excitedly began asking him questions about his progress and how he had managed to regain control over his body. Kai told them about drawing on the strength of his internal flame, but he made no mention of Azar, as he had promised to keep their connection a secret.

As they listened to Kai's story, Lyra, Elijah, and Alina marvelled at the determination and resilience their friend had shown. It was inspiring to see how far he had come in such a short amount of time.

"Kai, this is amazing," Alina said, finally breaking her silence. "I'm so happy for you."

Elijah nodded in agreement. "You've done what no one thought was possible. You should be proud."

Kai smiled, but he knew that he still had a long way to go. "Thank you, guys. But I'm not done yet. I still have a lot to learn, and I want to find a way to regain my sight, if possible."

Lyra placed a hand on his shoulder. "We'll be with you every step of the way, Kai. You're not alone in this. But remember, there's no rush!"

"You want to try to go for a walk?" Elijah said all of a sudden. "You've been stuck inside this room for so long you must be going crazy!"

As Kai nodded enthusiastically, he was sure that he heard a feint 'tell me about it' rumble up from Azar, but he ignored it.

For the next few hours, Kai explored The Pit with the help of his friends. They took turns guiding him through the corridors and narrating where they were going, helping him become familiar with his surroundings without the use of his sight.

"I've been thinking," he said hesitantly. "What if my internal flame has more capabilities than I know? What if it could help me regain my sight, or even enhance my magic?" I mean, I've learnt how to walk again already, so the possibilities are endless, aren't they?"

Elijah raised an eyebrow. "It's an interesting idea, but how would you go about finding out?"

Kai frowned, deep in thought. "I'm not sure. Maybe I could experiment, keep trying to push the limits of what I can do, I guess. With you guys helping me I bet I can do anything."

Lyra nodded thoughtfully. "It could be dangerous to push yourself too hard, Kai. But if you think it's worth trying, we'll support you. If it looks like you start causing yourself harm though, we won't let you continue, you know that, right?"

"It'll be OK I think," Kai muttered as they sat just outside the training grounds together. "I've come so far, and something tells me I have a lot more potential than I ever have before."

Lyra reached out and squeezed his hand. "Don't give up, Kai. You've already achieved so much. I believe that if anyone can find a way, it's you."

Her words brought a small smile to his face, and as he felt the warmth of his friends' support, he knew that he couldn't give up. No matter how long it took or how hard it was, he would keep pushing forward, exploring the depths of his internal flame and striving to unlock its full potential.

"What's potential really if it isn't just a lack of power right now?"

Kai immediately recognised Marcus' voice and his blood began to boil.

"Marcus," Kai said, his voice cold and restrained. "I didn't realise you were here."

Marcus stepped forward, a smug grin on his face. "Just happened to be passing by and overheard your little conversation. I must say, it's touching to see how supportive your friends are."

Elijah glared at Marcus. "What do you want, Marcus? Can't you see we're busy?"

"Oh, I just wanted to offer my... congratulations," Marcus said, the sarcasm dripping from his words. "It's truly inspiring to see someone like Kai, so weak and helpless, suddenly managing to stand on his own two feet again. But don't get your hopes up too high. You're still a long way from being a real mage."

Kai clenched his fists, anger bubbling up inside him. "I may be blind, Marcus, but I can still sense your arrogance from a mile away. And let me tell you something – I may not have my sight, but I have something you'll never have: true friends who support and believe in me. And that gives me the strength to keep moving forward."

Marcus scoffed. "Save your pathetic speech, Kai. You think your friends' support will make you a powerful mage? You're just as delusional as ever."

Lyra stepped in, her voice firm. "That's enough, Marcus. You have no idea what Kai has been through, or what he's capable of now. Your constant need to belittle others only shows how insecure you really are."

Marcus's face reddened with anger, but he held his tongue. After a tense moment, he turned and stormed off without another word.

"Damnit!" Elijah exclaimed. "If he wasn't Master-ranked I'd love to give him a good beating."

Kai took a deep breath, trying to calm himself. "It's not worth it, Elijah. Marcus may be powerful, but he'll never understand what true strength is. It's not just about raw power; it's about the bonds we form and the people we support."

Alina, who had been quiet until now, finally spoke up. "Kai's right. We shouldn't let Marcus get under our skin. We have each other, and that's what matters."

Lyra voiced her agreement. "We're a team, and we'll continue to grow and learn together. Let's focus on our own progress and not waste energy on people like Marcus."

Elijah sighed, relenting. "You're right, guys. We have our own path to follow, and we don't need to prove anything to Marcus or anyone else."

Kai smiled, grateful for his friends' unwavering support. "Thank you, all of you. Together, we'll become stronger than we ever thought possible."

The group was silent for a long moment before Elijah finally spoke again. "I bet it'd be fun to wipe that smile off his face though."

"I bet it'd be even more fun if I did it while wearing this blindfold though," Kai offered and Elijah laughed.

"Absolutely," Elijah agreed, grinning. "That would be one for the history books."

Alina chimed in, "We'll just have to keep training and getting better, together. We'll show everyone what we're capable of."

Lyra nodded enthusiastically. "Exactly. We'll become the best team The Pit has ever seen, and we'll do it our own way, without having to answer to anyone."

"Uh… what do you mean, 'team'?" Kai asked, not sure if he was grasping the meaning properly.

"Oh that's right!" Lyra exclaimed. "You haven't heard!"

"Heard what?" Kai asked impatiently.

"This week's tournament has been cancelled," Lyra said, "because next weekend, there's going to be a tournament held for all the Journeyman ranks, and the participants are going to be all in groups of four!"

"That sounds so cool!" Kai replied, and then he remembered two things that weren't so cool about the statement.

"Before you say…" Lyra said slowly, "there's something I have to tell you…" she hesitated for a long moment, and then said it quicker than Kai had ever heard her speak before. "I got promoted to Journeyman a couple of days ago. I got the hang of a heatwave spell and, well I didn't want to say anything because of how you were in such a bad way and…"

"Don't worry about it Lyra," Kai exclaimed. "You got promoted! That's awesome." Then his tone changed to one a little more somber, "but guys… I'm not a Journeyman rank… I don't have any spells…"

Lyra smiled gently. "Don't worry, Kai. We've got your back. We'll help you get there, and we'll do it together."

Elijah nodded in agreement. "Yeah, man. You've come so far already. You've got the talent and determination. It's just a matter of time before you catch up with us."

Alina added, "And besides, you have that internal flame of yours. I'm sure it'll help you find your own unique spells. If you don't make it this time, then we'll team up next time."

Kai felt a surge of gratitude towards his friends. "Thank you, guys. I'll do my best to catch up, and we'll enter that tournament as a team. If not, you'll just have to carry someone else through and we can group up with us next time!"

"It's too soon," Azar said to Kai from deep within. Kai waited for a moment to see if any of his friends had detected the voice, but none of them seemed as though they had.

Kai ignored Azar and turned his attention back to the group.

"Guys," he asked. "How bad do I look?"

No one answered for a long while, and then Elijah spoke up. You look terrible man. Your hair has totally burnt away, your skin's scarred, your eyes are completely red… I mean you really couldn't look worse if you tried."

Kai smiled. "Good. Then maybe our opponents will get scared, or disgusted. Maybe I won't be useless after all."

Lyra reached out and squeezed Kai's hand reassuringly. "You're far from useless, Kai. You have a determination that's unlike anything I've ever seen. And besides, true power doesn't come from how we look, but from what we're capable of."

Elijah added, "Exactly. Just remember how you surprised us when you started walking and talking again. Your appearance doesn't define you, and neither does your current level of magic. You'll prove that to everyone soon enough."

Alina agreed, "we believe in you, Kai. And when the time comes, we know you'll find a way to make a difference in our team.'

Kai's heart swelled with gratitude for his friends' unwavering faith in him. "Thank you, all of you. I promise I'll do everything in my power to be ready for the tournament. But hey, you think I can sleep in the dorm tonight?"

Elijah patted Kai's back. "Sorry pal, we rented your room out to some girl already."

Kai's heart sunk, but he did his best to keep a smile on his face.

Then he heard a thud and Elijah exclaim with an "ouch!"

"Of course you can come back," Lyra said. "Don't listen to Elijah he's just being an idiot as usual. Besides, if the dorm was three girls and Elijah, I think he'd be begging to leave already."

"You got that right," Elijah said playfully. "The ratio's already off now until you come back!"

Kai smiled. "OK, I'll take my room back if you want me that bad, but I'm going to need a little extra help for the time being. You know it's not easy being blind an all."

"Could be worse, we have to look at your terrible demon eyes and bald head," Elijah said. Kai again heard a thump as Lyra hit Elijah, followed by another "ouch."

The group helped Kai to his bed and as he settled down for the night, he couldn't help but let his mind wander.

As Kai lay in his bed, his mind drifted into a whirlwind of thoughts and emotions. He could feel the warmth of the familiar sheets beneath him, the soft murmur of his friends' voices in the distance, and the comforting presence of the dorm. Even without sight, he once again felt at home and safe.

Kai's thoughts shifted to his internal flame and the mysterious connection he had with Azar. He wondered why he had been chosen, what it meant, and if it was truly a blessing or a curse. The power he had discovered within himself was both exhilarating and terrifying, and he couldn't help but ponder the implications of that connection.

He also thought about the upcoming tournament and the immense pressure to prove himself. His friends had placed so much faith in him, and he didn't want to let them down. The desire to catch up to them, to stand beside them as an equal, was all-consuming. He knew he needed to push himself harder, to explore the depths of his power, but he couldn't shake the nagging feeling that he might be playing with fire – literally.

The sound of Azar's voice echoed through his mind, a constant reminder of the secret he carried. He wrestled with the idea of telling his friends about the ancient spirit, but he had made a promise to keep it a secret. He couldn't help but wonder if the knowledge would bring them closer together or drive them apart.

In the darkness of his mind, he imagined his friends standing beside him, their faces filled with determination and camaraderie. He saw Lyra, her eyes sparkling with intelligence and fire, Elijah, his grin wide and infectious, and Alina, her quiet strength shining like a beacon in the night.

Despite his blindness, Kai could see the love and support they offered him as though it had a physical presence, and he felt a surge of hope and determination. He knew that together, they could overcome anything – even the dark, mysterious power that dwelled within him.

As the night wore on, Kai drifted in and out of sleep, his dreams filled with images of fire and friendship, of hope and determination. And though the challenges ahead were daunting, he felt more prepared than ever to face them head-on, with his friends by his side.

The next morning, as the first light of dawn began to filter through the curtains to warm Kai's face, he awoke with a renewed sense of purpose.

And as he lay there, listening to the familiar sounds of his friends stirring in the dorm, he couldn't help but smile. For he knew that whatever the future held, they would face it together, as a team. A team that he very much wanted to be an active part of.

Chapter 15 – An Experiment

"We should try to add a little more power before we get up this morning, shouldn't we? Especially if I'm going to go train with the others today," Kai said inwardly to Azar.

Azar responded, his voice a calming presence in Kai's mind. "Indeed, we can attempt to harness more of our combined power. However, you must remember to be cautious and maintain control. We don't want to cause any harm. I will only push a tiny sliver of my power into this for now, otherwise it could knock you back into your bed for the day."

Kai nodded, even though he knew Azar couldn't see him. "I understand. Let's just go with a small increase, and see how it feels."

Closing his eyes, Kai focused on the flame that burned within him, feeling its warmth and energy. It had always been a tiny, non-imposing candle but ever since Azar had been feeding him his power, it seemed larger, brighter and had within it the look of a flame that simply wanted to grow.

Kai visualised allowing the flame to grow, with it becoming brighter and more intense, its power surging through him.

As he did so, he could feel Azar's presence, the ancient spirit lending its support and guidance and his latest sliver of power to add to his body. Together, they worked to build upon the flame's power, pushing the limits of what Kai had previously been able to achieve. It was almost second nature by now as they had done this on more than a few occasions, and even though the pain was still evident as the strands of their power weaved together, Kai was used to it. He could deal with it – and he felt he could deal with even more.

Gradually, Kai felt the increase in strength and vitality. It was subtle, but unmistakable. A sense of accomplishment filled him, knowing that he was taking the first steps towards becoming the mage he aspired to be.

Opening his eyes, he couldn't help but smile. "Thank you, Azar. I can feel the difference. It's small, but it's there."

Azar's voice was filled with a hint of pride. "You're making progress, Kai. Continue to work diligently, and you'll only grow stronger."

"Do you think if we try again, that maybe I'll get my eyesight back?"

Azar paused for a moment, though eventually a wave of sadness and sorrow washed over Kai. "I do not think so," Azar replied. "I have been trying to push my own power in that direction, but I think that your body is simply too damaged. The eyes are delicate and precise, and I do not know if I can wield my power in such a way that it can be properly directed. I am sorry, Kai."

Kai sighed, disappointment weighing heavily on his chest. "It's alright, Azar. I appreciate your efforts. I guess I'll just have to learn to adapt and make the best of my situation."

Azar's voice was gentle and reassuring. "You are strong, Kai, and I have no doubt that you will continue to grow and adapt. Your spirit and determination are your greatest assets."

Kai nodded, taking a deep breath. "You're right. I can't let my blindness hold me back. I'll just have to find new ways to harness my power and be a part of the team."

He thought about his friends – Lyra, Elijah, and Alina – and the unwavering support they had shown him. They believed in him, and he refused to let them down.

With renewed determination, Kai rose from his bed, eager to join his friends for the day's training. He knew that every step he took, every challenge he faced, brought him closer to realising his full potential.

As he exited his room, he found Lyra, Elijah, and Alina waiting for him, ready to begin their day together. They exchanged smiles and words of encouragement, each knowing that they were all working towards a common goal – to become stronger, both individually and as a team. Kai of course didn't see the smiles, but he felt the warmth and the friendship in the room and the feeling was infectious.

Together, they headed to the training grounds, their spirits high and their determination unwavering. As Kai walked beside his friends much easier now – although he was still guided - he couldn't help but feel a sense of belonging, a connection that transcended their individual abilities and bound them together as a family.

And with every step, Kai grew more and more certain that, with the help of his friends and the guidance of Azar, he would become the powerful mage he was meant to be.

Upon reaching the training sands, the group took a moment to assess their surroundings. The area was vast and not that Kai could see, it was set up with multiple stations set up for different types of training – from target practice for mages to obstacle courses for agility training. The air was filled with the sounds of other mages honing their skills, their determination palpable.

Kai couldn't see any of this, but he could sense the energy in the air, the heat from the spells and the excitement of his friends as they prepared for the day's training. He knew that they were there to support him, and it gave him the strength he needed to face the challenges ahead.

They decided to start with hand-to-hand combat, Lyra's favourite, as it would allow Kai to utilise his sense of touch and his no-doubt improved hearing to compensate for his lack of sight. Lyra, who was the group expert in grappling, took the lead in teaching Kai some basic techniques.

"Alright, Kai," Lyra began, positioning herself in front of Kai. "I want you to focus on feeling my movements and listening to the sounds around you. Use your other senses to predict where I'll be and when to strike."

Kai nodded, taking a deep breath as he prepared to engage in the exercise. He reached out his hands, feeling the air around him, and concentrated on the sounds of Lyra's breathing and footsteps.

As they began to move, Kai discovered that his hearing had indeed improved, allowing him to track Lyra's movements more accurately than he had anticipated. He was also pleasantly surprised to find that his strength and speed had increased, likely a result of Azar's power – a secret he still had to keep from his friends.

At first, Kai struggled to maintain his balance and coordination, but with each passing moment, he grew more confident in his abilities.

Then Lyra's open palm slapped into his face and he shook his head.

"Concentrate on my movements, Kai," Lyra berated Kai and he returned his attention to the training at hand.

Elijah and Alina watched in awe as Kai began to defend himself against Lyra, blocking a good portion of her attacks and even managing to land a few strikes of his own.

Elijah and Alina exchanged impressed glances, amazed at the progress their friend was making in such a short time. Especially after what he had been through and how fragile he looked.

"Wow, Kai," Lyra said, her voice filled with admiration. "You're really adapting to this quickly. I think you have a natural talent for feeling where I'm going to be!"

Alina nodded in agreement. "I've never seen someone learn so fast. You're truly remarkable, Kai."

Kai smiled, his cheeks flushing with pride. "Thanks, guys. Just lucky I guess."

The group continued to train for hours, focusing on grappling techniques, balance exercises, and even some basic self-defence moves. Kai found that he was able to learn and adapt to each new challenge, his body and mind working in harmony to overcome his limitations. He was still inferior to the others for sure, but it wasn't like before. Where before he'd lost every bout, every challenge and couldn't see any hope for the future, now he felt like he *knew* what he was supposed to do, and with each passing moment he was getting closer and closer to victory.

During a break, as they sat together on the edge of the training sands, Kai couldn't help but feel a sense of accomplishment. He had faced his fears and was beginning to thrive despite his blindness.

Elijah clapped Kai on the back. "You did great today, man. You're going to be an amazing fighter, no doubt about it."

Alina smiled warmly. "And you'll be an even more incredible mage once you've mastered your mana. We're so proud of you, Kai."

Lyra chimed in, her eyes shining with admiration. "You've shown us all what it means to be strong and resilient. You've inspired us to push ourselves even harder."

Kai felt his heart swell with gratitude for his friends' unwavering support. "Thank you, all of you. I couldn't ask for a better team."

After they had all regained their breath, Alina stood up and announced to the group. "I think it's time we showed Kai what we've been doing apart from the fighting."

Kai turned his head towards where he knew Alina was standing, awaiting the end of her statement.

"The spells, Kai. We won't win a tournament designed for mages to fight each other by fighting hand to hand!"

"Oh," Kai said, his heart sinking. Somewhere along the way he had forgotten that he was still unable to use his mana effectively. In fact, the one spell he actually could cast in the past – the tiny candle-like flame in the palm of his hand – he didn't know if he could still actually do. It'd been days since he'd even tried.

Lyra sensed Kai's sudden unease and quickly reassured him. "Don't worry, Kai. We're going to help you with your magic too. We've all been working on new spells and techniques, and we'll teach you everything we've learned."

Elijah nodded in agreement. "Yeah, man. We've got your back. Just take it one step at a time, and you'll be casting spells in no time."

Kai took a deep breath, trying to push aside his anxiety. He knew his friends were right – he couldn't let his fear of failure hold him back. With their support, he could learn to harness his mana and become the mage he was meant to be.

Determined to face this new challenge head-on, Kai stood up and joined his friends as they moved to a different part of the training sands, one more suited for magical practice. He could hear the sounds of other mages casting spells in the distance, their voices and the crackling of energy creating a symphony of power.

They began with basic spellcasting exercises, focusing on visualising their mana properly. Lyra guided Kai through her thought process as she engaged with her Eternal Flame, her voice steady and encouraging as she demonstrated the way in which she spoke to her mana. Kai listened intently, trying to mimic Lyra's instructions. Of course he'd tried this so many times before without any success, but the help of his friends, and the knowledge that a good portion of his Flame used to belong to Azar meant that this time he had a better chance, didn't he?

To his shock and surprise, slowly but surely, Kai began to feel a connection to his mana, a subtle thread of energy that seemed to hum with potential. With each attempt, he could sense the energy growing stronger, more tangible, the connection between him and his tiny candle of light turning from thin, tentative tendrils to a thick, unbreakable rope.

"Now I'm telling my mana that I want it to ignite in my hands, then curve the flame into a ball. Only small at first, but I can grow that later," Alina said as she watched conflicting expressions warring on Kai's face.

Then the entire group inhaled sharply as Kai's hands, no more than six inches apart began to glow, and between them, a swirling ball of fire grew into existence and stopped when it reached the size of a tennis ball.

The group erupted in cheers and congratulations, their faces beaming with pride and excitement. They couldn't believe that Kai had managed to create a fireball, a feat that had eluded him for so long. It was a testament to his determination and the progress he had made in harnessing his mana.

But their celebration was short-lived, as they soon realised that Kai faced a new challenge – aiming and throwing the new fireball. Without his sight to guide him, this would prove to be a daunting task.

Undeterred, Kai and his friends set up a simple target for him to practice on. They positioned him in front of the target, explaining its location and distance as accurately as possible. Kai took a deep breath, focusing his mind on the task at hand.

"Alright, Kai," Elijah said, his voice encouraging. "Just try to feel the target with your senses. Listen for any sounds, and imagine the path your fireball should take. You can do this."

Kai nodded, his brow furrowed in concentration. He could feel the heat of the fireball in his hands, the energy pulsing with potential. He listened intently, trying to pinpoint the exact location of the target. With a deep breath, he threw the fireball, hoping that his aim was true.

To their disappointment, the fireball sailed past the target, missing it by a significant margin. Kai sighed, his shoulders slumping, but his friends were quick to offer words of encouragement.

"Don't worry, Kai," Alina said, giving him a reassuring smile. "It's your first try. We'll keep practicing until you get it right."

Over the course of the afternoon, Kai attempted to hit the target again and again. With each throw, he inched closer and closer to his goal, his aim gradually improving. But despite his best efforts, he couldn't quite hit the target.

As the sun began to set, casting long shadows across the training sands, Kai and his friends reluctantly decided to call it a day. Although he had made significant progress, Kai couldn't shake the feeling of disappointment that gnawed at him. He had come so close, and yet the target still eluded him.

Lyra placed a comforting hand on his shoulder. "Don't be too hard on yourself, Kai. You've come a long way in a short time. Aiming without sight must be incredibly difficult, but we'll keep working on it together."

Elijah nodded in agreement. "Yeah, man. Rome wasn't built in a day. You'll get there. We have faith in you."

Kai managed a small, grateful smile. "Thanks, guys. I appreciate your support. I won't give up. I'll keep practicing until I can hit that target."

As they made their way back to their dorm, Kai couldn't help but feel a renewed sense of determination. He had faced countless challenges and had managed to overcome many of them. And though this particular hurdle still stood in his way, he knew that with the help of his friends and the guidance of Azar, he would eventually succeed.

Chapter 16 – Now You See Me

Kai lay in his bed, his thoughts swirling around the events of the day. He had made significant progress in his training, but there was still so much more to learn and achieve. As he lay there, contemplating his future, he felt a familiar presence in his mind – Azar.

"I must say, I am both surprised and pleased with how well you've adapted to the power I've shared with you," Azar said, his voice warm and encouraging. "You have shown remarkable resilience and determination."

Kai smiled, appreciative of the praise. "Thank you, Azar. I couldn't have done it without your help and guidance."

As their conversation continued, Kai couldn't help but bring up the one obstacle that still weighed heavily on his mind – his vision. "Azar, I know you said you couldn't restore my sight, but I've been thinking... is there any way I could use my mana to 'see' in some way?"

Azar was silent for a moment, considering Kai's question. "It's an interesting idea," he mused. "I have never encountered such a request before, but it's possible that we could find a way to help you sense the world around you using your mana in some way."

Kai felt a flicker of hope ignite within him. "Really? How would that work?"

Azar explained his thoughts. "We could try to extend your mana outward, like a sort of energy field. By sensing how the mana interacts with objects and living beings around you, it might give you a rudimentary form of 'vision'. But I can't be sure."

Kai's excitement grew as he listened to Azar's idea. "That sounds amazing. Can we try it now?"

"I do not know what the results could be, and I do not know if it is going to be painful. But I am willing to try this with you, if it is something that you truly desire," Azar said.

Kai took a deep breath, considering the potential risks and challenges. But his desire to find a way to 'see' and improve his abilities was stronger than his fear. "Yes, I want to try it, Azar. I understand the risks, but I believe this could be a real breakthrough for me."

Azar acknowledged Kai's determination and prepared to guide him through the process. "Very well, Kai. Focus your mind and gather your mana, then gently push it outward, creating a thin layer of energy around you. I will give you another portion of myself so that it may strengthen this spell – because you must understand, that is what this is."

Kai did as instructed, concentrating on his mana and slowly extending it outward. As the energy field began to envelop him, he felt a slight tingling sensation, but no pain. He could sense the mana interacting with the objects and living beings in his vicinity, eventually providing him with a crude form of 'vision.'

He could see his body, his hands and legs out on the bed before him. He could see the bed itself, the walls, his desk, the door and even to some degree beyond. It was amazing and as Kai looked about himself without even turning his head, he realised two things: One, that everything he 'saw' this way was a deep red colour as his mana interacted with it, with different objects appearing in different shades of the colour, and two, that he could only see in a radius of about three metres all around himself.

It was an incredible experience; unlike anything he had ever felt before. As he began to practice and home in on specific objects around him, Kai internally decided to keep his blindfold on, both as a reminder of his journey and to focus his newfound ability without distraction. Besides, if his eyes truly did look demonic, it was probably for the best.

The other thing, was that without Kai's brain trying to decipher all the usual things in the small field of vision that his eyes had been so dependent on, it meant that he could see all around himself in a complete sphere, and it wasn't as dizzying as he might've thought previously.

Azar's voice echoed in his mind, filled with amazement and pride, shocking Kai back to the situation at hand. "This is extraordinary, Kai. I never imagined this would be possible, but you have proven once again that you are a remarkable individual."

Kai grinned, his heart swelling with gratitude. "Thank you, Azar. I couldn't have done this without you. I know we still have a long way to go, but with your guidance and support, I believe we can achieve great things."

Together, Kai and Azar continued to test this new ability, working to improve its range and accuracy. As Kai grew more adept at manipulating his mana field, he found that he could focus on specific objects with greater precision, as well as detect more subtle variations in the shades of red that represented the world around him. The one thing he couldn't seem to manage yet though, was to 'see' past a few metres. He didn't know if there was simply too much interference past this point or if he simply wasn't powerful enough yet, but he knew that he would keep trying, keep pushing to be better, stronger even, and his road ahead was getting less and less windy, and straighter with every day that passed.

Of course, it was not true sight as he had had previously, but this newfound perception provided Kai with a valuable tool in his quest to become a powerful mage. And in some ways, he thought that this could be even better. Just imagine being able to see someone sneaking up on him from behind, three metres away, what they held in their hands, the expression on their face without him even having to move an inch. Yes, in some ways this was going to be so much better than being able to see normally.

Once Kai had exhausted himself testing out this new ability, he eventually drifted off to sleep, his mind filled with the possibilities that lay ahead, he knew that he was no longer defined by his blindness. When he woke up, he'd have something new to show off to his friends. Or would he? He hadn't yet decided how to break the news to them, but he was sure he'd think of something.

The next morning as the group travelled to the great hall for breakfast, Kai had allowed his friends to take his arms to help him once again. He said not a word about the fact that he could now see all of them with relative red clarity and he took to the bench between Lyra and Elijah, who placed a plate of food before him.

Kai then reached out searching for a salt-shaker and began to feel all around the table in a mock mild frustration. His intentions, to him, were going to result in a hilarious situation.

Suddenly, he pulled his arms away from the table, announced "Ah, there it is," and picked up the illusive shaker without so much as a hesitation and effortlessly poured the perfect amount onto his food, all without giving any indication that he could actually see what he was doing.

The table fell silent, everyone staring at Kai in surprise. Finally, Alina broke the silence. "Kai, did you... how did you know exactly where the salt was?"

Kai couldn't contain his excitement any longer and beamed at his friends, looking directly at them each in turn.

"I have some news, everyone. Last night I… I developed a new way to 'see' using my mana. It's not perfect, but I have a way of seeing things as kind of a spell I think…"

His friends exchanged shocked looks before they broke into wide grins, excited and amazed by Kai's revelation. Lyra reached out and squeezed his hand. "That's incredible, Kai! You really are full of surprises."

"How?" Elijah said loudly after swallowing the food that had filled his mouth.

Kai chuckled at their reactions and began to explain, "Well, last night, I had an idea. What if I could extend my mana outward, like an energy field? I can sense how the mana interacts with objects and living beings around me, giving me a sort of 'vision.' Everything I 'see' is in shades of red, and my range is limited to about three meters, but it's definitely an improvement."

Kai watched as each of his friends' mouths hung agape at his explanation and smiled again, beginning to shovel food into his mouth without any issues.

"Can we all do it?" Alina asked with wide eyes.

"No idea," Kai said. "Try it, I'll walk you through what I do."

So, one by one, Kai attempted to walk his friends through the process of extending their mana outward as an energy field. He explained how to focus their minds, gather their mana, and push it outward gently, creating a thin layer of energy around themselves.

However, as each of his friends tried the technique, they couldn't quite get it to work. They furrowed their brows, attempting to sense their surroundings with their mana, but their functioning eyes seemed to interfere with their ability to perceive the world in the way that Kai could.

After several attempts, Lyra sighed in frustration. "I just can't seem to get it to work, Kai. It's like my eyes are too busy processing the world around me, and I can't focus on sensing my mana."

Elijah nodded in agreement. "I think that's the problem, Lyra. Our eyes are so used to interpreting the world for us that it's difficult to switch to an entirely different way of perceiving things."

Kai couldn't help but feel a little disheartened that his friends couldn't share in his new ability, but he also understood that his unique circumstances had allowed him to develop this skill. "I guess it's something that came about because of my blindness," he admitted. "Maybe my brain had to find a new way to perceive the world, and my connection to mana allowed for that to happen."

Alina placed a comforting hand on Kai's shoulder. "Don't be upset, Kai. This ability is unique to you, and it's an incredible gift. You've managed to turn a weakness into a strength, and that's something to be proud of."

As the group finished their breakfast, they decided to head out to the training arena to work on their fireball spell and with Kai's newfound ability to see, he wondered just how good he could possibly get.

The sun was shining brightly, casting a warm glow over the training arena through the open ceiling, and the place was already alive with the sounds of groups of mages practicing their spells.

Upon arriving at the training arena, Kai and his friends found an open space to practice. Kai felt a mixture of excitement and trepidation as he prepared to put his newfound ability to the test. He could 'see' the targets around him, their red shades standing out against the dark background. He took a deep breath and focused, determined to make the most of this opportunity.

Kai began by working on his fireball spell, concentrating his mana into a small, fiery orb between his open hands. He then extended his mana field to encompass the targets, sensing their positions and the distance between them as they moved back and forth. He knew he could do more than simply hit one target – he could focus on multiple targets all around himself. With his enhanced perception, he was able to track the targets' position and calculate the trajectory of his fireball with precision, without so much as turning his head.

His friends watched in awe as Kai launched a series of fireballs at the targets, his accuracy improving with each attempt. The fireballs flew through the air, leaving a trail of smoke and heat in their wake, and collided with the targets, causing them each to burst into flames. Kai's control over his mana and his new way of seeing the world had allowed him to anticipate the targets' movements and make split-second adjustments to his aim.

"Are you kidding me?" Elijah announced loudly. "You're the only person who could come back from what you did and have it turn out for the best!"

"Way to go Kai!" Lyra cheered, and Alina tapped Kai on the back.

"This is amazing Kai, keep going!"

As the training session progressed, Kai continued to push himself, refining his control over the fireball spell and experimenting with different techniques. He discovered that by adjusting the intensity of his mana field, he could focus on specific areas or expand it to encompass a larger area, giving him greater awareness of his surroundings. This newfound ability allowed him to not only direct the fireball towards a single target but to also split his focus and send fireballs towards multiple targets simultaneously.

Kai's friends couldn't help but be impressed by his progress. They practiced alongside him, honing their own skills and providing words of encouragement and support. As the training session continued, they all felt a sense of camaraderie and teamwork, knowing that they were all working towards a common goal.

As the day wore on and the sun began to set, casting long shadows across the training arena, Kai and his friends finally decided to call it a day. They were exhausted but exhilarated, their faces flushed with excitement and the heat of their magical exertions. As they turned to leave though, a familiar voice caused them to stop on their tracks.

"Can you come with me, please?" Grandmaster Orthos said to Kai. Kai could tell though that it wasn't as much of a request, as it was an order.

Kai glanced at his friends, who all shared a mix of concern and curiosity in their expressions. He nodded to the Grandmaster and followed him as they walked away from the group, leaving his friends to exchange worried glances.

Grandmaster Orthos led Kai to his office, the room still filled with bookshelves, artefacts, and the large, ornate desk covered with scrolls and parchment. He gestured for Kai to take a seat, and the young mage did as he was told, feeling a knot of anxiety in his stomach.

"I've been watching your progress, Kai," the Grandmaster began, his eyes studying Kai intently. "Your new ability to use your mana is truly remarkable. You have managed to turn a disadvantage into a powerful tool, and that is no small feat. I'm proud of you, Kai. This is what you always wanted."

Kai swallowed hard, unsure of where the conversation was going. "Thank you, Grandmaster," he replied, trying to keep his voice steady.

The Grandmaster leaned back in his chair, his fingers steepled in front of him. "Your progress has not gone unnoticed, Kai. The way you've harnessed your unique situation and applied it to your magical training is impressive. You've shown dedication and adaptability, and these are qualities we value in a mage."

Kai felt a flicker of hope, but he remained silent, waiting for the Grandmaster to continue.

"As such," Grandmaster Orthos said, "I have decided to promote you back to your previous rank of Journeyman. You have proven that you are capable of overcoming obstacles and adapting to new challenges, and I believe you have earned this recognition."

Kai's eyes widened, and he felt a wave of relief and joy wash over him.

"Thank you, Grandmaster," he said, his voice thick with emotion. "I won't let you down."

"I know you won't," the Grandmaster replied, a hint of a smile playing at the corners of his mouth. " I expect you to continue your training and exploration of this gift, and I look forward to seeing what you can achieve."

Kai nodded, determination burning in his chest. "I will do my best, Grandmaster."

As they stood up to leave the office, the Grandmaster placed a hand on Kai's shoulder. "Remember, Kai," he said, his voice firm but encouraging, "your strength lies not only in your magic but also in your determination and resourcefulness. Never forget that."

Kai nodded, feeling a newfound sense of purpose and resolve. "I won't, Grandmaster. Thank you for your faith in me."

With that, they left the office, and Kai returned to his friends, who were eagerly waiting for news. As he shared the Grandmaster's decision with them, their faces lit up with pride and happiness.

Chapter 17 – Preliminaries

With only a few days to go before the first round of the upcoming tournament, the group decided to do what they had become very good at in their time in The Pit: they were going to train. But this time, they decided to see what they could do to work as a team. To combine their fire magic with their increasing skills in hand-to-hand combat, thanks mainly to Lyra.

The training grounds were bustling with activity as the other mages prepared for the tournament as well. The anticipation and excitement were palpable, and Kai and his friends could feel the energy in the air. As usual, they found an area to practice, away from the other groups, and began discussing their strategy.

"Alright, guys," Lyra began, taking the lead as she had become accustomed to doing during their hand-to-hand combat training, "we need to figure out how to combine our fire magic and combat skills effectively and to work as a team. We've been working on them separately, but now it's time to bring it all together."

Alina nodded in agreement. "Lyra's right. We should be able to use our fire magic to enhance our physical abilities and surprise our opponents."

Elijah chimed in, "And we can also use our hand-to-hand skills to create openings for our magic attacks."

Kai, feeling confident with his new ability, said, "I think I can use my mana vision to help us coordinate our attacks and keep track of our opponents' movements. That way, we can avoid being blindsided and stay one step ahead."

His friends agreed, and they began devising a plan that would take advantage of each of their unique strengths. They practiced various combinations, working on timing and coordination, and learning how to anticipate each other's moves.

As they trained, they quickly discovered that their individual skills complemented each other perfectly. Lyra's agility and speed made her a formidable fighter, able to dodge and weave around her opponents while landing quick, powerful strikes. Elijah's brute strength allowed him to overpower his opponents, giving him the opportunity to deliver crushing blows.

Alina's keen analytical mind enabled her to predict their opponents' movements and devise clever counterattacks, while her mastery of fire magic allowed her to do something that filled Kai's vision with so much mana that he had to concentrate to stop it from blinding him. In his absence, Alina had found a way to make the walls of fire that were always so effective in shepherding opponents around the battlefield.

Kai, with his mana vision, acted as the group's eyes and ears, guiding the group through the chaos of battle and helping them stay in sync. It would mean they were effectively a man light because he wasn't right there in the thick of it, but if they could all work together properly, he didn't think it would matter.

As the group continued practicing their new strategies and techniques, they became more and more confident in their abilities to work together as a team. The synergy between them was apparent, and they could feel the progress they had made. They were excited to put their skills to the test in the upcoming tournament, but little did they know that they would face a challenge sooner than expected.

As they wrapped up one of their practice rounds, a familiar voice called out to them, dripping with disdain. "Well, if it isn't the misfit group trying to play with the big kids," Marcus sneered, his eyes scanning the group with contempt.

Marcus, being a Master-ranked mage was not participating in the upcoming group matches, but apparently that didn't stop him from making his presence felt. As he approached the group, his gaze settled on Kai, his lips curling into a cruel smile.

"What are you even doing here, Kai?" he taunted. "From what I can see, you're not doing anything useful. You're just standing there, pretending to be important."

Kai clenched his fists, struggling to control his anger. His friends stepped in, trying to defend him.

"Kai's been working hard to overcome his disability," Alina shot back.

"He's been a huge help to us so why don't you just leave us alone."

Lyra chimed in, her eyes narrowed in defiance. "Kai is a vital part of our team, Marcus. We wouldn't be where we are without him."

Marcus simply laughed, his eyes cold and unfeeling. "Oh, please. As if any of you stand a chance in the tournament. You're all just wasting your time. I could take on all of you on my own and still come out on top."

The group exchanged glances, their resolve hardening. They knew that Marcus was trying to get under their skin, but they refused to let him get the better of them.

"Fine," Elijah said, his voice steady and determined. "If you think you're so much better than us, then prove it. Let's have a little friendly competition, shall we?"

Marcus raised an eyebrow, a smug grin spreading across his face. "You're serious? Very well. I'll show you just how outclassed you are."

The group quickly prepared themselves, their hearts pounding with a mix of nerves and excitement as they stood facing their superior opponent. They knew that Marcus was a formidable mage, but they also had faith in their own abilities and in each other. Either way, they would win or they would lose and besides, they really needed to see what they could do whilst working together as a team.

As the impromptu match began, Kai took his position behind the rest of the group, using his mana vision to track Marcus's movements and make sure he wasn't doing anything out of the ordinary. They moved as a cohesive unit, their training together allowing them to anticipate each other's actions and coordinate their attacks.

Marcus stood across from them, his posture relaxed but confident, a smug grin still plastered on his face. As the battle commenced, it was clear that Marcus wasn't going to hold back. He raised his hands, and a wave of fire erupted from his palms, hurtling towards the group with incredible force like a column of flame.

Alina quickly reacted, creating a barrier of her own fire magic to shield them from the worst of the flames. Despite her efforts, the sheer power of Marcus's attack pushed them back, the heat from the flames making it difficult for the group to breathe.

Regaining their footing, Lyra and Elijah charged at Marcus, hoping to use their hand-to-hand skills to pressure him. Lyra darted around him, her agility and speed allowing her to evade his fiery attacks. She landed a quick strike on Marcus's side, but it seemed to barely faze him.

Elijah, on the other hand, relied on his brute strength to try and overpower Marcus. He launched a series of heavy punches, but Marcus nimbly dodged each one, countering with a well-placed fireball that sent Elijah sprawling to the ground.

Meanwhile, Alina kept her distance, conjuring walls of fire to keep Marcus contained in one area, while searching for an opening to strike for herself. Marcus, however, was unfazed by her efforts, his mastery of fire magic allowing him to easily dissipate her walls with blasts of heat and fire, and continue his relentless assault on the group.

It became increasingly clear that Marcus held the upper hand. His fire magic was far more potent than any of theirs, and his experience as a Master-ranked mage gave him an edge in both strategy and combat skills.

Kai, doing his best to guide the group through the chaos of the battle, felt a growing sense of frustration and helplessness. He could see Marcus's attacks coming, growing within his body before erupting like a volcano, but their combined efforts still weren't enough to gain the upper hand.

Desperate for a win, the group attempted one last coordinated assault. Lyra and Elijah, bruised but determined, launched themselves at Marcus once more, while Alina prepared a powerful fire spell.

Kai, focusing all his energy into his mana vision, tried to find an opening in Marcus's defenced, saw a brief moment of vulnerability as the mana left Marcus' body and he was drawing in more for anther spell. Without hesitation, Kai shouted, "Now, Alina!"

Alina didn't need to be told twice. She unleashed her spell, a massive fireball that rocketed towards Marcus with incredible speed. For a moment, it seemed as if their attacks might land, but Marcus simply smirked, raising his hands and conjuring an enormous firestorm, picking up the fireball as it approached and it joined hundreds more as they began to swirl around Marcus like they were caught within this orbit.

The firestorm roared and expanded to all around them, the heat and pressure threatening to crush the group. They could only watch in horror as their last-ditch effort failed.

Just as they were about to be consumed by the flames, Marcus lowered his hands, and the firestorm dissipated. The group, battered and exhausted, collapsed to the ground, their defeat undeniable.

Marcus stood over them, his smug grin wider than ever. "I told you, I could take you all on and still come out on top." He sneered, before walking away, leaving them to lick their wounds.

"Wait!" Kai called after Marcus. "Is that all you've got?"

Marcus stopped in his tracks, turning back to face Kai with a look of surprise and annoyance. "Excuse me?" he asked, his voice dripping with disdain.

"Is that all you've got, Marcus? I mean, we're just a group of Journeymen, and you barely broke a sweat. But if that's all you can do, then maybe you're not as impressive as you think you are."

Kai's friends looked at him in shock, unsure of what he was trying to achieve by provoking Marcus further.

Marcus's expression darkened, his smug grin replaced by a scowl. "You dare to challenge me further? Fine, I'll show you just how powerful I really am." With a quick motion, he raised his hands, summoning a massive wave of fire that threatened to engulf the entire group momentarily.

But Kai was ready for it. Drawing on every ounce of his Eternal Flame within, he focused on the fire. He watched as his friends dived out of the way of the powerful spell, but Kai simply stood there and awaited the arrival of the wave.

The flame came closer and closer, and brought with it the heat of a raging inferno, but Kai didn't budge. He simply stood there unmoving.

"Kai!" Elijah called out to his friend.

But it was too late. The inferno engulfed Kai and he disappeared from view as it raged all around him.

Kai though, could feel a lack of danger in the spell. Something deep within told him that there was something more he could do with these flames.

He watched as his friends gasped and covered their mouths and eyes and as they did so, Kai raised his arms to his sides and began to *draw in* the cyclone of fire that had wrapped itself around him.

Kai felt no pain, rather as the fire entered into his body it was as though it reached Azar deep within, and the powerful spirit of the mage he housed simply extinguished the attack without having to so much as raise a little finger.

The group watched in awe as the fire dissipated, leaving Kai unscathed and nothing but smoke and steam rising from his body. Marcus, his face a mixture of shock and fury, stared at Kai, unable to comprehend how he had managed to counter his attack.

Kai, breathing heavily but standing tall, stared back at Marcus. "Like I said, maybe you're not as impressive as you think you are."

After Marcus had left, the group gathered around Kai, bombarding him with questions and expressions of awe.

"Kai, how did you do that?" Lyra asked, her eyes wide with astonishment.

"Yeah, I've never seen anything like it," added Elijah, shaking his head in disbelief.

Kai hesitated, unsure of how to explain what had just happened. "I'm not entirely sure," he admitted, rubbing the back of his neck sheepishly. "When the fire was about to hit me, I felt this strange connection to it, like I could control it somehow. It's like something within me was helping me to extinguish the flames."

Alina, who had been quietly observing the conversation, finally spoke up. "It's possible that your connection to your mana has grown stronger since you've been able to use your mana vision. It's not unheard of for mages to develop unique abilities based on their bond with their magical spirit."

Kai considered her words, wondering if that could be the key to understanding his newfound ability. "So, you're saying that my connection to my Eternal Flame has evolved, allowing me to absorb and control fire?"

Alina nodded thoughtfully. "It's definitely a possibility. We'll have to do more research and testing to be sure, but it could be a game-changer for our team."

The group exchanged excited glances, the prospect of a new and powerful ability boosting their confidence even further.

Over the next few hours, the group continued to train tirelessly, honing their individual skills and working to strengthen their newfound teamwork. They researched and experimented with Kai's new ability to absorb and control fire, gradually incorporating it into their strategies and tactics.

As night fell, the group gathered around a small fire that they had brought into being a few inches off the tabletop in their common area. They were discussing their experiences and the implications of Kai's newfound ability. The warm glow of the fire cast flickering shadows on their faces, illuminating their excitement and determination.

"We've come a long way in such a short time," Elijah mused, poking at the fire with a stick. "I never thought we'd be able to stand up to someone like Marcus, but we did. And now, with Kai's new power, we're even stronger."

Lyra nodded in agreement. "We've grown so much, both as individuals and as a team. It's incredible what we can achieve when we put our minds to it."

Alina, ever the strategist, couldn't help but think about the future. "We still have a lot of work ahead of us, though. We need to perfect our teamwork and make sure we're ready for whatever challenges come our way. But I believe in us. I know we can do it."

"I feel like we already won," Elijah said. "I can't think of any better sight than Marcus' face as you absorbed his spell. Please, I'll pay you everything I have if you ever do that again!"

Kai couldn't help but chuckle at Elijah's enthusiasm. "I appreciate the offer, but I'll do it for free next time. Seeing the shock on Marcus's face was worth more than any amount of money."

The group shared a laugh, the tension of their recent battle and the upcoming challenges momentarily forgotten.

As the laughter died down, Lyra spoke up, her voice filled with conviction. "We've come a long way, but we can't rest on our laurels. We need to keep pushing ourselves, improving our skills and teamwork, so that when the time comes, we can stand up to anyone, not just Marcus."

Alina nodded in agreement. "You're right, Lyra. Our success so far is just the beginning. We have the potential to achieve even greater things, and we owe it to ourselves to pursue that potential to the fullest."

So with the day out, the group left the common area to their rooms. They knew that in just a couple of days, they'd be watched by the whole of The Pit, and they needed their rest if they were going to stand a chance of actually winning the tournament.

Chapter 18 – The Tournament

As the day of the tournament finally arrived, the group felt more prepared and united than ever before. The anticipation and excitement of the event were palpable, as mages from all over the academy gathered to compete for glory and prestige.

In the stands, spectators of all ranks buzzed with excitement, discussing the various competitors and their chances of victory. Among them, whispers began to spread about the underdog team of Journeymen who had stood up to Marcus, the Master-ranked mage, and survived. Everyone knew who Kai was after he had caused himself pain and suffering almost to the point of death once he had sat in the torture chair, but most of the group remained a mystery to the others, who'd been far more concerned with their own training and progress. Alina was a little more recognisable than the rest though, having won the Journeyman ranked tournament already.

As the day of the tournament began, Kai, Elijah, Lyra and Alina took their places in the stands, their hearts pounding with a mix of nerves and determination.

"Do we know who we're supposed to fight against?" Kai asked as he remembered that he hadn't checked to see if the brackets had been announced the day before as usual.

"Nah," Elijah replied. "This one's being kept a secret, so no one could get any unfair advantages."

That seemed fair to Kai. But he couldn't help but wonder who in the Journeyman-ranked mages would've teamed up together.

But to cut into his pondering, Grandmaster Orthos walked out into the centre of the sands, and cleared his throat. The vocalisation must've been so quiet in reality, but his voice carried around the stands and the arena, causing everyone present to be silent.

"Good morning Brotherhood of the Flame!" Orthos announced loudly. "The time has finally come, where we will pit the Journeyman mages against each other in battle, in groups of four!"

A loud cheer erupted from the crowd.

"This tournament has been designed so that you may see how different a fight can be when there is another mage by your side, one who you must trust with your life. This is what it is like in the real world, and what it is going to be like the day that we all fight together as one force to overthrow the oppressive reign of King Roderick and his army!"

Again another cheer erupted from the crowds.

"This week, the Apprentices will not fight. The Masters and Archmages will not fight, but the Journeymen will surely put on a display, the likes of which have never before been seen within The Pit!"

Cheers from the crowds now practically deafened Kai, and he couldn't help but join in.

"But I am sure that you are all eagerly awaiting confirmation of the groupings, and who you will be fighting against in this tournament!"

Kai couldn't stop himself from leaning forwards now, eager to hear who had been grouped up, but more importantly, who his group was going to face in the coming first round.

The Grandmaster then raised his hands to the air and above the arena sands, burning with a bright intensity appeared a tournament bracket with ten groups of four pit against each other in a knockout system. On the left were all ten groups in a line, with the progression lines etched into the air to show who they would fight in each round. Because there were ten teams though, it meant that one team would get an automatic bye through to the final after their second fight. The other participants would have to reach the final with three wins, putting them all at a definite disadvantage.

Kai scanned the brackets for the teams, and he saw that his group were to fight in the third contest, against Mia, Theo, Charlotte and Zack. Their position in the brackets also meant that they would not be the lucky team getting the bye to the final.

The group of Nathan, Dex, Owen and Aiden – of whom Nathan and Owen were Marcus' friends – were to fight last against Henry, Emma, Hunter and Lucas, which meant that if they won their first two fights, they would arrive in the final against Kai and his friends. Kai couldn't help feeling that it was a little unfair, though he knew that to be the best, you had to be prepared to face off against anyone.

"So without any further fanfare," the Grandmaster spoke again, "I invite the first two teams into the arena of battle, to test their combined might against each other! I must remind you though, as usual it is not permitted to land a purposeful killing blow on your opponents, and once one team has been left with no members able to continue, the victors will be announced."

Kai watched as eight people descended the stands to stand in two groups of four. On the one side, Theo, Kylian, Lionel and Levi, four young boys who looked very sure of themselves and on the other, Anthony, Lex, Justin and Beatrice. This group looked a little more worried about the contest and truth be told, Kai didn't truly recognise any of them. Not because everyone looked a little different as he watched through his mana visior, rather because at least a few of these Journeymen mages must have been relatively new to the Brotherhood.

The Grandmaster retreated from the sands and sent up a great burst of flame to indicate the beginning of the battle.

Kai watched intently for the first moves.

Theo's group, who had certainly practised together by the way they fanned out, leaving an even handful of metres between each of them were the first to move, where Anthony's group huddled together as though if they spread out, they would present themselves as easy targets.

Theo and his three partners, seeing their opponent's reluctance to engage with them properly, quickly moved to surround the group of worried-looking mages and when they were in place, they each exchanged a short nod.

Kai saw the mana build up inside of them before the crowds gasped, signalling the first spells being cast in the tournament. Theo, Kylian, Lionel and Levi all raised their hands towards their opponents and as one unleashed four identical bursts of bright orange flame. They walked forwards menacingly as their jets of orange burning heat threatened to end the battle before it had even begun, and Kai couldn't help but grit his teeth.

The flames caused sweat to bead on the faces of the huddled mages and Kai wondered if the Grandmaster was going to stop this madness, when he saw a new burst of mana building up from within the huddle. A second later, a wall of flame burst up from the ground and intercepted the incoming flamethrowers. The flames joined and flickered high up into the air as the walls remained in place, but the advancing mages did not let their spells drop. It looked like it was going to be a battle of attrition, where offence would meet defence and eventually one would have to falter.

The walls continued to absorb to terrible flamethrowers emanating from the four mages, who by the looks on their faces, already thought they had won this fight. Kai watched as the blazing inferno rose up and even though he was using his mana vision to see through the flames, it was so bright and the arena so full of mana that he couldn't see what was happening behind the walls. The flames simply obscured his sight and he wondered if the four were even still alive in there.

His question was then answered, as the four mages stepped closer and closer until eventually he was sure that nothing could survive inside their attack.

All of a sudden though, two of the mages from within leapt through the flames and launched fireballs from point-blank range into the faces of two of their opponents. Their flamethrowers were immediately extinguished and the battle had swung from a certain loss in Kai's eyes, to a four on two.

The two remaining mages, Theo and Kylian dropped their spells for a moment, looking at each other as though they were unsure of what to do next. Their moment of hesitation though, would ultimately cause them the fight.

As Theo and Kylian hesitated, the four mages who had just turned the tide of the battle wasted no time in capitalising on their opponents' confusion. They quickly dropped the walls of flame from around themselves and launched a coordinated attack, with each mage casting a different spell that targeted their two opponents.

Anthony created some kind of intense heat around Kylian that closed ever inwards and intensified moment after moment, making it difficult for him to maintain his focus. Meanwhile, Lex sent a series of fireballs aimed at Theo, forcing him to constantly dodge and left him no time to counterattack. Justin controlled small walls of flame that moved around his teammates, creating protective barriers of fire to ward off any attempts from their opponents, and Beatrice summoned a swirling mass of fire that descended from above to catch the two remaining mages off-guard.

Theo and Kylian, overwhelmed and outmatched, tried their best to defend themselves, but their attempts were futile against the well-coordinated onslaught. Within moments, they were both incapacitated, their bodies lying smoking on the arena sands.

The crowd, initially stunned by the unexpected turn of events, roared with excitement and approval. The underdogs had triumphed, proving that teamwork and strategy could outshine sheer power if properly executed.

The Grandmaster raised his arms, signalling the end of the battle, and announced the victors. "Anthony, Lex, Justin, and Beatrice have emerged victorious! Let us all applaud their impressive display of teamwork and skill."

Kai, still in the stands, couldn't help but feel a mixture of awe and excitement. The first battle had been nothing short of thrilling, and he knew that his own group would need to be just as well-prepared and coordinated if they hoped to succeed in their upcoming match.

As the victorious team left the arena to the cheers of the crowd, the next set of competitors began to make their way onto the sands.

The battle that followed was over far quicker than the first had been, with one team moving to the offence from the beginning. Just like in the first battle, the team that took this stance looked as though they were going to steamroll their opponent, but in contrast to the first, the defending team didn't have much to offer. They were soundly beaten in less than two minutes and the crowd didn't offer too much in the way of applause.

That meant that next up, was Kai and his friends.

Kai felt the excitement in the air grow as he stood up and began to descend the steps to the arena and as he did so, he watched as the spectators turned to watch the mage who could not see, the mage with the blindfold tied around his head, work his way towards the arena of battle to be tested against mages he had never once been able to stand up against.

Kai, Elijah, Alina and Lyra stood shoulder to shoulder as they looked across the arena sands at their opponents. Mia, Charlotte, Theo and Zack stared back at them, their faces a mix of confidence and determination. Kai could sense the mana radiating from each of them, their mastery of fire magic evident. He knew that his team would have to work together seamlessly if they were to stand a chance.

As the Grandmaster signalled the start of the battle, both teams immediately sprang into action. Mia and Charlotte sent streams of fire towards Kai's team, attempting to force them onto the defensive. Kai, thankful for his mana vision, expertly dodged the incoming flames and called out to his teammates, guiding them as they evaded the fiery assault.

Elijah and Alina countered with their own fire spells, creating a barrier of fire to shield them from their opponents' attacks and Lyra launched fireballs at Theo and Zack, forcing them to split up and divide their attention.

Both teams exchanging spells in a more conventional manner than had been evident in the tournament so far, and both attempted time after time to gain an advantage. It was clear that their opponents were skilled fire mages, and Kai's team had to rely on their teamwork and strategy to stay in the fight.

In a bold move, Kai and Elijah decided to close the distance between themselves and their opponents, using their recently honed hand-to-hand combat skills in combination with their fire magic. As they neared Mia and Charlotte, they both unleashed a torrent of fire from their hands, momentarily blinding their opponents with the intense heat and light.

Seizing the opportunity, Kai and Elijah rushed forward, ducked down low and shot in to take the two girls down with double-leg takedowns, dumping them to the ground simultaneously. They then swiftly applied their armbars, using their physical strength and practised technique to quickly change the odds for the rest of the fight. Despite Mia and Charlotte's attempts to break free, Kai and Elijah maintained their grips, finally forcing them to yield.

With Mia and Charlotte out of the fight, Kai's team now had the advantage. They all turned their focus to Theo and Zack, who had been momentarily distracted by the surprising turn of events. Lyra and Alina pressed the attack, sending waves of fire and heat in sequence towards their remaining opponents and forcing them on the defensive.

As Theo and Zack struggled to counter the relentless assault, Kai and Elijah moved in to support their teammates. Elijah managed to create a vortex of flames that swirled around their opponents, while Kai peppered them with tennis-ball sized fireballs. It was still one of the few things that he could actually pull off.

With no means of escape, Theo and Zack were left with no choice but to defend themselves as best as they could. They tried to extinguish the flames surrounding them with their own blasts and walls of heat, but their efforts were futile against the combined might of Kai's team.

Seeing their opponents weakening, Kai's team increased the speed and intensity of their assault, the vortex of flames growing hotter and fiercer and the fireballs now coming quicker and quicker.

Finally, unable to withstand the overwhelming heat and pressure, Theo and Zack succumbed, falling to the ground in defeat.

The crowd, who had been holding their breath throughout the intense battle, erupted in cheers and applause as the Grandmaster raised his arms, signalling the end of the match. "Kai, Elijah, Alina, and Lyra have emerged victorious! Let us all celebrate their incredible display of teamwork, strategy, and skill!"

As Kai and his friends left the arena, their hearts pounding with adrenaline and pride, they knew that they had proven themselves as a formidable team, but they knew that their next opponents would've been watching, so the same tricks weren't going to work for a second time.

Chapter 19 – Round 2

The four friends made their way back to their seats in the stands, mentally preparing themselves for the challenges that lay ahead. As they watched the last battle in the first round unfold, they couldn't help but analyse the techniques and strategies employed by the last two teams, searching for potential weaknesses they could exploit in future matches if they had to face these opponents.

The battle turned out to be the longest so far, and as the minutes progressed, the level of skill and intensity displayed by the participating mages only seemed to increase. Each round of attacks and defences brought new surprises and thrilling moments that left the crowd on the edge of their seats. This new style of competition was surely about to become everyone's favourite.

Kai and his friends discussed their observations and strategized for their upcoming match. They knew they couldn't rely on the same tactics that had brought them victory in their first battle. Instead, they would need to adapt and evolve, constantly refining their teamwork and honing their individual skills. They also knew that their opponents, Oliver, Henry, Oscar and Sara had already proven that they were a formidable group and if they fought like they had in the first round, they would be looking for a quick victory.

As the second round of the tournament began, the first battle between two of the previous round's winning teams took place. Kai, Elijah, Alina, and Lyra watched intently, eager to learn from the ongoing fight and use that knowledge to their advantage in their upcoming match.

"That team has excellent coordination," Alina observed, as one of the mages launched a perfectly timed fireball that managed to break through their opponents' defences. "We'll need to step up our own teamwork if we want to stand a chance against them."

"You're right," Lyra agreed. "But did you notice how their fire spells seem to be weaker on the defensive? If we can keep up the pressure, we might be able to find an opening."

Kai listened carefully to his friends' comments, his mana vision allowing him to 'see' the battle in a way that others could not.

"Their defensive tends to favour creating walls of flame. If we can find a way to breach those walls or bypass them altogether, we might be able to catch them off guard," Alina continued.

Kai in fact, had already noticed this. It seemed like as soon as one group had used defensive walls, it was all anyone could do to imitate them.

Alina nodded, taking note of the opposing team's weaknesses. "We should also work on improving our own defensive spells. It's clear that the competition is only getting fiercer, and we'll need to be prepared for anything."

"We should try to come up with something that isn't a wall of flames or a blast of heat, something that'll really surprise people," Kai said.

As the bout continued, the friends went on discussing their observations, dissecting each team's strategy and technique. They tried to predict the outcome of the fight and offered suggestions on how they would counter specific moves if they were in the same situation.

Gradually, the battle reached its climax, with both teams launching one final, desperate attack against each other. In the end, it was the team with superior coordination and adaptability that emerged victorious, a lesson that Kai and his friends took to heart.

As their own match drew closer, the friends walked down from the stands again and gathered at the edge of the arena, away from the noise and excitement of the crowd. They knew that it was crucial for them to remain focused and composed if they wanted to have any chance of advancing to the next round.

Elijah, who had been relatively quiet up until this point, finally spoke up. "I've been thinking about our defensive options. Since we're all fire mages, we should find a way to diversify our fire spells to create a more effective barrier that can work offensively as well as defensively. What if we could manipulate the intensity and behaviour of our flames to make them harder to predict and penetrate, but also send out burst of flames when anyone comes close?"

"That's a great idea, Elijah," Lyra said, nodding enthusiastically. "And we can experiment with different fire properties, like creating a swirling vortex of flames or something that would be difficult for opponents to navigate or using rapidly oscillating temperatures to throw them off. It's just that… if we do this against Arlo's team, then if we make it through to the final, we'll have to face two more teams and no doubt they'll be watching us."

Kai considered Lyra's concern and nodded in agreement. "You're right, Lyra. We need to strike a balance between showcasing our strength and keeping some tricks up our sleeves for the future battles. We can start by implementing Elijah's idea of manipulating the intensity and behaviour of our flames, but let's keep the swirling vortex and rapidly oscillating temperatures as secret weapons for later rounds."

Alina chimed in, "That's a good plan. We can also practice and improve our communication and adaptability during the battle. That way, we can adjust our strategy on the fly if needed without giving away all our secrets."

When it was finally time for their second-round match against Oliver, Henry, Sara, and Oscar's team, Kai, Elijah, Alina, and Lyra felt prepared and focused.

As the Grandmaster called out the names of the two teams, the atmosphere in the arena became electrified with anticipation. Kai, Elijah, Alina, and Lyra stood tall, once again shoulder to shoulder, eyes locked on their opponents, who were mirroring their determined stance. Grandmaster Orthos swiftly raised his hand, signalling the start of the match.

Without a moment's hesitation, both teams sprang into action. Oliver and Henry, both clearly skilled Journeymen as Kai had seen from their previous bout, launched a barrage of fiery projectiles towards Kai and his friends, hoping to catch them off guard with a quick and aggressive opening move. However, the four friends had anticipated this strategy and immediately responded with their own counterattack.

Elijah, putting his earlier idea into practice, pulled a wall of flames up before the group and manipulated the intensity of his flames to create a flexible and dynamic barrier that bent and seemed to absorb the incoming fireballs as they impacted his spell. If anything, as the balls of flames hit, the wall seemed to grow slightly larger and hotter. The flames in the barrier danced and flickered unpredictably, making it difficult for the opposing team to discern any pattern or weakness in the wall. As an added touch, Elijah then incorporated small bursts of fire that shot out tiny balls of fire from the barrier towards their opponents, though it was clear that these caused little harm as when Oliver allowed the balls to hit him, they splashed into tiny puffs of smoke without any damage caused.

Kai and Alina then began to focus on the offensive, launching a coordinated assault on Oliver and Henry. Working together, Lyra sent a powerful wave of fire towards the duo, forcing them to split up and break their formation and Kai ran at Henry as quickly as his legs would carry him. He couldn't help but smile at the surprise on Henry's face at the speed with which Kai could move, regardless of the fact that he still wore a blindfold tied around his face.

Kai barrelled into Henry, though the boy had seen Kai's group use the same double-leg takedown in the last match and he managed to get out of the way of Kai's attack at the last moment, throwing Kai to the ground.

But Kai was unfazed by the setback. Using his momentum, he rolled back to his feet in one swift motion, and he could see within Henry that he was already summoning his mana for a counterattack, so he focused his energy and unleashed a small ball of fire directly at Henry's face.

Henry, clearly not expecting Kai to recover so quickly nor be able to cast a spell with such speed and accuracy, narrowly dodged the flames. As he regained his footing, he looked up just in time to see Lyra advancing on him with her hands raised, forcing him to retreat further.

Oliver was doing his best to handle the assault from Elijah and Alina. He managed to deflect some of their attacks and returned with a few of his own, but it was clear that the relentless pressure was starting to wear him down. Sweat beaded on his forehead as he struggled to keep up with their rapid-fire spells and eventually, he called out to his friends for assistance.

Lyra launched a volley of precise, high-speed fire bolts at Henry as he stepped back further and further, unrelenting in her desire to end the fight quickly. Kai too joined in with a few fireballs of his own but Henry managed to bat them all away fairly consistently with a combination of small, precise walls of flame and bursts of intense heat.

Sara and Oscar quickly came to Henry's aid and helped him by creating a solid defensive barrier of their own. However, their barrier was more conventional and lacked the innovative features of Elijah's creation. Recognising the changing tide of battle, Alina shouted out to her teammates.

"Concentrate your attacks on the barrier, with enough force it'll fall!"

Kai, Lyra, and Alina immediately focused their efforts on Sara and Oscar's barrier. The three of them bombarded the defensive wall with a relentless barrage of fire spells, the heat and intensity increasing with each passing second. Elijah, seeing an opportunity, joined in the assault, adding his own powerful flames to the mix and the battle quickly changed to a clear four-on-four attack versus defence.

The barrier, strong as it was, began to show signs of faltering under the intense pressure. Sara and Oscar, struggling to maintain the wall, desperately tried to reinforce it, but it was clear that they were fighting a losing battle.

As the barrier continued to weaken, small cracks appeared in the wall of flames, allowing Kai and his friends to catch glimpses of their opponents on the other side as the flames flickered and began to die down. They could see the determination etched on their opponent's faces, but also the strain of trying to maintain the defensive spell.

Sensing that the barrier was on the verge of collapse and seeing the magic begin to fail, Kai gave a nod to his teammates, and they unleashed a combined firestorm of immense power. The sheer force of their combined attack shattered the barrier, sending a shockwave of heat and light throughout the arena and throwing their opponents back and to the ground.

With their defensive wall gone, Oliver, Henry, Sara, and Oscar were clearly left exposed and vulnerable. Kai and his friends didn't hesitate to press their advantage, launching a series of rapid attacks that forced their opponents to roll back away from them and throw up weak, hasty defensive spells as they went.

Oliver, trying to regain control of the situation, called out to his teammates.

"Regroup! Bring the wall back up!" he shouted. But the relentless onslaught from Kai, Elijah, Alina, and Lyra left little room for their opponents to mount a coordinated response.

Henry was the first combatant in the battle to fall. With a final burst of energy, he managed to deflect one last attack before succumbing to exhaustion, collapsing to the ground in defeat. Nobody sent any more spells his way as he walked from the arena sands and sat down on the edge, watching with hope as his comrades continued to fight.

Sara and Oscar, seeing their teammate removed from the battle, knew they needed to act quickly if they were to have any chance of turning the tide. They attempted to launch a counterattack of their own, but their efforts were met with fierce resistance from Alina and Elijah, who expertly shrugged off their weakened and hasty spells while maintaining their own offensive pressure.

Kai's own spells were clearly weaker than the rest of his teammates, being behind in his training and it became clear that Sara, Oscar and Oliver were taking the brunt of the enemy advances whenever they had the chance to counterattack. Seizing the opportunity to catch the other team off-guard, Kai began to skirt the battlefield as the other six traded spells back and forth. Eventually he made it to the side of the opposing team and sent two small fireballs simultaneously into the faces of Sara and Oscar. They didn't even see it coming.

The fireballs blinded their targets for a split second and it was all the opportunity that Elijah, Alina and Lyra needed to imitate what they had already seen happen in this tournament; they changed tact in their spells from fireball to flamethrower and within moments, Sara and Oscar were ingulfed in flames and heat.

The pair fell to the ground as the flames abated, removed from the battle and clearly soundly beaten.

Oliver, now the last remaining member of his team still standing, made a desperate attempt to fight back against the overwhelming force of Kai and his friends. He mustered a huge amount of strength and unleashed a powerful wave of fire all around himself, but Kai shouted a warning before the spell had even arrived and the group countered it as one with a combined blast of their own.

The audience watched in silence as the arena filled with a sense of foreboding, Kai's team slowly moving to surround Oliver as he stood, waiting for the final barrage of flames coming in his direction.

It didn't come though.

Kai's team was expecting Oliver to submit, being clearly beaten but he stood there, defiant to the end.

Then suddenly as Kai watched the mana surge within his one last opponent, Oliver mustered all of his remaining strength and unleashed a second powerful wave of fire all around him and in all directions. Elijah, Alina and Lyra all threw a burst of intense heat at Oliver in response and the two opposing forces of fire met, creating a spectacular display of cyclonic, swirling flames and intense heat. For a moment, it seemed as though the outcome of the battle hung in the balance, but it quickly became apparent that Kai's team's attack was simply too powerful for Oliver's to withstand.

As the flames died down, Oliver dropped to his knees, exhausted and defeated. The crowd, which had been holding its breath during the final clash, erupted into cheers and applause as the Grandmaster declared Kai, Elijah, Alina, and Lyra the winners.

Kai, Elijah, Alina, and Lyra stood victorious in the centre of the arena, their faces flushed with the heat of battle and their chests heaving as they caught their breath. As the applause from the crowd washed over them, they exchanged glances of relief and pride, knowing that they had given everything they had in that battle and emerged triumphant.

Grandmaster Orthos approached the group, a smile playing on his lips as he regarded the four young Pyromancers. "That was an impressive display of skill, teamwork, and determination," he said, his voice carrying across the arena. "You have shown great promise, and I look forward to seeing how you fare in the rest of the tournament."

Kai, Elijah, Alina, and Lyra bowed respectfully to the Grandmaster, their hearts swelling with gratitude for his acknowledgment. As they turned to leave the arena, they saw Oliver and his teammates waiting for them, their expressions a mix of disappointment and respect.

Oliver stepped forward, extending his hand towards Kai. "Well fought," he said, his voice hoarse from the exertion of battle. "You and your team were the better fighters today. Good luck in the rest of the tournament."

Kai grasped Oliver's hand firmly, giving him a nod of appreciation. "Thank you," he replied. "Your team put up a strong fight as well. I'm sure we'll see you again in future battles."

Oliver stared at Kai's blindfold for a long moment before letting his gaze drop, and with that, the two teams parted ways, each knowing that they had learned valuable lessons from the fierce competition.

Finally, having won the chance to rest for a moment, Kai's team made their way back to the stands to rest and watch the next round between Arlo, Harper, Elsa and Freya, and Rosie, Flo, Freddie and Jaxon.

Chapter 20 – An Easy Win

The next battle moved along quickly with Arlo's team winning with relative ease, and it now meant that in the next round, Kai's team would face off against Arlo's team, and then against the team of Nathan, Owen, Dex and Aiden providing they won that round. After that would come the final, where they would face one of the other two remaining teams.

It wasn't exactly fair, because Nathan's team would be able to rest for longer, having received a bye into the next round, but Kai wouldn't let anything as silly as that get to him.

As they watched Arlo's team celebrate their victory, Kai and his friends knew they would have to prepare themselves for an even more challenging battle ahead. They exchanged determined glances, silently agreeing to give their all in the upcoming match. Not that they hadn't already been giving it their all, but they had been holding a little something of themselves back, just so they didn't give all their secrets away right from the beginning. But they all knew that in the end, the tournament was about more than just winning; it was about proving themselves as skilled fire mages and growing together as a team.

As they continued to watch from the stands, Kai turned to his friends and spoke up. "Alright, guys, we need to come up with a solid plan for our match against Arlo's team. They won that last round easily, and we can't afford to take them lightly."

Lyra was the first to reply, "That's a good idea. We should also work on improving our communication during the battle. If we're more in sync with each other, we'll be more effective as a team. So far it's been alright, but I think we're going to have to work together more."

Alina added, "And let's not forget about our own individual strengths. We need to make sure we're all at our best when we face them. That means using everything we know, not just relying on the spur of the moment stuff."

Kai nodded, appreciating his friends' input. "You're all right. We have some time before our next match, so let's make the most of it. We'll study our opponents and come up with a solid strategy. And remember, no matter what happens, we're in this together."

His friends nodded, their determination evident in their expressions. They knew that the challenge would be tough, but they were ready to face it as a team. And with their unwavering dedication and strong bond, there was no doubt that they would give their all in the upcoming battles.

As the next round of matches commenced, Kai and his team observed their potential opponents closely. They couldn't help but notice the ruthless fighting style of Nathan, Owen, Dex, and Aiden. It quickly became clear that their tactics went beyond winning; they seemed to revel in causing pain and suffering to their opponents.

As Nathan's team faced off against Henry, Emma, Hunter and Lucas, the crowd initially cheered enthusiastically, excited to see a display of impressive magic. However, their excitement soon turned to shock and dismay as Nathan and Owen relentlessly attacked their opponents without pause, even after it was clear they had won the match and their opponents had surrendered.

Nathan and Owen focused their fire spells on their opponents' weak spots, aiming to inflict maximum pain and damage. It was as if they had no regard for the spirit of the tournament, and their cruelty was on full display for everyone to see.

Dex and Aiden, though not as ruthless as their teammates, seemed to have no qualms about following Nathan and Owen's lead. They, too, pummelled their opponents relentlessly, showing no mercy or compassion.

The crowd's cheers gradually turned into boos and jeers as they witnessed the unnecessary brutality. They could no longer support the cruel tactics being employed by Nathan's team. The Grandmaster, watching the match with a frown, appeared to be considering whether or not to intervene.

As the match continued, Kai, Elijah, Lyra, and Alina exchanged concerned glances. They knew that if they faced Nathan's team in the upcoming rounds, they would have to be prepared for a much darker and more dangerous battle than they had anticipated.

Seeing their opponents finally collapse under the relentless onslaught, Nathan and Owen smirked, clearly pleased with their performance and held their hands up in the air in arrogant victory. Even as the fallen members of The Brotherhood doubled over in pain and dropped to the ground before they could leave the field of battle, Nathan and Owen continued to launch a few more fireballs at them, as if to prove a point.

The Grandmaster, having seen enough, finally stepped forward and raised his arms to the air. With a wave of his hand, he extinguishing the flames that still burned within the arena, putting an end to the carnage.

He then sternly and loudly addressed Nathan, Owen, Dex, and Aiden.

"I will not tolerate this level of cruelty in my tournament. You have won this match, but let this serve as a warning: should you continue to fight with such malice and disregard for your fellow competitors, you will be disqualified and removed from the competition."

Nathan and Owen exchanged a defiant glance before nodding reluctantly, acknowledging the Grandmaster's warning. As they left the arena to the jeers and boos of the crowd, Kai's team couldn't help but feel a growing sense of unease.

After the incident, Kai and his friends regrouped, discussing how they would approach their future matches, particularly if they had to face Nathan's team soon. They knew they had to be ready for anything, but they also knew they couldn't let fear or anger guide them. Instead, they had to rely on their bond and their skills, and most importantly, they had to keep to the principles they had already begun to hold dear.

As the tournament progressed, the group continued to watch the other teams closely, learning from their strategies and techniques, taking mental notes of what they could do to best each opponent or team.

Their next match against Arlo's team, in the end, proved to be an easy one in contrast to what they had anticipated. Where they thought that they would have to coordinate their attacks to defeat their opponents with superior skill and planning, they found that their unwavering focus and superior skill were enough to secure a victory without even having to break much of a sweat. Through effective communication and teamwork, they managed to outmanoeuvre Arlo's team from the very beginning and defeat them without any trouble after bombarding their opponents from all angles with their most basic spells.

As they moved back into position on the sands, ready to face Nathan's team immediately following their victory, they couldn't shake the memory of the cruelty they had witnessed by this group in the last round.

They knew they had to be prepared for anything, but they also knew they couldn't let fear of what could happen influence their actions. Instead, they had to rely on their bond and their skills, and most importantly, they had to ignore the fact that this group really needed a good beating, and face off against them as they would any other.

The tension in the arena was palpable as the two teams faced off, each sizing up their opponents. It was clear that Nathan's team, with their raw power and cruel tactics, appeared to have the advantage and Kai could see the arrogance in all of their faces with his mana vision. However, Kai's was confident in the abilities of his friends and their teamwork, which could prove to be the deciding factor in the battle.

The Grandmaster announced the beginning of the match and immediately, Nathan's team lurched forward. A flurry of fireballs flew across the battlefield with Nathan's team focused on overwhelming their opponents with powerful attacks, while Kai's team worked in tandem to evade the flames and shield each other as the spells arrived.

Kai was able to detect the magical energy of his opponents' spells and anticipate their movements. He skilfully dodged and redirected the incoming fireballs, despite only being able to cast small ones himself. His teammates, noticing the effectiveness of his mana vision, took advantage of the openings he created and began to send hasty fireballs back at their opponents in response. It entirely to attack, rather to keep them off balance and unable to mount an effective coordinated attack.

Elijah, deciding to put his close-quarters combat techniques to good use took advantage of the ferocity of the battle and closed the distance between himself and Dex, catching his target guard. With a swift and precise movement, Elijah bundled Dex to the ground, momentarily neutralising him.

Anya and Lyra, seeing the success of Elijah's strategy, followed suit and began to run towards their own targets on Nathan's team, all the time throwing fireballs as they moved to cover their advance. They engaged Owen and Aiden in close combat with ferocious punches before leaning into their grappling techniques to try to subdue their respective opponents.

Nathan, realising that his team's lack of coordination was costing them the match, attempted to rally his teammates. However, their individualistic fighting styles, combined with their desire to be the best member of the team prevented them from working together effectively, leaving them vulnerable to the coordinated attacks of Kai's team.

As the battle continued, it became increasingly evident that Nathan's team's raw power was not enough to secure a victory. Kai's team, with their superior teamwork and strategic approach, began to gain the upper hand. All of this was new to Nathan and his team, having not had any real opportunities to learn hand-to-hand combat, focussing mainly on powerful fire spells were being manhandled and forced about the arena in a way they'd never experienced.

Despite their mounting advantage, Kai's team did not let their guard down. They knew that their opponents were still dangerous, and they couldn't afford to make any mistakes or the tide of battle could quickly change. They continued to press their advantage, using their grappling techniques and teamwork to keep their opponents off balance and constantly trying to retreat to a safe distance to cast their spells.

Eventually, Aiden managed to create some distance between himself and Lyra by creating a bright white flash of flame and rolling backwards. Immediately, he was relentless in his attacks, hurling fireballs towards the smaller girl. However, Lyra remained calm and used her speed and agility to evade his fireballs as she moved towards Aiden. When she was close enough, she executed a well-timed takedown, throwing Aiden to the ground and temporarily incapacitating him. This time though, she leapt into full mount and held his arms out by his sides.

Elijah continued to engage Dex, using his own quick reflexes and grappling expertise to keep his opponent on the defensive. Dex, growing increasingly frustrated by his inability to land a hit on Elijah, became more reckless in his attacks, leaving himself vulnerable to a decisive counter from Elijah.

As Dex lunged forward with a wild swing, Elijah swiftly sidestepped the attack and grabbed Dex's arm, twisting it behind his back and using his opponent's momentum to bring him to the ground. With Dex effectively pinned, Elijah maintained his hold, preventing Dex from breaking free and continuing the fight.

With Aiden and Dex incapacitated, the battle now came down to Kai, Elijah, Lyra and Alina, versus Owen and Nathan, but it wasn't going to be an easy fight, regardless of their advantage.

Nathan, his pride wounded and clearly growing increasingly desperate and angry, started to unleash a barrage of powerful fireballs in a last-ditch attempt to turn the tide of the battle. Owen, realising too that they were outnumbered and outmatched, struggled to join in with the barrage of attacks by casting fireballs of his own, though they were smaller and weaker than Nathan's, fatigue clearly playing a part in their power.

Kai, however, remained composed, utilising his mana vision to anticipate the string of combined attacks and exploit the openings they created. He deftly dodged fireballs and started to close the distance between him and Owen. His small fireballs, though not as powerful as anyone else's on the field once again proving to be more effective due to their accuracy and the element of surprise they provided.

The rest of the group, watching Kai, decided to all follow suit. They sent fireballs into the gap between them and their opponents and ducked and weaved as they approached, ready to put their grappling skills to good use once again.

Nathan and Owen moved subtly closer together as Kai and his team approached, though it made no difference. Kai was the first to hit, taking Nathan down to the ground, followed swiftly by Lyra who easily bundled Owen over.

The group quickly pulled their opponents into submission holds, but something was wrong. It was all too easy. Then they realised: Nathan and Own had seen Kai's team carry out these tactics in previous matches already – they were expecting this to happen.

No matter how hard Kai's team pulled their submission holds on, neither Nathan nor Owen would yield. Then Kai noticed something. Inside each of the pair, their mana was building, growing and it was far brighter than any he had seen in the tournament so far.

"Careful! Something's happening!" Kai shouted to alert his friends to the impending danger.

As the warning rang out, Nathan and Owen's mana reached a crescendo. Their bodies, now glowing with the intense energy, suddenly released a powerful shockwave, blasting Kai's team away from them. Kai, Elijah, Lyra, and Alina were sent sprawling, momentarily dazed from the unexpected counterattack.

As they struggled to regain their footing, they saw Nathan and Owen rise to their feet, their eyes glowing with a fierce red glow and an anger dwarfing any Kai had seen from them before. It was evident that they had been holding back, waiting for the perfect moment to reveal their true power.

Kai quickly assessed the situation, realising that they needed to adapt their strategy and quickly. He could see that Nathan and Owen's mana was now far more potent than before, and that meant their attacks would be even more dangerous.

He called out to his friends, "We can't take them head-on anymore! We need to be more tactical. Let's split up and use hit-and-run tactics. Keep them off-balance and don't let them regain their footing!"

Kai's team nodded in agreement, and they sprang into action. They began to move more fluidly, evading the powerful fireballs that Nathan and Owen hurled at them while responding with their own quick, accurate counterattacks. It was clear that the balance of power had well and truly shifted though, as neither of their opponents seemed dazed by the inconvenient attacks.

Where Kai's team had been focussed on dodging the usual attacks aimed at their heads and chests, Nathan and Owen now changed tact. Their fireballs hurtles along the ground at ankle-height and it was only a matter of time before Alina and Elijah were both hit, falling to the ground with a cry from each.

Both of Kai's teammates held their hands up in surrender as huge fireballs began to reign down from above, taking them out of the battle. The Grandmaster saw fit to extinguish the final blows in puffs of black smoke so that the pair could leave the field of battle unscathed.

Kai could see the desire in the eyes of both Nathan and Owen to hit them again, he even saw the mana within them begin to build up, but remembering the words of the Grandmaster, they didn't attack Kai's friends after they'd surrendered, and after the Grandmaster had already intervened.

In the lull of battle when two of her teammates had fallen, Lyra took the opportunity to try to take Nathan down again. Kai though had seen what was unfolding and couldn't help but shout: "Lyra, NO!"

But it was too late. What Kai had seen, was that the power that had built up inside both Nathan and Owen hadn't dissipated. In fact, the pair had held onto it when they hadn't sent final blows towards Elijah and Alina, and now it glowed within them with a terrible brightness.

As one, the pair released their mana in the form of two jet-streams of bright orange and black fire, right into the face of the approaching Lyra, who screamed, then fell to the ground unmoving.

Nathan and Owen, clearly revelling in their newfound advantage, turned their attention to Kai, who was now the last member of his team standing. They stalked toward him menacingly, with Nathan on his left and Owen on his right. As they drew closer, they reached out and grabbed one of his arms each, their hands crackling with fiery energy.

Holding onto Kai tightly, their touch began to burn Kai's skin, the pain coursing through his body like electricity. Yet, despite the agony, Kai refused to submit. He clenched his jaw, closed his eyes and focussed on the determination burning brighter than the flames that enveloped him.

He had been through worse than this. This was nothing. That was what he kept telling himself over and over as he set his mind to endure.

After what felt like minutes to Kai, seeing that their torture wasn't breaking him, his opponents changed tactics. They released Kai's arms as one and stepped back, creating some distance between them. Then, in unison, the mana within each of them began to build again. Kai knew he could do nothing, and so he simply stood and awaited their attack.

Then the pair unleashed their combined power, which took the form of a massive cyclone of fire that surrounded Kai, trapping him inside the blazing inferno.

The crowd gasped in horror, convinced that this would be the end for Kai. But to everyone's astonishment, something unexpected began to happen.

As the flames spun around Kai and licked at his body, Kai started to rise from the ground, his body levitating within the fiery whirlwind. The fire that had been meant to destroy him now seemed to be imbuing him with strength and power, his eyes glowing with a fierce red intensity through his cloth blindfold for all to see.

Before long, Kai had absorbed so much of the fire that he became a living embodiment of its power, his entire form emanating a bright, fiery glow. The cyclone of fire around him started to dissipate as he absorbed its energy, and the once-deafening roar of the flames began to quiet down leaving the entire arena quiet in astonishment.

Witnessing this incredible display of strength and resilience, the crowd sat in stunned silence, unsure of what would happen next. It was clear that Kai was no ordinary Journeyman mage, and the power he now wielded was beyond anything anyone had ever seen from his rank. But not only that, it was different.

At this critical moment, Grandmaster Orthos decided to intervene. He could see that the battle had reached a dangerous point, and he needed to protect Kai, his opponents, and the integrity of the tournament.

Stepping into the arena, Grandmaster Orthos raised his arms, and with a powerful blast of mana, he extinguished the remaining flames, bringing an end to the battle. The arena was filled with the sound of the audience's collective exhale as the tension was released.

"Enough!" Grandmaster Orthos' voice boomed, echoing throughout the arena. "I hereby declare this match over. Both teams have shown great skill and determination, but this battle has gone too far. I will not allow any further harm to come to these young mages."

As Nathan and Owen stared at Kai in disbelief, they reluctantly backed away, knowing that they had no choice but to accept the Grandmaster's decision.

Kai, still hovering slightly above the ground, felt the intensity of the fire within him starting to fade. As he lowered himself back to the ground, he wondered what had happened that had caused the Grandmaster to interfere.

"Take your blindfold off," Orthos said to Kai as he approached, and Kai hesitated for a moment. Then, knowing he had no choice, he reached back and removed his blindfold and watched as the Grandmaster peered into his pure red eyes.

Chapter 21 – An Eye For An Eye

"Is there anything you want to tell me, Kai?" The Grandmaster asked quietly. "Anything that you perhaps think that you shouldn't?"

Kai stared back at the Grandmaster with his mana vision, trying to determine if Orthos was asking about Azar, who lived as Kai's Eternal Flame deep down inside his soul or if perhaps he just thought that Kai had been cheating somehow.

Kai hesitated for a moment, carefully considering his response. "I'm not sure what you mean, Grandmaster," he replied, a faint quiver in his voice betraying his anxiety.

Orthos gave Kai a knowing look. "Very well," he said, nodding slowly. "I want the Archmages to oversee the rest of the tournament. I believe it is time for you and me to have a little chat." The Grandmaster then turned to address the other mages. "I trust you can manage without me for a while?"

The Archmages exchanged glances, then nodded in unison. "Of course, Grandmaster," one of them replied, her fiery red hair flickering like a living flame. "We will ensure the tournament proceeds without any issues."

"Good," Orthos said, then gestured for Kai to follow him. Together, they left the bustling arena and made their way to the Grandmaster's office.

As they walked, Kai couldn't help but play through all of the scenarios in his head. Was it possible that the Grandmaster knew about Azar? Could he sense the Eternal Flame that burned within Kai's soul? And what would Kai do, would he continue to keep his secret?

Once they reached the office, Orthos closed the door behind them, the sound echoing in the silence of the room. He moved to sit behind his large wooden desk, gesturing for Kai to take a seat across from him. Kai obeyed, feeling the heat emanating from the various fire-related artifacts that decorated the room.

Orthos leaned forward, his eyes fixed on Kai. "You must understand, Kai, that as Grandmaster of the Fire mages, I have a responsibility to ensure the safety and well-being of all those under my tutelage. I have brought you here now because I have reason to believe that there's something… unusual about you. Something you've been keeping hidden."

Kai swallowed hard, feeling the weight of Azar's presence within him. "I assure you, Grandmaster, I have no secrets that would put anyone in danger."

Azar remained silent deep within, and Kai could sense that he was doing his best to steer well clear of this conversation, and any scrutiny.

The Grandmaster's eyes narrowed slightly. "I never said anything about danger, Kai. But I can sense a power within you – a power that is not entirely your own. And I believe that power is connected to your ordeal with the chair. Do not forget, I have already told you that I too, have sat in that very chair and I, too, experienced what it has to offer."

Kai stuttered, trying to decide what would be best to say to the Grandmaster. He knew he shouldn't lie to the man, but also he'd made a promise to Azar that he wouldn't reveal his presence.

"It is OK, Kai," Azar's voice finally came from deep within him, along with the strong sensation of acceptance. "If you do not tell him about me, he will never trust you again. I believe that he already knows to a degree, but we have little to gain or lose either way."

Kai took a deep breath, gathering his courage. "Grandmaster, there is something I need to tell you," he began, his voice barely more than a whisper. "When I sat in the chair, I encountered an entity, a being of fire. His name is Azar, and he is my Eternal Flame... I think"

Orthos' expression remained stoic, but his eyes seemed to hold a hint of understanding. "Go on," he urged.

Kai continued, "Azar bonded with me, becoming a part of my soul. He has been with me ever since, providing guidance and enhancing my abilities as a fire mage. He has not harmed me, nor has he sought to harm others. I believe he is just trying to help, though I don't truly know why. Without him I'd be blind, and powerless like I was before."

The Grandmaster leaned back in his chair, his gaze never leaving Kai's face. "I suspected as much," he said quietly. "I could sense the power within you, a power similar to the one that I too gained from the chair. It is a gift and a burden, one that we must bear with responsibility."

Kai looked up at Orthos, relief flooding through him. "So, you're not angry with me?"

The Grandmaster shook his head. "No, Kai. I am not angry. I understand the need for secrecy. But now that I know, we must work together to ensure that Azar's presence does not pose a threat to you or to others."

Kai nodded, grateful for the Grandmaster's understanding. "I will do my best, Grandmaster. I promise."

Orthos smiled, his eyes warm with compassion. "I know you will, Kai. And remember, you are not alone in this. As your mentor, I will help guide you and ensure that your bond with Azar becomes a source of strength and wisdom, not danger."

"Grandmaster?" Kai asked. "What did you mean when you said that you received this power too? Does your Eternal Flame contain an entity that you too can communicate with?"

Orthos sighed and was silent for a long moment. "There was an entity…" he said slowly. "But it sought to harm others and cause pain wherever I went… it is no longer within me…"

Kai furrowed his brow, concern filling his expression. "What happened to it?" he asked cautiously, wondering if there was a chance that Azar might someday become a malevolent force like the one Orthos had paired with.

The Grandmaster's eyes darkened, and he looked away for a moment before answering. "It was a difficult battle, both physically and mentally. I had to confront the entity within myself and sever the connection between us. I won't lie to you, Kai. It was a painful experience, and it left a mark on my soul. But ultimately, it was necessary for the safety of those around me and for my own growth as a fire mage."

Kai listened intently, his heart heavy with the weight of the revelation. "I'm sorry you had to go through that, Grandmaster," he said softly.

Orthos offered a small, sad smile. "Thank you, Kai. But my experience serves as a reminder that we must always be vigilant and mindful of the powers we wield. Not all Eternal Flames are benevolent like your Azar seems to be, and I do not believe that many are sentient. Regardless of where they come from though, we must learn to control and harness their energy without allowing it to consume us."

Kai nodded, determined to learn from Orthos' experience. "I will do everything I can to ensure that my bond with Azar remains a positive force."

The Grandmaster placed a hand on Kai's shoulder, his expression turning resolute. "Together, we will make sure of it. Now, let's return to the tournament. We have much to do and many lessons to learn. But Kai… if anything changes, I want you to tell me immediately, OK?"

Kai simply nodded. There was nothing more that he could do, but as they walked back to the arena, He felt a newfound sense of purpose and camaraderie with the Grandmaster. He was no longer alone in his journey as a fire mage with a terrible secret, and he was determined to grow stronger and wiser under Orthos' guidance, always remaining vigilant against the potential darkness within.

Back at the arena, as the final match approached, it was clear that Nathan's team was the crowd's least favourite. However, their undeniable skill and power had carried them through the competition, and they now stood at the cusp of victory. Kai was annoyed that his team had been removed from the competition, but he knew that it didn't really matter; he had proven his point to the rest of The Brotherhood.

The atmosphere in the arena was tense as the final battle commenced. Nathan's team showed no signs of faltering, quickly gaining the upper hand against their opponents. The crowd's boos and jeers intensified, but it seemed to have no effect on Nathan and his teammates as they pressed their advantage.

Despite the crowd's disdain, Nathan's team managed to secure their victory, and along with it, the championship title. The crowd's reaction was mixed – some applauded their skill, while others continued to voice their disapproval.

As the Grandmaster stepped forward to present the winning team, he addressed the crowd. "Today, we have seen incredible displays of skill and power from all of our competitors. But in the end, it is Journeymen Nathan, Owen, Dex and Aiden who have proven themselves a worthy team, and it is they who have emerged victorious. Let us put aside our personal feelings and recognise their achievement!"

The crowd reluctantly applauded, their respect for the Grandmaster's authority outweighing their disdain for Nathan's team.

With the tournament over and as the crowd began to disperse, the Grandmaster raised his hands, calling for everyone's attention. "Wait, my friends! Before you leave, I have a surprise announcement."

The arena fell silent, curiosity piqued.

"I am granting special permission for the winning team to challenge a Master-ranked mage to a battle. A unique opportunity to test their skills and showcase the power of a Master."

Whispers rippled through the crowd, the excitement growing as everyone realised the significance of this challenge.

"I present to you, Marcus, an incredibly skilled fire mage here in the Brotherhood. This will be a great chance to see him in action, demonstrating the vast difference between a Master and a Journeyman and perhaps an opportunity for many of you to learn something from him."

Marcus stepped forward, an air of confidence surrounding him. He scanned the crowd, his gaze intense, as if daring anyone to accept the challenge.

Nathan's team exchanged glances, and after a brief, whispered conversation, they decided to announce that they would abstain from the battle, having no desire to fight against their friend and fellow fire mage. To Kai, it looked like Marcus was actually a little disappointed.

The team they had beaten in the final, Oliver, Sara, Henry, and Oscar, were in no condition to face Marcus either, their bodies battered and exhausted from the intense competition.

A hush settled over the crowd, the tension palpable. It seemed as if Marcus had been brought out for nothing.

Suddenly, Kai stood up in the stands, his voice ringing out clear and strong. "We accept the challenge, Marcus!" Elijah had tried to stop him, to pull him back down, but it was too late. Kai had accepted the challenge and there was nothing he could do to take it back.

A murmur of surprise rippled through the spectators. Kai's courage and determination were evident, and they were traits that everyone in The Pit held dear.

Marcus turned his attention to Kai, his eyes narrowing in contemplation. He considered the challenge for a moment before nodding in acceptance. "Very well, Kai. Gather your team, and we shall see what you're truly made of."

Kai's friends, Elijah, Alina, and Lyra exchanged apprehensive glances, though Kai could see at least a little excitement in them too. They knew the risks, but they were not about to let their friend face Marcus alone. They stood by Kai, ready to fight alongside him. And besides, the Grandmaster would never let them put themselves in any real danger, would he?

As the four friends made their way to the arena floor once again, the crowd's energy shifted. A sense of anticipation filled the air, the excitement reaching a fever pitch. This would be a battle unlike any other, pitting the skill and determination of four Journeymen against the power and experience of a Master.

The Grandmaster presiding over the match with his voice solemn, announced the rules. "This will be a single round, with no time limit. The battle will continue until one side concedes or is incapacitated. Use your skills wisely and may the best team win."

With a wave of his hand, the Grandmaster moved away, signalling the start of the battle.

Chapter 22 – Master Ranked

Marcus wasted no time, immediately unleashing a torrent of flames towards Kai's team, the size of which was at least double of what they'd seen in the Journeyman tournament and Kai heard the crowd gasp at the impressive spell. The four friends barely managed to dodge the attack by diving to the sides, their hearts pounding with adrenaline before they even hit the ground.

Kai called out to his friends, coordinating their movements and spells as they counterattacked. Elijah and Alina created a barrier of fire to shield them from Marcus's continued relentless onslaught, while Lyra hurled fireballs to keep the Master at least a little occupied.

For a time, it seemed that their teamwork might be enough to hold Marcus back. However, the Master's skill and experience soon became apparent, as he easily shrugged off and countered their attacks, showcasing his superiority. It was like their spells mean nothing to him. Smaller fireballs he flicked away with his hands and they careened off in all directions and larger ones he expelled with either blasts of heat, or small shields of flame that seemed to appear out of nowhere and with no thought or effort.

Kai used his mana-vision to watch Marcus, though the mana moved within the mage so freely and so quickly it was almost impossible for him to follow.

As time passed and they couldn't find an effective way to participate in the battle, Kai's team began to tire, their spells weakening under the strain. They knew they had to change their strategy if they had any hope of victory.

Slowly but surely, Marcus began to wear down Kai's team. The gap in their abilities was too vast, and their stamina was running low. Despite their best efforts, they were unable to break through Marcus's defences.

Kai knew that they couldn't keep up the fight much longer. His heart ached at the thought of admitting defeat, but he also knew that he had to protect his friends. But this fight had been his idea and it was his responsibility to ensure their safety.

"Cover me!" Lyra shouted above the sounds of battle and Kai watched in horror as his friend darted towards Marcus behind a torrent of fireballs. He knew that she was about to attempt a takedown, being an expert grappler, but Kai knew that this wasn't something you should be doing against a powerful Master-ranked mage, especially not this one.

Kai watched the mana shift within Marcus, from deep inside his chest, past his shoulder and down into his right arm. He barely had the chance to shout a warning as Lyra entered into his range.

Marcus' arm ignited as he cocked, and then launched his fist at Lyra. It moved so quickly and with so much force that she took the impact and flew back ten feet to the ground before she could even begin her manoeuvre.

Alina screamed and ran over to Lyra, but was struck down by an expertly aimed fireball along the way.

Kai's heart raced as he watched his friends fall, one after another. It was clear that they were no match for Marcus, and he had to find a way to end this battle before anyone else got hurt. Winning wasn't the point anymore, surviving without lasting damage was the issue.

Desperation surged through Kai, and he knew he had to act quickly. He watched the mana flowing through Marcus as the Master prepared another devastating attack and Kai gathered all the remaining strength within him and called within himself to Azar, seeking the spirit's guidance.

"Azar, I need your help," he pleaded. "We can't keep fighting like this. What can we do?"

The spirit's voice resonated within Kai, soothing and wise. "Kai, you must trust in your own abilities and the strength of your friends. Even when things seem impossible, believe in yourself and in them."

With renewed determination, Kai focussed, formulating the beginnings of a plan after he realised what Azar was saying to him. His friends would be the key in all of this, he was sure of it. He turned to Elijah, who was still standing but visibly exhausted as he attempted to cast protective walls between the Journeymen and the Master.

"Elijah, I need you to create a massive smokescreen. Give us some cover, can you do that?"

Elijah looked unsure for a moment and then nodded confidently, understanding the urgency of the situation. He gathered his remaining energy and unleashed a thick, billowing cloud of smoke from his hands that enveloped the arena, obscuring their movements from Marcus. The crowd gasped loudly. It was the first time that Kai had ever seen a spell like this cast, and by the look on Elijah's face, he could tell that he was just as surprised by it as the crowd was.

Kai then rushed to Alina and Lyra, helping them back to their feet one at a time. They were both hurt, but they both assured him they could continue.

"We can't keep going like this," he whispered urgently. "We need to regroup and find a way to end this battle without risking any more harm."

"Let me do it," Lyra said confidently, though her breathing was laboured and she was clearly in a fair amount of pain. "With this smokescreen he'll never see it coming, and you can guide me, can't you?"

Kai's immediate reaction was to tell her 'no way', but as he looked around, he noticed that Lyra was correct; Kai had no trouble seeing Marcus through the smoke, his mana shining like a beacon as he stood still in the centre of the arena, waiting to brush off whatever was to come next.

"Oh Journeymen…" Marcus cooed loudly in a very sweet and sickly voice. "You know you can run, but you cant hide!"

The sound of Marcus' voice made Kai grit his teeth and with no other option, he nodded to Lyra.

"We'll skirt the outside of the arena, and you can take him from behind. He won't see you coming this time. Just take him down quickly, OK?"

Lyra nodded, though Kai couldn't help but see a tiny amount of apprehension in her face.

The group as one, then slowly moved around the arena as quietly as they could manage and once Kai nodded to Lyra again and pointed her in the right direction, she set off at a run. The smoke swirled behind her as she moved, leaving a corridor open for Kai, Elijah and Alina to watch her as she moved to make her attack.

Kai watched everything as it unfolded. Marcus still unaware that Lyra silently approached, his friend getting closer and closer.

Until she was there, within striking distance.

Marcus then showed Kai exactly what a Master-ranked mage could do. He spun on the spot in the blink of an eye, faster than Kai had ever seen anything move and launched Lyra twenty feet into the air with a swift strike of his empowered fist.

Lyra screamed as she rose and the three friends immediately ran into a position that would allow them to catch Lyra when she fell.

Marcus seemed to stand in waiting for Lyra to be caught, though as soon as she was in the arms of the three, Kai saw his mana rising up again and he instinctively rolled out of the way.

A ring of flames emanated from Marcus, tearing up the sand as it quickly expanded towards Kai and his friends. Kai had seen it coming, the rest had not.

Kai leapt just in time to avoid the flames, but as he turned to look at his friends, he saw them all engulfed by the attack. They were now totally out of action, their unconscious bodies lying on the ground with smoke rising from them, and now Kai was alone, facing off against an opponent that wasn't even playing the same game as he was, let alone in the same league.

Kai turned to look to see where Marcus was, having lost a track of the battle momentarily. Elijah's black smoke still covered most of the arena, which should've been an issue for Marcus, though as soon as Kai turned his head, he found himself face to face with Marcus, and Marcus' eyes were glowing with a deep red hatred for Kai.

"You think that you are even worthy to stand on the same battlefield as me?" Marcus growled. "You think that you can keep trying to best me, to make yourself feel better? Well, this is it Kai, this is your end. You've flown too close to the sun and now it's time for your wings to finally be burnt off."

"Don't you think you're taking this all a little too seriously?" Kai quipped. "I mean, aren't we all on the same team here?"

Marcus scoffed. "There are no teams. There's survival and there's death. Unfortunately for you, there are two of us, and two results to be had here today. And the best part of it is that with all this smoke around, I'll just say it was an accident. You'll be mourned, but eventually you'll be forgotten."

"You're going to try to actually kill me?" Kai asked in disbelief. He knew Marcus hated him and all and he must've had his own reasons for that, but to actually want to murder someone else was all kinds of next level.

"Yes Kai, I'm going to kill you. Because weakness will not be tolerated in the Brotherhood of the Flame. Weakness in one is weakness for all, and we need all the strength we can get for when we take war to the city. King Roderick will fall, and people like you are just going to get in the way."

Kai could tell there would be no talking Marcus down from this ledge, but he wouldn't get the chance anyway. Before Kai could speak another word, Marcus wrapped a single hand around Kai's throat.

Kai instinctively brought his hands up to Marcus' forearm and tried to pull himself away, but Kai could see the mana reinforcing Marcus' strength in his arm and in his grip. Kai couldn't even move Marcus away from him by an inch and with every second that passed, he felt himself growing weaker and weaker.

Gasping for one single life-saving breath, and as his vision began to fade, Kai desperately sought a way out of his impending doom. The flow of mana within Marcus seemed to pulsate, growing stronger with each passing moment. It was then that he realised the horrifying truth: he was going to die at Marcus' hands and there was nothing that he could do about it.

In a last-ditch effort, Kai cried out to Azar internally, hoping that the Eternal Flame within him would respond. "Azar, help me," he pleaded, his thoughts frantic. "I don't want to die. There must be something we can do."

Azar's voice echoed within Kai's mind, surprisingly calm despite the dire situation. "There is a way, Kai, but it comes with great risk. You can attempt to reverse the flow of mana, draining Marcus of his Eternal Flame. It may be enough to save your life, but it could also leave him in a weakened, vulnerable state."

Kai weighed his options in an instant, aware that he was running out of time. With a shaky breath, he made his decision. "I'll do it," he whispered, hoping that he could even muster the strength required for such a feat.

Focusing all of his energy, Kai reached out with his mana vision, locking onto the flow of mana within Marcus. With Azar's guidance, he began to manipulate the mana currents, reversing the flow and drawing the energy back into himself.

The process was slow and painstaking, and Kai could feel the strain on his body as the intense power started to course through him. As the seconds ticked by, Marcus' grip on his throat began to loosen, his face contorted in pain and confusion as he felt his own strength being drained away.

Finally after a long while as Kai and Marcus strained against each other, locked in their battle of will and determination, the last of Marcus' Eternal Flame was absorbed into Kai, and the Master-ranked mage fell back, collapsing onto the ground. Kai slumped forward, gasping for breath as the smoke around them cleared.

Around them, the other mages could now see the result of the battle and they watched in shock, trying to process what had just occurred. There, in the centre of the battlefield, Kai knelt over Marcus' unconscious form, the once powerful mage's eyes now a dull grey and staring straight upwards as though he'd been entirely petrified.

Marcus was alive, but it was clear that something was very, very wrong. The balance of power had shifted, and Kai had somehow managed to survive a seemingly impossible situation.

Kai's heart raced as he looked around at the stunned faces of his fellow mages. He knew that what he had done was risky, and he wasn't entirely sure of the consequences. But one thing was clear: he had managed to defy the odds and escape death's grasp, at least for now.

As whispers of disbelief and awe rippled through the crowd, Grandmaster Orthos quickly approached Kai, his eyes filled with concern and curiosity. "What happened here, Kai?" he asked, his voice low and measured.

Kai hesitated, knowing that explaining the events that had just transpired would not be easy. But he also knew that he owed it to the Grandmaster, and to himself, to tell the truth. And so, with a deep breath, he began to recount the harrowing ordeal that had just unfolded, and the role that Azar had played in saving his life.

Grandmaster Orthos listened intently as Kai recounted his brush with death and when Kai had finished, the Grandmaster's expression was a mixture of concern and disappointment.

"Kai," he began, his voice heavy with the weight of his decision, "what transpired here today should never have been possible. The fact that Marcus sought to kill you and that you were forced to use such drastic measures to save your own life is a serious breach of our code."

Kai nodded solemnly, understanding the gravity of the situation. He was still shaken by the events that had unfolded, the realisation that he could have killed someone weighing heavily on his conscience.

"In light of this," Orthos continued, "I have no choice but to detain you for the time being. We must investigate this matter further and determine the appropriate course of action."

Kai swallowed hard, his heart racing in his chest. "I don't understand, Grandmaster. What did I do?" his voice barely above a whisper.

"Later Kai," Orthos replied. "Please, do as you are told and we will talk later."

As he was led away by a pair of solemn-faced mages, Kai tried to reach out to Azar again, hoping to find some solace in the presence of his Eternal Flame. However, to his surprise, he found that he could not communicate with Azar as he usually did.

Instead, Azar sent Kai a series of visions, images of a ferocious battle between the powerful fire mage and an equally formidable opponent. The two mages stood on opposite sides of a vast, scorched battlefield, their robes billowing in the heat of the flames that surrounded them.

Azar's opponent was a tall, imposing figure, his face obscured by a hood that cast his features in shadow. The air around him shimmered with heat, and his eyes glowed like molten gold, burning with intensity and determination.

The battle between the two fire mages was fierce and unrelenting. Azar unleashed a torrent of flame, a massive wall of fire that roared across the battlefield toward his enemy. But the hooded mage was not deterred, countering with a gust of searing wind that dispersed the flames, sending them spiralling into the sky above.

Undaunted, Azar gathered his strength and launched another attack, this time summoning a series of fiery tendrils that lashed out at his opponent like a whip. The hooded mage deflected the assault with ease, his hands glowing with an intense heat as he manipulated the fire, bending it to his will.

Their battle continued, neither mage willing to back down or concede defeat. As they fought, the very earth beneath them began to crack and smoulder, the heat of their conflict taking a tangible toll on their surroundings.

With each attack and counterattack, Azar and the hooded mage seemed to grow more powerful, their control over the flames becoming more refined and precise. It was clear that this was not a mere contest of strength, but a battle of wits and strategy as well.

As the visions unfolded before Kai's eyes, he could not help but be captivated by the ferocity and skill displayed by both combatants. But he also found himself wondering about the purpose of this battle and why Azar had chosen to share it with him now, in the aftermath of his own near-death experience.

Could it be a warning, a reminder of the dangers that lay in the unchecked power of fire magic? Or perhaps it was a lesson, a glimpse into the potential that Kai himself could achieve if he continued to hone his skills and strengthen his bond with Azar?

As the visions faded and Kai was left alone with his thoughts, he realised that the answers to these questions would have to wait. For now, he had more pressing concerns to deal with, as he faced the consequences of his actions and the uncertainty of his future within the Brotherhood of the Flame.

As Kai was led to his temporary confinement, he couldn't help but feel a gnawing sense of dread. He knew that his actions had been necessary for his survival, but he still didn't know what he'd actually done, and why it was such a big deal. He'd defended himself and beaten a Master-ranked mage, surely that was to be celebrated, not punished.

Once locked inside a small, windowless chamber, Kai tried to talk to the Grandmaster again, but was met with an outstretched hand and nothing more than silence. Then the Grandmaster left Kai alone, and the young mage could do nothing more than sit down on the cold stone floor, his mind racing with thoughts and questions. He worried about the consequences of whatever this was, and what it would mean for his future as a fire mage.

In the darkness, Kai found himself turning to the only thing he could assess, reflecting on the visions Azar had shared with him. The intensity and skill of the battle between Azar and the hooded mage served as a stark reminder of the power that fire magic could wield, and the responsibility that came with wielding it.

As the hours passed, Kai resolved to learn from the experiences he had faced, both in his own battle against Marcus and in the visions shared by Azar. He knew that he had much to learn and even more to prove, not only to himself but also to the Brotherhood and to Grandmaster Orthos, regardless of the reason for his punishment.

Chapter 23 – Deflating

"Kai?" the voice that woke Kai from his sleep was, without a doubt, his mother's. She and his father must've returned from their duty and been immediately told about what'd happened.

In the hours that'd passed, he was unable to speak with Azar, or even receive any further images or feelings from the being that inhabited his soul.

"Mom?" Kai asked, blinking sleepily as he looked up at her worried face. Her eyes were red-rimmed, and he could tell she had been crying. Beside her stood his father, his face a mixture of concern and confusion.

"Kai, we just heard what happened," his mother said, her voice trembling. "Are you alright?"

Kai nodded, trying to put on a brave face for his parents. "I'm okay, Mom. Just... shaken up, I guess."

His father stepped forward, placing a reassuring hand on Kai's shoulder. "Son, we're here to support you no matter what. But we need to know what really happened out there."

Kai took a deep breath, readying himself to recount the events once more. He knew his parents deserved to know the truth, and he trusted them implicitly. So, he told them everything – from his near-death experience with Marcus to the role Azar played in his survival, and even the visions he had received.

As he spoke, his parents listened with rapt attention, their expressions shifting from shock to disbelief to concern. When he finished, his mother hugged him tightly, her voice choked with emotion. "Oh, Kai, I'm so relieved you're okay. But this... this changes everything."

His father's face was solemn, his brow furrowed in thought. "We'll have to talk to Grandmaster Orthos about this. It's clear that the Brotherhood needs to address these issues, and we need to make sure you're safe."

"What? Why?" Kai asked, still not sure what was happening.

"Just… don't you worry Kai, we're going to go and speak with the Grandmaster right now and get this mess cleaned up. Just… stay strong Kai, we'll be back soon," his father replied.

In the days that followed, Kai's parents didn't return to his cell, though they spoke with Grandmaster Orthos, advocating for their son and demanding an investigation into Marcus' actions, as well as Kai's release. Though Kai was still confined to his small chamber, he could feel the tension within the Brotherhood mounting as the investigation unfolded.

During this time, Kai was left with little to do but reflect on the visions Azar had sent him and work on strengthening his connection with his Eternal Flame. Though he still couldn't communicate with Azar directly, he found solace in the knowledge that they were at least still linked by their shared power.

He worried about his parents though, and the fact that they hadn't come to visit him again since they'd left.

His friends had visited him regularly though, and it made him think back to the time when he'd been recovering from his ordeal in the chair. They spoke about what they were doing, even told Kai about new spells they'd figured out on their own and in some cases, strategized for any future group tournaments. Their visits made Kai feel useful, and gave him the feeling that in the future, things were going to go back to normal. They didn't speak of what was happening surrounding his ordeal though, telling him each time that the Grandmaster was 'working something out' and eventually he had no choice but to simply leave it.

The time came though, when the Grandmaster returned to Kai's confinement, and Kai could see that something weighed heavily on him.

"What's wrong?" Kai asked. "Can I go? Have I been kicked out of The Brotherhood?"

Grandmaster Orthos exhaled loudly. "Has anything changed, since you've been in here Kai, in this cell, I mean?"

Kai wondered what he could possibly have witnessed change, being confined to a small room, and then it hit him. Something *had* changed.

"Actually… yes," he said slowly. "I haven't been able to communicate with Azar at all. Is that what you meant? He sent me images… visions of a fight between him and some other fire mage… I don't know what's happening but I don't think it's good."

Orthos shut his eyes tightly, as though this was not the answer that he wanted to hear.

"Has anyone told you what's happened to Marcus?" the Grandmaster asked.

"Happened?" Kai replied, not knowing exactly where he was going with this. In truth, he hadn't even thought about Marcus.

"Marcus… Marcus is no longer a member of the Brotherhood," Orthos said. "Actually, he's no longer a mage at all. He has already left The Pit and is heading back to the city."

"No longer a mage?" Kai asked with wide eyes.

"I believe that when you drained his power from him, that the change was permanent…" the Grandmaster began to explain.

Kai's heart sank at the realisation of what he had done. "I never meant for that to happen, Grandmaster. I only wanted to save myself…" It was clear to Kai now why he had been locked away; taking someone's ability to call upon their mana was the worst thing that he could think of.

"I know, Kai," Orthos said, his voice softening. "Marcus will have to find a new path in life, one that does not involve the Brotherhood, or magic. I believe that what you have told me is the truth, that your actions were unintentional. Trust me when I say that if this were not the case – if it was your Eternal Flame that caused this intentionally, our conversation would be very different. This is why you have remained here thus far; if your Azar wished for you to break free, he would've attempted to do so already."

Kai struggled to find the right words to express his guilt and remorse. "I'm so sorry. I'll do whatever it takes to make things right. And I know it doesn't mean much, but I trust Azar; he saved my life."

Grandmaster Orthos shook his head. "You cannot undo what has been done, Kai. But you can learn from this experience and grow as a person and a mage. Let this serve as a reminder of the responsibility that comes with wielding such great power. What it means to work with an Eternal Flame that can do something like this to others. But Kai, no matter what, you must never attempt this again."

Kai nodded solemnly, understanding the gravity of the situation. "You're right, Grandmaster. I won't let this happen again. I'll work harder than ever to ensure that I can control my power and use it responsibly, I promise. And I know Azar will help, when I can speak to him again."

Orthos placed a reassuring hand on Kai's shoulder. "That is all we can ask of you, Kai. We will continue your training, and together, we will find a way to ensure that your connection with Azar does not pose a threat to yourself or others. But that leads us onto our next issue, Kai."

Kai barely heard what the Grandmaster had said after he'd told Kai about Marcus. The guy was an ass, but that didn't give Kai the right to change his entire life, did it?

"Kai. From what you have told me, there is a reason that I believe you haven't been able to communicate with Azar. I believe that when you absorbed Marcus' power, you have taken within you his own Eternal Flame, and it is at war with Azar inside of you. It is not possible for a mage to contain two Eternal Flames, and if left unchecked, I do not know what will happen to you." Grandmaster Orthos continued, "I will help you by sapping Marcus' Eternal Flame piece by piece. I have done something similar before, but it will be painful for both of us, so we can only do it a little at a time, day by day."

Kai listened intently, anxiety welling up inside him.

"During this process, you must be extremely cautious, Kai. If you call on your mana to cast a powerful spell, it could backfire due to the instability caused by the two Eternal Flames within you. Until we've resolved this issue, you must practice restraint and control. It would be too risky to allow you back into practise, let alone a tournament whilst you are in this state."

Kai understood the severity of the situation and the potential danger he was in. He nodded, determination filling his eyes. "I'll do whatever it takes, Grandmaster. I won't let this destroy me or hurt anyone else."

Grandmaster Orthos nodded approvingly. "That's the spirit, Kai. Together, we will face this challenge and overcome it. You have the support of the Brotherhood, and we will do everything in our power to help you."

"Can we start now?" Kai asked hopefully. "I mean… is it something that we can just *do*?"

The Grandmaster nodded solemnly, and placed a hand on Kai's shoulder again. Kai could see the mana swelling within Orthos, and began to feel very, very nervous.

The atmosphere in the cell suddenly turned heavy with anticipation, as both of them knew the pain that they were about to endure.

"Kai, I need you to trust me completely and focus on your breathing. The more relaxed and focused you are, the easier the process will be for both of us," Orthos instructed, his voice steady and calming.

Kai nodded, closing his eyes and taking deep breaths as he tried to centre himself. Through his mana vision though, he saw a warm, red light emanating from the Grandmaster's palms, enveloping Kai's body in an instant.

As the extraction process commenced, Kai immediately felt a searing pain spreading from his chest throughout his body. It was as if a thousand needles were piercing his very soul, threatening to tear him apart from the inside. He clenched his teeth, fighting the urge to cry out in agony.

Orthos' face contorted with pain as well, beads of sweat forming on his brow. He gritted his teeth and continued the process. It was clear that as he tried to drag the unwanted Eternal Flame from within Kai, he was experiencing no less hardship than Kai was himself.

Kai's breathing grew rapid and shallow as the pain intensified. He felt as if he really was being torn in two, the conflicting energies of Azar's and Marcus' Eternal Flame clashing violently within him. He balled his fists as tightly as he could, his knuckles turning white.

The room grew hotter and hotter as the extraction continued, the air itself pregnant with energy. Despite the unbearable pain, Kai focused on the sound of Orthos' voice as he began to speak quietly, using it as an anchor to keep himself from being swept away by the storm of agony raging inside him.

Minutes felt like hours, and with every passing moment, the pain seemed to grow exponentially. Kai's mana vision blurred and flickered on and off, and he fought to remain conscious, knowing that if he lost control, the consequences could be disastrous.

Finally, after what felt like an eternity, the red light surrounding Kai began to recede, and with it, the pain started to subside. The Grandmaster slumped back in exhaustion, sweat dripping from his face, and his breathing laboured.

Kai, too, felt drained, both physically and emotionally. The pain, though lessened, still lingered in his body like the memory of a bad dream. He then used his mana vision to check over Orthos with a mixture of gratitude and concern. The Grandmaster was practically glowing with energy.

"Are you alright, Grandmaster ?" he asked, his voice shaky.

Orthos nodded weakly, managing a small smile. "Yes, Kai. We've done it. The first extraction is complete. But we must continue this process, day by day, until Marcus' Eternal Flame is entirely gone from you."

Kai nodded, understanding the long road ahead of them. Despite the lingering pain, he felt a small sense of relief, as if a heavy burden had been lifted from his shoulders. He could feel the foreign flame slightly dimmer now within him.

"Can I leave this cell?" he asked in a very small voice.

The Grandmaster seemed to think about the question for a moment before replying. "I think that you have already been through enough, Kai. Please, return to your dorm and do not attempt to cast any powerful spells. I will find you when we are both ready for the next extraction."

It took Kai longer than he expected to return to himself fully. He hadn't spoken to another soul, retreating immediately to his room. That night, as he lay in his own bed, he attempted to reach out to Azar once again. To his surprise, he felt a faint flicker of connection, as if a thin thread of communication had been re-established between them.

Kai focused on that thread, trying to tentatively push a little mana into the connection to try to strengthen it, and suddenly, he found himself immersed in a vivid, dream-like landscape. There, standing before him, was Azar, the powerful mage he had come to know so well. However, Azar appeared to be struggling, as if he were still locked in a fierce battle.

"Azar!" Kai called out, concerned for his friend.

Azar turned his head, and his eyes met Kai's, a mixture of relief and worry gleaming in them. "Kai, you can hear me. Thank the stars," Azar said, his voice strained.

"What's going on?" Kai asked, alarmed by the sight of his friend in distress.

Azar looked away for a moment, as if gathering his thoughts. "When you absorbed Marcus' Eternal Flame, you didn't just take in a powerful source of mana," he began, his voice filled with urgency. "His flame... it's sentient, and it's been fighting me since the moment it entered you."

Kai's eyes widened in shock. "Sentient? You mean, it has a mind of its own?"

Azar nodded gravely. "Yes, and it's violent and hate-filled. It's trying to consume me, to take control of the power within you. I've been doing my best to hold it back, but it's been a constant struggle. I don't know how much longer I can hold it for."

Kai's heart ached for his friend, who had apparently been silently battling this malicious force within him. "Azar, I'm so sorry. I had no idea."

The mage shook his head. "It's not your fault, Kai. You couldn't have known. But the process Grandmaster Orthos has started, sapping Marcus' Eternal Flame from you piece by piece... it's helping. With the extraction, I'm able to push back against the darkness, to regain some control."

Kai felt a surge of determination, fuelled by his desire to protect his friend and rid himself of the dangerous force that threatened them both. "We'll keep going, Azar. We'll do whatever it takes to get rid of Marcus flame and free you from this battle."

Azar's eyes held gratitude, but also a note of caution. "Kai, you must be careful. While the flame is still within you, you'll need to guard against its influence. It may be why Marcus was the way he was, consumed by anger and hatred. Don't let it take hold of you."

Kai nodded, his jaw set with resolve. "I won't, Azar. I promise. Together, we'll overcome this."

They stood there for a moment, the bond between them stronger than ever. As they prepared to face the challenges ahead, Azar shared a final piece of advice with Kai: "Remember, the most powerful force you have against the darkness is the light within you. Hold onto that, and let it guide you through the days to come."

With that, the connection between them began to fade, and Kai found himself back in his bed, the room silent and still.

Chapter 24 – Enemy At The Gates

Kai didn't know how many hours had passed, but due to the lack of sounds coming from within The Pit, he could only assume that it was still night time. He didn't know what had caused him to stir, but he was almost positive that he'd heard *something* to rip him from his sleep.

His questions were answered shortly afterwards, when his thoughts were interrupted by a loud banging noise, followed by the unmistakable sound of an explosion. Kai sat bolt upright, his heart racing as adrenaline coursed through his veins, jolting him fully awake. He leaped out of bed and rushed to the door, pulling it open and finding nobody there to await him.

"Hey!" he shouted, pounding on the door. "What's going on out there?"

There was no response, only the distant sound of chaos and more explosions echoing through the fort. Fear clawed at Kai's insides, and he desperately tried to come up with a plan. He had the feeling that with every passing moment, the situation outside seemed to grow increasingly dire.

Just as he was about to run to where he thought the sound was coming from, he heard footsteps approaching him. Kai tensed, unsure if the newcomers were friend or foe and unwanting to push his mana into expanding his vision, he simply waited. A moment later, Kai let out a breath as his friends rounded a corned into view.

"Kai, come on! We have to go!" Elijah urged, grabbing Kai's arm and pulling him back the way they'd come.

"What's happening?" Kai asked, his voice shaking. "And where have you been?"

"There's no time Kai, An army of air mages and soldiers have reached The Pit," Lyra explained, her eyes filled with fear. "They're here to kill us all."

Kai's heart dropped at her words, but he pushed down the terror that threatened to paralyze him. This was not the time for fear – he had to stay strong for his friends and the Brotherhood that had become his family. "We need to find anyone else and get everyone to safety," he said, his voice firm and resolute.

They nodded, voicing their agreement, and together, the four friends – Kai, Elijah, Lyra, and Alina – sprinted through the dimly lit hallways of The Pit.

The sounds of battle grew louder as they made their way through the labyrinthine fort, though as explosions rang out louder and louder it was clear that the very building itself was under siege. They had to dodge falling debris and flashes of magical energy as they moved and Kai wondered for exactly how long The Pit could remain standing.

As they turned another corner, they stumbled upon a group of injured mages. Lyra quickly moved to their side and began administering aid as best she could under the circumstances, but not having any magic or spells to do so, all she could do was to tell them to put pressure on any wounds and to see if they could escape The Pit before it was too late.

"We need to find the Grandmaster," Alina said, her eyes scanning the chaos around them. "He'll know what to do."

Elijah nodded, his expression determined. "Kai, you and Alina go find Grandmaster Orthos. Lyra and I will stay here and help these injured mages. We'll try to get them out, I don't care if we have to carry them."

Kai hesitated for a moment, not wanting to leave his friends behind, but knew that finding the Grandmaster was going to be crucial to their survival. He nodded at Elijah and Alina, and the two of them set off in search of Orthos, following the sounds of battle and destruction.

As they raced through the halls, they almost bundled in to a large group of several enemy soldiers and what Kai knew immediately were air mages. Kai, mindful of the danger posed by the two Eternal Flames within him and the warning that he shouldn't use any powerful spells, focused on just getting through to the Grandmaster's office rather than fighting these new enemy combatants. So instead of standing and fighting, the pair turned back to find another path.

Finally, and after a mixture of sprinting and hiding, they reached the Grandmaster's chambers. The door had been blown open, and inside they found Orthos battling several soldiers simultaneously.

With a powerful display of fire magic, Orthos sent the soldiers flying back against the walls, their armour glowing red from the intense heat. However, even the Grandmaster was showing signs of fatigue, his normally controlled movements becoming increasingly laboured. He must've been fighting for a very long time.

"Grandmaster!" Kai called out, his voice filled with concern.

Orthos glanced in their direction, his eyes filled with relief at the sight of them. "Kai, Alina, you're safe," he said, before felling another soldier with a precise burst of flame. "We must regroup and devise a plan to repel this attack. Gather everyone you can and meet me in the central courtyard."

Kai and Alina nodded, knowing that every moment counted. They quickly made their way back through The Pit, alerting everyone they encountered about the plan to meet in the central courtyard and doing their best to remain out of any fights. In some cases they were too late though, with the bodies of fire mages, soldiers and air mages littering the ground where there had clearly been intense battles.

The air stank of smoke and death, but Kai ignored everything he could to simply keep moving. He had to, he had no time to waste. He had no time to feel fear or sadness.

As they hurried through the chaos, the pair once again found Elijah and Lyra, who had managed to help the injured mages find cover and had moved on to helping others who hadn't yet perished.

Kai explained the headmaster's orders and quickly, together, the group continued to make their way through the fort, still evading enemy soldiers and air mages while assisting their fellow fire mages whenever possible. Finally, they reached the central courtyard, where they found Grandmaster Orthos already rallying the Brotherhood, his voice commanding and filled with determination.

"We cannot let these invaders destroy our home!" he shouted, his voice carrying across the courtyard. "We must stand together and fight as one! This is our sanctuary, and we will defend it with every fibre of our being!"

The fire mages around him roared in agreement, their spirits ignited by the Grandmaster's words. Despite the overwhelming odds, a sense of unity and determination spread throughout the crowd. Even Kai felt a warmth resonating in his soul, as though he was ready to defend his home to the very last breath.

Grandmaster Orthos quickly assessed their forces and began organising the defence.

"Kai, Elijah, Alina, and Lyra, I need you to lead a team to the eastern wall. It's one of their main points of attack. Hold the line and push them back. I'll stay here and coordinate the defence on this front."

The four friends nodded, ready to take on the responsibility entrusted to them. They knew that the Masters and Archmages had surely been tasked with something more difficult and were no doubt already in the thick of battle, but they felt that if they could do anything that could make a difference, then they were going to do it to the best of their ability.

As they moved, they gathered a group of fire mages, bolstering their ranks with the most experienced and skilled fighters they could find from the Journeyman-rankers. Together, they made their way to the eastern wall, their hearts pounding with anticipation.

As they reached their destination, they found themselves faced with an onslaught of air mages and soldiers, the battle raging fiercely already, with members of the Brotherhood doing their best to repel the combined forces of the air mages and the city soldiers. Kai took a deep breath, focusing on the light within him, as Azar had advised. He couldn't risk using his full power, but he knew that eventually he wasn't going to be left with a choice but to do something. Either he would die at the hands of these enemies, or he would die from his pair of Eternal Flames tearing him in two.

Elijah, Lyra, and Alina each tapped into their own inner strength and determination. Together, they stood facing the front line of the battle, already using their fire magic to repel the attackers as best they could. Flames danced and roared around them, a testament to the fierce resolve of the fire mages defending The Pit.

Kai watched as his friends fought with all their might, the ferocity of their flames driving back the enemy forces. He felt torn between his desire to fight alongside them and the need to abstain from using his powers, as he knew that he couldn't control the two Eternal Flames within him. He knew that if he lost control, the consequences could be catastrophic for his friends and the Brotherhood.

But there were so many enemies, and so many bodies already on the ground. It was clear that both sides were taking heavy losses, but the intense heat that he felt from his allies was dropping slowly, and each time one of The Brotherhood fell, the shining mana he could see was dimming. He had to do something. He had to help.

Kai focused on doing what he could to support his friends and the other fire mages. He provided strategic guidance, identified weaknesses in the enemy's formations, and offered encouragement to those around him. He knew that he wasn't directly participating in the battle, but he was still determined to contribute in any way that he could.

Elijah, Lyra, and Alina fought relentlessly, their flames growing stronger with each passing moment. They channelled their fury and desperation into their magic, becoming a formidable force against the invading air mages and soldiers. The Brotherhood's forces slowly began to push the enemy back, inch by inch, refusing to let them breach the eastern wall.

As the tide of the battle began to turn in their favour, the fire mages grew more resolute, their spirits lifted by the progress they were making. But the enemy was relentless, and they continued to launch wave after wave of attacks against the Brotherhood's defences. Like sonic booms and cutting hurricanes that the fire mages were unfamiliar in dealing with.

Suddenly, a massive explosion rocked the battlefield, sending a shockwave through the air that knocked many of the fire mages off their feet, including Kai and his friends. As they scrambled to regain their footing, they saw that the source of the explosion was a powerful air mage, one who appeared to be the leader of the invading forces.

The air mage's eyes were cold and ruthless, and it was clear that he would stop at nothing to see the Brotherhood defeated. He raised his hands, preparing to unleash another devastating attack on the already weakened eastern wall.

Kai knew that they couldn't withstand another assault like that, and he felt a surge of desperation course through him. He looked at his friends, who were all struggling to stand, and realised that the time had come for him to make a decision. He couldn't stand by any longer, watching as everything he held dear was destroyed.

The golden mana within the air mage stirred again and it glowed like a beacon to Kai. The time was now.

Taking a deep breath, Kai drew upon the light within him, focusing on the bond he shared with Azar and the strength it provided. He called upon his fire magic, but did his best to mentally and carefully control the flow of power from the two Eternal Flames within him, doing his best to harness their energy without letting them consume him.

As Kai's flames roared to life, he felt a surge of hope; it was working, he was using his mana, fuelled by his desire to protect his friends and his home. He turned his attention to the powerful air mage, knowing that he needed to act quickly if they were to have any chance of survival.

With a fearsome battle cry, Kai unleashed a torrent of fire, the flames blazing with a ferocity that seemed to surprise even the air mage. The enemy leader attempted to counter the attack and redirect the flames, but Kai's spell was evidently too powerful, and they broke through the air mage's defences, engulfing him in a searing inferno. The air mage let out a scream of pain and rage before collapsing to the ground, quicky defeated by Kai's unexpected display of power.

The sudden defeat of their leader sent a shockwave of fear and uncertainty through the ranks of the invading forces. The fire mages, sensing their advantage again, pressed forward with renewed vigour driving back their enemy.

Kai, exhausted but determined, continued to fight alongside his friends, using his fire magic in more of a controlled and focused manner. He was constantly aware of the dual threat within him, but the connection to Azar and the support of his friends helped him maintain control over the two Eternal Flames. He wouldn't take any unnecessary risks though; he remembered what he had been told and he needed to remain in this fight, to help, not to become another thing for his friends to worry about.

The battle seemed to last for hours, but eventually, the invading forces were pushed back and forced to retreat. The Brotherhood had successfully defended The Pit, although the cost had been high. Many fire mages had been injured, some fatally, and parts of the fortress had been badly damaged in the conflict that would no doubt take years to put back together.

As the enemy forces retreated, Kai and his friends finally allowed themselves a moment to catch their breath. They were bruised, battered, and utterly exhausted, but they were alive, and they had stood together to protect their home.

A few moments later, the Grandmaster arrived at the eastern wall, looking at the damage and the fallen with a heavy heart and sadness in his eyes. He approached Kai and his friends, placing a hand on each of their shoulders. "You all fought bravely," he said, his voice filled with pride and gratitude. "I'm proud of you. Together, we managed to protect our sanctuary. The enemy has left our walls… but I doubt that we will not see them again soon."

Kai nodded, his heart swelling with a mixture of pride and relief. "We did it, Grandmaster. We defended our home. And we'll do it again if we have to."

Orthos looked out over the battlefield, his eyes filled with determination. "Yes, we did. But I have already received word that more soldiers are on the way, and more powerful air mages. I do not know why these mages have chosen to work with the tyrant King, but we must be prepared to fight them until the very end."

Chapter 25 – Retaliation

"We have to go out and meet them on the battlefield before they get here," Kai said to his friends as they watched the headmaster walking away. "If the mages and the soldiers make it here again, we risk losing everything we have, and the Apprentice mages aren't ready to fight yet. People will die, so many people."

Elijah shook his head slowly, his expression serious. "You're right, Kai. We can't afford to wait for them to attack us again. We need to take the fight to them and try to put an end to this conflict once and for all... but it's just us? What can we do against an army?"

Lyra and Alina shared a determined look before adding their own words of support. "We'll stand by you," Lyra said, her voice full of conviction. "We're stronger together, and we can't let the tyrant King and his air mage allies continue their reign of terror."

"We need help if we're going to do this," Kai said. "We aren't going to be stupid and run straight at an enemy we cant beat. We'll speak to Orthos, raise an army and put a stop to all this."

The four friends agreed, and then quickly caught up with the Grandmaster and told him what they thought. After some deliberation and a small argument for the safety of his students, he agreed that a counterattack was now the only way to protect both The Pit and the Brotherhood.

"We'll gather all the Journeyman-ranks and above, and head out to confront the enemy," Orthos declared. "Kai, Elijah, Lyra, and Alina, you've proven yourselves to be exceptional leaders and fighters. I want you all to come with me, but I wont force anyone to fight. If you want to run, to save yourselves then now is the time."

The group accepted the responsibility without even a second thought; there was no way that they would be running when faced with this oppression. They each knew that the fate of their home and their fellow fire mages rested in their hands, and they were going to do whatever they could to help.

Once rounded up into a veritable army, the huge group of mages ventured out from The Pit and into the arid desert beyond and to the east. Kai and his friends couldn't help but feel the weight of their task. They knew that the enemy forces were growing stronger and more numerous, and they had to find a way to stop them before it was too late.

The fire mages marched towards the waiting army, ready to meet them head-on. As they grew closer to the enemy, the tension in the air was palpable. They knew that the upcoming battle would be brutal and that many lives would be lost, but they were determined to fight for their home and their people. Kai was shocked at how brightly the mana shone, almost blinding him again with the sheer power that had been amassed by the two opposing forces.

Mages of all levels up to the Grandmaster himself walked slowly out into the field of battle and each of them looked as though they were ready to defend their friends, families and home.

Kai couldn't help but feel inferior. Of course most of the group were Journeyman-ranked like himself, though there were a handful of Masters, four Archmages and the Grandmaster leading the charge.

As the two armies finally faced each other on the battlefield, they stopped and stared, sizing up their opponents. The fire mages and the air mages locked eyes, their faces reflecting a mixture of anger, fear, and defiance.

The bald and weary leader of the air mages, stepped forward, his royal white tunic flapping in the breeze. His eyes scanned the ranks of the fire mages, finally coming to rest on Kai and his friends. "My name is Captain Ren, and I offer you a choice!" he called out, his voice carrying across the battlefield with ease. "Surrender now, and we'll take you alive as prisoners. Resist, and we'll show you no mercy."

The fire mages exchanged uneasy glances, the tension in the air growing ever thicker. Grandmaster Orthos stepped forward, his gaze never wavering from Captain Ren's. "We will not surrender," he replied firmly, his voice full of conviction. "We are prepared to fight to protect our home and our people."

Captain Ren's eyes narrowed, and his expression hardened. "Very well," he said, his voice cold and devoid of emotion. "You have made your choice. Say your goodbyes to your friends and loved ones, and prepare to face the consequences."

The two armies stood there for a moment, the air thick with anticipation and anxiety. The fire mages visibly braced themselves, their hands glowing with the flickering flames of their power. The air mages, led by Captain Ren, readied their own magic, the air around them crackling with energy.

The battlefield was silent for a moment, each side waiting for the other to make the first move. The tension between the fire and air mages was palpable, a taut string ready to snap at any moment.

Finally, with a shrill battle cry, Captain Ren launched an attack. The fire mages felt what had happened in an instant, but Kai *saw* it. The air around his allies filled with a bright golden glow, and the fire mana within them all seemed to be suppressed somehow. He watched as a few of The Brotherhood tried to cast their spells, but the mana hit the golden aura and simply dissipated. It was clear that Captain Ren was manipulating the space around the fire mages somehow so that they couldn't cast their spells. Then the air mages followed suit, unleashing a torrent of wind and pressure on their opponents that seemed unaffected by Captain Ren's spell.

Kai and his friends fought against the oppressive force, struggling to maintain their footing and regain control of their magic. They knew that they couldn't let Captain Ren's tactics render them powerless. They needed to adapt, to find a way to fight back. But he was just so strong.

Kai had never felt a spell like this before. It wasn't a tangible force like a fireball, rather he could see with his mana vision that the usual red auras of his friends and fellow mages had been suppressed to a point where they were now almost invisible.

He could still see the glow within them though, so he knew that the mana had not been entirely quashed.

Desperation began to take hold as Kai racked his brain for a solution. As the air mages continued to press their advantage, the fire mages found themselves pushed back, struggling to mount an effective counterattack.

Kai glanced at Elijah, Lyra, and Alina, their faces etched with determination and grit. They couldn't give up now; they had to find a way to break through Captain Ren's manipulation. As he stared at his friends, an idea began to form in his mind.

"Guys," he called out as he realised what he needed to do, "we need to combine our powers! If we can focus our fire magic together, maybe we can break through the control and push back against the spell!"

His friends hesitated for a moment, but then nodded, understanding the urgency of the situation. With renewed determination, they took a hold of each other's hands, each of them beginning to focus their fire magic into a single, concentrated point.

It wasn't something that they'd practised before, but they had talked about it and just as they'd theorised, Kai watched as their mana began to twist and weave together as though it was growing stronger and thicker.

As they pooled their energy, flames began to grow from their hands and as moments passed, they grew in intensity and power, reaching an almost blinding brightness. The fire mages, inspired by Kai and his friends' defiance, followed suit, each and every one of them taking the hand of the mage to their sides and pushing their mana into combinations that far outweighed the sum of their parts.

Kai watched as the mana within them all grew, spurred on by each of their connections.

The battlefield was suddenly awash with the light and heat of dozens of combined fire magic attacks, each one more powerful than the last. The air mages, taken aback by the sudden surge of power, found themselves struggling to maintain their own control over the space around the fire mages.

Captain Ren, realising the danger posed by this new tactic, frantically tried to reinforce his own spell, but it was too late. With a collective shout, Kai and his friends released their combined fire magic, the force of the attack blasting through the golden aura and through the air mages' defences.

The other fire mages again followed suit, unleashing a torrent of powerful, combined flames that tore quickly through the ranks of the air mages. Captain Ren, overwhelmed by the sheer force of the fire mages' retaliation, was unable to maintain his spatial manipulation spell any longer and the fire mages' own red auras flared back to life, their magic returning to them in full force.

What had been moments before, a totally one-sided and mostly quiet battlefield suddenly turned into an inferno of heat, flames and smoke, a battlefield of death and destruction.

The fire mages capitalised on their regained power, launching a variety of devastating spells at their enemies. One group of fire mages, standing shoulder to shoulder, unleashed a wall of flames that surged forwards like a tidal wave. The heat was so intense that it melted the very ground beneath it, creating a river of molten earth that flowed towards the air mages and soldiers. Some of the air mages managed to redirect the spell with powerful gusts of wind, though the soldiers that stood in its wake were quickly removed from the enemy ranks with not much more that cries of pain and anger.

Another fire mage unleashed a flurry of fireballs, each one a large whirling sphere of searing heat and raw power. The fireballs streaked through the air, leaving trails of smoke in their wake as they found their targets, causing explosions of flame and destruction among the enemy ranks and sending bodies flying everywhere. Soldiers and a few of the unfortunate air mages were thrown high into the air and across the battlefield as though they'd been thrown by a giant.

It was when one of the Archmages cast his first spell that Kai really saw a glimpse of what pure power was. A massive, serpentine dragon made entirely of fire, its form twisting and writhing as it soared through the sky flew from the side of the fire mages and out into the space between the warring armies. For a moment it seemed as though everyone had stopped to watch the majestic creature, trying to figure out not only where it was going to strike, but also when and how.

The fire dragon swooped down upon the soldiers and air mages, its blazing maw opening wide to unleash torrents of fire that incinerated everything in its path. The attack was devastating and Kai couldn't help but think that if the Archmage was *that* powerful, then what could the Grandmaster do.

Within just a few moments, the battlefield had become a chaotic maelstrom of fire and smoke, the air mages and soldiers finding themselves hard-pressed to defend against the relentless onslaught of the fire mages. Soldiers who had been overconfident and unwary found themselves consumed by the fire spells, their armour unable to protect them from the intense heat. Less powerful air mages, caught off guard by the sudden ferocity of the fire mages' counterattack, were similarly engulfed by the flames, their air shields insufficient to ward off the powerful spells of the well trained fire mages. After all, The Pit was designed to turn these mages into fighters, and it was clear that it had been effective.

The fire mages continued their relentless assault, throwing everything they had at their enemy and refusing to give them a single moment's respite. Their combined magic had shifted the tide of the battle, but they knew they had to keep pressing forward, using the full extent of their power to drive back the air mages and soldiers who sought to destroy their home.

With every spell cast and every enemy felled, the fire mages inched closer to victory, fuelled by their determination to protect their people and their sanctuary. The sound of fire magic filled the air, a cacophony that echoed across the battlefield as the two armies fought for dominance.

"Enough!" the shout had come from Captain Ren, who'd steeled himself and now stood tall afront his army. "If you wish to fight, lose your friends and comrades on this day then we shall oblige. But do not think that you have bested us!"

Captain Ren then raised his hands high above his head and clapped his hands together once. Time stood still.

Kai *saw* the effects of the spell before anything actually happened. He had watched as the mana had risen within the Captain, and he saw the golden shockwave that spanned the battlefield in an instant, extinguishing each and every flame that the members of the Brotherhood had wielded to their advantage. What was more, was that once the shockwave hit the Brotherhood of the Flame, it sent every single mage flying back and down to the sand.

Kai heard the sound of a rushing army before he saw it coming. The soldiers now bore down on them in the wake of Captain Ren's spell and if they weren't quick to right themselves, the soldiers would be able to take them down the old-fashioned way without response.

Kai quickly returned to his feet in time to see Grandmaster Orthos standing alone between the fire mages and the onrushing soldiers, with his hands down by his sides as though he didn't have a care in the world.

"Grandmaster! What are you doing?" Kai managed to call out, knowing that if Orthos didn't do something quickly, then he would be killed without a doubt.

But then Kai watched as the Grandmaster clenched his fists, and the soldiers rushing towards him began to slow down. Some of them even dropped their swords to the ground and it took Kai a moment to realise what was happening. Every piece of metal on the battlefield before the Grandmaster had turned a cherry-red, as it superheated as a result of whatever the Grandmaster's spell was. Soldiers wearing metal cuirasses fell to the ground, trying feebly to pull the leather straps away from them to prevent themselves from being cooked alive and others simply fell to the ground screaming in agony, already past the point of reason.

It was all over so fast. Once the Grandmaster unclenched his fists, all that was left was a field of either dead or dying soldiers, twenty or so air mages including Captain Ren, and around forty fire mages of the Brotherhood of the Flame. The Grandmaster alone had been enough to put a stop to this fight.

But Captain Ren was still smiling.

"It's been a long time since I've managed to find someone worthy of my personal attention," the Captain said. "Why don't we make this more interesting? You and I will battle one on one, and if you defeat me, my mages will leave this place and promise never to return. But if I defeat you, then all of your…" his face twisted into an expression of disgust, "…fire mages, will accompany me willingly back to the city, where they will face trial, and punishment for their crimes."

"You mean the crime of being a mage?" Lyra shouted out from beside Kai. The ferocity of her tone made Kai jump, but he really couldn't have said it better himself.

Grandmaster Orthos regarded Captain Ren with a steely gaze, ignoring Lyra's shout. It was clear that he was weighing the risks of accepting such a challenge. He knew the stakes were high, but if there was a chance to end this conflict without further bloodshed, the Grandmaster had to take it, didn't he? Eventually, with a deep breath, he nodded. "Very well, Captain Ren. I accept your challenge."

The two leaders squared off, their eyes locked in a battle of wills even before the first spell was cast. The remaining mages and soldiers on the battlefield formed a wide circle around them, the tension in the air thick enough to cut with a knife.

As the battle began, Grandmaster Orthos and Captain Ren exchanged a flurry of powerful spells, each one more potent than the last. Orthos summoned a searing torrent of flames that roared towards Ren, who countered by creating a whirling vortex of air that snuffed out the fire before it could reach him.

Ren retaliated with a series of lightning-fast air blades, slicing through the air towards the Grandmaster. Orthos managed to deflect most of them with a barrier of flame, but a few slipped through, leaving shallow cuts on his arms and chest.

Kai couldn't believe that the Grandmaster had allowed an attack to get through, to be hit in battle. But then he realised something he hadn't noticed before. The mana within the Grandmaster, although fierce was still being subdued by Captain Ren and his ability to suppress magic.

Kai's eyes widened as he realised what was happening. The Grandmaster although was still forcing his mana to bend to his will, it was as though the flow was through treacle. Captain Ren's mana on the other hand, Kai could see was free flowing with an almost blinding yellow gold glow.

"Grandmaster!" Kai shouted out as Orthos dispelled a fresh wave of air blades but only barely. "He's suppressing your mana!"

The Grandmaster didn't respond, determined to keep his attention on the fight, but Kai saw that he begun cycling his mana to test the limits of what he still had left.

As Kai watched, Captain Ren's mana stirred. It began to shine brightly as though whatever was going to happen next, was going to be the most powerful spell that Kai had ever seen.

Kai knew that he had to act quickly to prevent Captain Ren from unleashing this devastating spell. He looked around at his friends and fellow mages, each of them staring at the battle with a mixture of awe and concern.

"We have to do something!" Kai urged, his voice desperate. "We can't let the Grandmaster fight this battle alone!"

Elijah, Lyra, and Alina exchanged glances, understanding the gravity of the situation. They nodded in unison, ready to support Kai and their Grandmaster in any way they could.

Kai's mind raced as he tried to come up with a plan. Then, recalling how they had combined their powers earlier in the battle, an idea began to form. "Elijah, can you make that smokescreen again?" he asked quickly.

Elijah thought for a moment as he checked on his mana. It was clear that there was still a level of suppression holding him back, but he replied with a determined expression. "Yeah I can," he said.

"Right, do it. I'll go and talk to Orthos while Ren can't see and Alina and Lyra, do whatever you can to keep him away from us. Try to keep in the smoke though, and attack from one place, together, so he doesn't know we've joined in."

The team all nodded as one and Elijah extended his fingers to begin the process of covering the entire battlefield with his dark grey smoke.

Kai could still see Captain Ren throwing spells out as the Grandmaster, but from what he could see he was still building up to something huge, the spells merely a distraction until he was ready to unleash whatever it was that would surely end the fight once and for all.

Kai sprinted towards the Grandmaster as Elijah began to create the smokescreen. Lyra and Alina prepared themselves, concentrating their fire magic into powerful fireballs that they would hurl at Captain Ren once the smokescreen enveloped the battlefield.

As the smokescreen thickened and the view of the battlefield was well and truly gone, Kai reached the Grandmaster's side. "Grandmaster, I can see it in his mana! He's preparing a massive spell that will devastate us all. We need to act fast!"

The Grandmaster, his face etched with pain and exhaustion, glanced at Kai, his eyes filled with sadness and acceptance. "I can't hold him back much longer, Kai. You must all flee while there's still time!"

But something within Kai wouldn't accept that solution. A fierce anger surged through him, and he refused to let the Grandmaster face this battle alone. Kai reached out and grabbed the Grandmaster's arm, feeling an intense surge of energy as he tapped into Orthos' mana.

Kai didn't know what made him do it, but he focussed on the flow of mana coursing through the Grandmaster. He didn't know if it was something that he could do anyway, or if he could only do this right now because of the Grandmaster's weakened state. Either way it didn't matter, Kai focussed everything he could on the Grandmaster's power and drew it into himself. Every last drop.

It only took a moment, but the power that Kai now held was immense, and he felt as though he could channel it to overcome Captain Ren's suppression if he so wished. His soul burnt with an intensity he hadn't experienced before, but in contrary to when he'd done this to Marcus, this time it felt right. It felt *good*.

Kai turned to the Grandmaster, his voice full of strength and conviction. "We won't abandon you. We'll fight together until the end!"

The Grandmaster, looking weak and pale, like he'd aged thirty years was taken aback by Kai's determination and newfound power. He looked a little confused at first, but then he nodded slowly as he realised what had happened. Both of them knew that the Grandmaster was no longer a mage, but wasn't that better than being dead? Or the entire Brotherhood wiped from existence? Kai couldn't know it, but the Grandmaster would make this trade each and every day, if it meant that his students, and The Brotherhood would go on.

Chapter 26 – Surrender

"Get everyone away from here," Kai ordered as he felt Orthos' power begin to flow through him. It wasn't like when he tapped into Azar's power. Azar's power had been strong and volatile, perhaps even oppressive, where the Grandmaster's was calmer and free flowing. Nevertheless, Kai felt it filling his soul more and more with every second that passed, until he could take no more.

He looked down at the Grandmaster. His skin had turned pale, and the man looked as though he stood at death's door, ready to walk through.

Suddenly, the Grandmaster cried out in pain, his body wracked with intense agony and as Kai watched, he saw the last flickering flames of the power within the Grandmaster fade away to nothing. Kai's eyes widened in horror as he realised what had happened.

"Grandmaster, I didn't know! You didn't tell me!" Kai's voice was filled with panic as he tried to reverse the flow of power back into the Grandmaster, but it was as if some invisible force held him there, preventing him from letting go of the Grandmaster's life force.

The Grandmaster, his face contorted with pain, gritted his teeth and managed to speak through the torment. "Kai, you must find a way to use this new power. My time is over but I sense within you the determination to turn the tide in this war..."

But determined to do what he could to save the Grandmaster, Kai closed his eyes and focused on the connection between them. He could feel the relentless flow of power coursing through him, and he willed himself to stop it, to release the Grandmaster from this torturous bond and return to him his Eternal Flame.

As Kai struggled with the unseen force, Lyra and Alina continued to launch fireballs at Captain Ren, their faces set with determination. Elijah's smokescreen swirled around them, obscuring their movements and providing them with the cover they needed to remain safe from the Captain's power.

With sweat dripping down his forehead, Kai felt a sudden shift within himself, as if a barrier had been broken. He could finally sense the force that had been holding him captive, and with a surge of willpower, he finally severed the connection between himself and the Grandmaster.

The moment the connection was broken, Kai stumbled back, breathing heavily. The Grandmaster, now freed from Kai's unintentional drain, collapsed back to the ground, his face pale and his breaths shallow. As Kai searched, he could see the tiniest flicker of mana deep within the Grandmaster. He knew there was nothing he could do, so he turned his attention inwards.

Kai's ordeal though, was far from over.

The power within his was burning him from the inside out. His skin had turned a vibrant red and simply existing pained him. He wanted to grit his teeth, but all that he could manage was an ear-piercing scream of pain as his body began to involuntarily lift from the ground and float five feet in the air.

Captain Ren, apparently hearing this change in circumstance behind the smokescreen summoned up a swift whirlwind that immediately cleared the battlefield to reveal the downed form of the Grandmaster, Elijah, Anya and Lyra standing nervously still and Kai floating in mid-air, glowing his violent shade of red.

After a few seconds passed, Captain Ren simply laughed.

"Well, well, well," Captain Ren taunted, a wicked grin spreading across his face. "It seems our little friend here has bitten off more than he can chew. What a shame."

Despite the pain and the overwhelming energy inside him, Kai knew he couldn't let Captain Ren win. He had to find a way to harness the Grandmaster's power and use it against the enemy. But it was just too much. With every effort that he made to turn his attention to anything other than keeping the pain at a manageable level, he felt like he wanted to die a thousand deaths. His mana vision was overwhelmed and regardless of the sheer power he felt within, he felt helpless.

His friends could only watch in horror as Kai floated there, his body wracked with pain. Elijah, Lyra, and Alina knew they couldn't just stand by and do nothing. They had to do *something*.

The three of them quickly formed a plan. Elijah would try and stabilise Kai, while Lyra and Alina would focus their fire magic on Captain Ren, keeping him at bay while they dealt with the situation.

Elijah began to summon a gentle cushion of warmth, carefully directing it around Kai, attempting to give him some support and time to regain control over his body. At the same time, Lyra and Alina launched a barrage of fireballs at Captain Ren, forcing him to focus on deflecting their attacks. It was feeble though, with Captain Ren seemingly laughing his way through the weak attacks, letting some hit him harmlessly, and flicking others away as though they were annoying gnats.

Kai, though, was already miles away. He could barely hear his friends as they tried in vain to keep Captain Ren away from him and the Grandmaster, and all the while, the Captain laughed, revelling in their feeble attempt to save themselves.

Then the Captain abruptly decided that he'd had enough.

"I am sorry," he said with a sneer in the lull of battle "But your time has finally come to an end. I would say that you fought valiantly, though as the annoying insect, your lives too must come to their early conclusions.

If Kai had been paying attention and not having to deal with the pain enveloping his body, he would've seen that the Captain finally released the mana that had been building up within him.

His eyes glowed a brilliant golden hue as he swung his arms forward, and then the spell began.

At first, a small cyclone wafted into existence before Captain Ren, but as it was fed by his mana, it quickly grew and grew until it reached high up into the sky before him. The sound that it gave off was deafening as it carried the very atmosphere around them with it.

"Kai!" Elijah shouted to try to get his attention. "We need to go!" his voice was strained and it was clear that he was both exhausted and terrified, but Kai made no motions to betray the fact that he could hear his friend. Kai's world was silent.

There was no time for escape though.

Captain Ren clapped his hands together once and the cyclone fell to the ground as though it had been detonated from its base.

Elijah, Lyra, Alina, the rest of the mages of the Brotherhood of the Flame, along with the soldiers of the king's army had but a single second to watch the column of air fall, and then explode outwards, sending everyone and everything flying high into the air and far away from the battlefield.

The air cleared around the sands and Captain Ren turned to speak to the remaining air mages behind him.

"Well, I guess that put an end to all of that," he said with a smile. "I doubt that any would survive when they do eventually land, but if they do… then they won't be any fit state to fight, wouldn't you agree?"

To his surprise though, no one seemed to answer the Captain and when he looked to see what had taken their attention, he slowly turned to see Kai still there, levitating now even higher at ten feet off the ground, his skin burnt and blistered, surrounded by a luminous red glow.

Then Kai opened his eyes.

Within those eyes, Captain Ren did not see a frightened young boy. He saw the kind of anger that could only have been nurtured over decades, or perhaps even longer, and a power the likes of which he had never seen in any other being before.

Kai's voice, ragged and filled with pain, cut through the air. "You think you've won? You think you can just destroy everything we've built and walk away?"

Captain Ren looked at him, forced amusement flickering in his eyes, but also a hint of unease. "You're still here? You should be grateful you're alive, boy. Now, know your place and stay down." As he spoke, Kai felt a pressure in the air bearing down on him, as though the Captain was forcing him to kneel. But he fought back against it, and remained in place.

Kai's eyes narrowed, the power coursing through him igniting a newfound strength. "No. You've taken too much from us, and now it's time for *you* to pay."

The red glow surrounding Kai intensified, and the air around him crackled with energy.

With a roar, Kai unleashed a torrent of raw energy, the force of it so great that it sent a bright beam of pure red light high into the sky and when it touched the clouds, the sky turned instantly black. Red tendrils of mana forked through the sky and after a short pause, the first meteor fell, accompanied by the smash of red lightning.

Behind it came countless more. Each meteor the size of ten men and burning with white-hot flames that trailed behind each before they slammed into the ground in a cacophony of explosions.

They slammed into Captain Ren and his air mages who all tried to run, or cast protective shells around themselves, but the sheer power of Kai's attack was too much for them to handle and within a moment the devastation was evident.

The air mages were sent flying, their bodies battered and broken by the force of Kai's fury.

Captain Ren, however, was not so easily defeated. With a grunt of effort, he managed to hold his ground, barely maintaining a protective barrier around himself. Kai could see now though, that the Captain was bleeding, and he had cuts all over his body, blood staining his royal white robes.

But Kai wasn't done. He drew upon every last ounce of strength within him, the power of the Grandmaster, Azar and Marcus' mana fuelling his final assault. The red glow around him grew brighter and more intense, and he let out another guttural scream as he launched a second, even more powerful attack.

Captain Ren's eyes widened in horror as the wave of heat bore down on him, causing the entire world to turn wavy as it approached. He knew that now he could do nothing to avoid the attack and so he held his arms out wide and welcomed his end.

When Kai's spell hit Ren's barrier, it shattered like glass under the immense force, and he was engulfed in the heat before his body crashed into the ground with a sickening thud.

The battlefield fell silent as the dust settled. Kai, exhausted and in immense pain, slowly lowered himself to the ground and looked at the devastation all around. The spell had destroyed everything it had touched, including The Pit, which was once again nothing more than an old ruin, a relic of the past.

Kai's chest heaved as he tried to catch his breath. He had never imagined he could wield such power, and the consequences of his actions weighed heavily on him. The battlefield was unrecognisable, a wasteland of scorched earth and smouldering craters.

He tried to reach for the magic within him, the familiar warmth that had been his constant companion. But now, it was different. The power felt distant, as if it had retreated to somewhere deep within him. He sensed that it would take time before he could access it again, but he knew he couldn't afford to wait. He had to find the survivors, his friends, and his family.

With a grim determination, Kai began to stumble through the wreckage, his body aching with every step. Each fallen comrade he encountered filled him with a mix of sorrow and resolve. They had fought bravely, and he wouldn't let their sacrifices be in vain.

As he searched, the scale of the devastation became all too clear. The land was veritably littered with the bodies of the fallen, both friend and foe. And yet, amidst the carnage, there was a glimmer of hope – Captain Ren had finally been defeated, and his reign of terror was over. Or at least that's what Kai thought, because in his searching of the battlefield for his friends, he hadn't spared another moment to worry about the fate of Captain Ren.

Kai's heart swelled with a mix of pride and sadness as he thought of the Grandmaster, whose power had helped turn the tide of the battle. The man had given so much, even when it threatened his own life, to protect the people he cared about. Kai knew he owed him a great debt.

He also thought of Elijah, Lyra, Alina, and the other mages of the Brotherhood of the Flame. They had stood by him, fought alongside him, and shared in his struggles. The thought of them being miles away, injured or worse, spurred Kai to keep moving forward.

As he ventured further from the battlefield, the first signs of life began to appear. Here and there, he found injured mages and soldiers, dazed and confused, slowly trying to get back on their feet. With each survivor he encountered, Kai felt a surge of relief, but he also knew that there were many more he had yet to find.

For days, Kai journeyed across the land, searching tirelessly for any sign of his friends and the other mages. Along the way, he encountered both familiar faces and strangers, all of whom had been touched by the devastating spell that had ended the battle. Each time he found a survivor, he offered what aid he could, his own strength waning with every passing moment.

As the days turned into weeks, Kai's resolve was tested, but he refused to give up. He knew that he had a responsibility to those who had fought beside him and had put their lives on the line. The thought of his friends and family, who might still be out there, waiting for him to find them, was all the motivation he needed to keep going.

Finally, after weeks of searching, Kai began to reunite with the people he had been so desperate to find. Some had been injured, others had somehow escaped the worst of the devastation, but they were all alive. One by one, the survivors came together, bound by their shared experiences and the knowledge that they had fought to protect something precious.

With each reunion, Kai's spirits were lifted, but he knew that there was still much to be done. The Brotherhood of the Flame and the home they had defended had been forever changed by the events that had unfolded, and it would take time to heal and rebuild. But together, they had survived, and they would face the future as one. That future though, would no doubt be to take war to the city, and put an end to King Roderick once and for all.

As he looked out across the ragtag group of survivors, Kai felt a newfound sense of purpose. They had lost much, but they had also gained something invaluable: the knowledge that they could stand up against tyranny and prevail. In their hearts, they carried the memories of those who had fallen, and they would honour their sacrifices by building a better future.

With the end of the battle behind them and the long road of recovery ahead, Kai made a promise to himself and to his friends: They would rebuild, they would heal, and they would never forget the lessons they had learned. They would face the future with courage and determination, knowing that they were stronger together.

And so, as the sun set on the horizon, Kai set off once more, his friends and family at his side, determined to find every last survivor and bring them home. They had triumphed over Captain Ren, but their journey was far from over. Together, they would face whatever challenges lay ahead and forge a new path for themselves and for the generations to come.

A Thankyou

Again, your investment of your own time and money is always well appreciated and again, I ask that you **rate** and **review** everything that you read – and not just this book, so that lesser-known authors can grow their audience and gain the credibility that they deserve for their hard work.

Also, check out my website, it's usually kept up to date with current works, reviews and a few extra little bits. You'll find it at:

www.davidlingard.com

Thank you